ANY POT IN A STORM

Also by Sandra Balzo

The Maggy Thorsen mysteries

UNCOMMON GROUNDS
GROUNDS FOR MURDER *
BEAN THERE, DONE THAT *
BREWED, CRUDE AND TATTOOED *
FROM THE GROUNDS UP *
A CUP OF JO *
TRIPLE SHOT *
MURDER ON THE ORIENT ESPRESSO *
TO THE LAST DROP *
THE IMPORTANCE OF BEING URNEST *
MURDER A LA MOCHA *
DEATH OF A BEAN COUNTER *
FLAT WHITE *
THE BIG STEEP *
FRENCH ROAST *

The Main Street Murders mystery series

RUNNING ON EMPTY *
DEAD ENDS *
HIT AND RUN *

* *available from Severn House*

ANY POT IN A STORM

Sandra Balzo

SEVERN
HOUSE

First world edition published in Great Britain and the USA in 2023
by Severn House, an imprint of Canongate Books Ltd,
14 High Street, Edinburgh EH1 1TE.

severnhouse.com

British Library Cataloguing-in-Publication Data
A CIP catalogue record for this title is available from the British Library.

ISBN-13: 978-1-4483-0674-9 (cased)
ISBN-13: 978-1-4483-0679-4 (e-book)

All Severn House titles are printed on acid-free paper.

Typeset by Palimpsest Book Production Ltd.,
Falkirk, Stirlingshire, Scotland.
Printed and bound in Great Britain by
TJ Books, Padstow, Cornwall.

Praise for Sandra Balzo

"Vividly drawn characters and dialogue crackling with wit"
Publishers Weekly on *French Roast*

"Balzo's latest will keep readers on their toes . . . Solid cozy fare"
Booklist on *French Roast*

"The body count rises quickly as Balzo's quirky cozy turns darker than a freshly brewed espresso"
Kirkus Reviews on *French Roast*

"Lively, intelligent characters . . . make this stand out from the cozy pack"
Publishers Weekly on *The Big Steep*

"Connecting murders past and present provides a welcome challenge for coffeehouse cozy fans"
Kirkus Reviews on *The Big Steep*

"Numerous plot twists, nicely delineated characters, dry humor . . . Suggest to those who enjoy Laura Childs' 'Tea Shop' mysteries"
Booklist on *Flat White*

"Readers who like their heroines on the spunky side will enjoy Maggy's company"
Publishers Weekly on *Flat White*

"Balzo smoothly blends eccentric characters, lively dialogue, and a fair-play plot with a touch of discreet romance. Cozy fans will happily keep turning the pages"
Publishers Weekly on *Death of a Bean Counter*

About the author

Sandra Balzo built an impressive career as a public relations consultant before authoring the successful 'Maggy Thorsen' coffeehouse mysteries, the first of which, *Uncommon Grounds*, was published to stellar reviews and nominated for an Anthony and Macavity Award. She is also the author of the 'Main Street Murders' mystery series published by Severn House.

www.sandrabalzo.com

ONE

'Ohhh, Kate, this is just too perfect,' antique shop owner Clare Twohig cooed, trundling her bag along the gravel path between forty-foot-high balsams and through the door of the massive log cabin. 'This place just oozes charm. And inspiration.'

'I think you'll find' – Sarah Kingston swiped her finger on one of the logs and peered at it – 'that what Payne Lodge is oozing is sap.'

Sarah and I owned Uncommon Grounds, a coffeehouse in Brookhills, Wisconsin, roughly six and a half hours south-east of where we now stood. Payne Lodge was 'Up North,' as we Wisconsinites put it, almost to the tip of the ring finger of our mitten-shaped state and nearly touching Lake Superior. I hadn't been this far north since I was a kid and, from what I recalled of that visit, northern Wisconsin hadn't changed much. It was . . . woodsy. And animally. And – I slapped at my leg – buggy.

You might say I'm not an outdoorsy person.

'Property backs onto 860,000 acres of national forest,' Kate McNamara was saying as she came up behind me. 'When Lita told me her grandparents had left her the lodge and she wasn't sure what to do with it, I knew it could be just what the Brookhills Writers' Club – hell, any writer or artist – needs. A retreat – a creative workspace away from the distractions of everyday life.'

Kate McNamara was the editor of our weekly newspaper, the *Brookhills Observer*, and president of the Brookhills Writers' Club. From what I could gather, her friend Lita had given her a great deal on the lodge for the weekend. Which explained why the writers were retreating all the way up here, rather than to a nice bed and breakfast in our own little town of Brookhills or even a conference facility in Milwaukee, just fifteen miles to our east, or Madison, sixty miles to our west.

It's not like we didn't have 'creative workspaces.' They just weren't plunked down in the middle of the woods. Which, honestly, was exactly how I felt right now.

Plunked.

Something unseen rustled through the underbrush by my feet and I backed away from the door, nearly colliding with Kate, who pushed around me with an exasperated sigh. I was sure she also rolled her eyes, but I was too busy dodging the fir-tree branches she sent snapping back at me in her wake.

'Well, let's just hope bears and wolves are conducive to creativity,' I grumbled, trying to center my red wheelie bag on the gravel walkway so as not to disturb whatever deadly fauna might be lurking in the likely poisonous flora. 'I would hate to get mauled for nothing.'

'Stop being a drama queen, Maggy,' Kate said, turning. 'The most dangerous animal up here is the mosquito.'

Somebody had been reading the Middle-of-Nowhere Chamber of Commerce's hype, apparently. Me, I had opted for a deep dive into the black hole of the Internet before embarking on this trip. 'That's because they carry Lyme disease,' I retorted. 'It doesn't mean there aren't vicious—'

'You're both half right.' Clare liked to keep the peace, her sweet vintage glass eternally half-full.

Mine on the other hand, remained half-empty. At least today. 'How is that?'

She smiled. 'It's deer – or deer ticks, to be precise – that carry Lyme disease, which would probably make the tick the most dangerous animal in Wisconsin.'

'Ticks.' I ducked away from the overhanging branches and ran my hand through my hair, searching for the ugly little bloodsuckers. 'I think I would prefer bears.'

At least with bears you had the whole 'don't have to outrun the bear you just have to outrun the guy with you' thing. And with us, we not only had a couple of senior citizens but also Kate who, despite the black leggings and white dry-fit T-shirt, I didn't fancy as a runner.

Kate picked up on the theme. 'You might want to have your

roommate do a tick check before bed, Maggy.' She grinned. 'Just in case.'

Roommate? Would this hell never end? 'We don't have our own—'

Kate interrupted before I could get my question out. 'Oh, for God's sake, Maggy. I know you're not a participant in the workshop, but please try to get into the spirit of the weekend.'

'Yeah, Maggy.' My partner, of course, had to give us her two cents' worth. 'The whole idea is for us to get out of our comfort zones, per se.'

'I am definitely that,' I said, pulling a twig from the handle of my suitcase. 'Per se or not.'

'Case in point,' Kate said, gesturing at my now dirt-smudged wheelie. 'You brought a roller bag to the woods, when there's nothing really to roll it on.'

'But I say good for you, Maggy,' Sarah chimed in again. 'This is how we learn.'

I wasn't sure if she was trying to help in her own perverted way, or simply piling on. I was leaning toward piling on.

Kate was surveying me. 'Lesson one. If you're so afraid of a little mosquito or big, bad tick – oh, and don't forget poison oak and ivy – then wearing short-shorts up here wasn't your best . . .' she grimaced, '. . . fashion choice.'

'They're not short-shorts,' I snapped, willing myself not to pull down the crotch of my blue shorts. They admittedly had been a little shorter than I remembered when I pulled them on this morning. Tighter, too, making the long van ride up uncomfortable enough without Kate rubbing it in, too. 'Since it's unseasonably warm for September, I—'

'Whatever, Maggy.' Kate flapped her hand, dismissing me and my shorts as she turned away. 'But you are in your forties now.'

Yes, but not exactly dead yet. And I would damn well wear what I wanted to wear, including shorts. Even if they crawled up my butt.

I scrunched sideways and gave them a discreet tug.

'Lift your leg much?' Sarah's voice was in my ear.

'What is your and Kate's fixation with my legs all of a sudden?'

'They are very, very white.' She stepped back to take in the entirety of me. 'It's kind of hard to look away.'

I stared her down.

Sarah rolled her eyes. 'I was speaking figuratively, and you know it. I go to the trouble of arranging this gig – with all its possibilities – and all you can do is lift your leg on it.'

As the proud owner of Frank, male sheepdog, and Mocha, dominant female chihuahua who lifted her own leg on everything Frank marked, I understood the concept. 'Fair enough, but this "gig" is for Tien and me.'

Tien Romano provided the food and baked goods at our shop and had agreed to do the same at Payne Lodge this weekend, thank God. As pretty much anybody who knew me would attest, I could brew coffee, but cooking was not my thing. And ordering out didn't appear to be an option up here.

'But not to worry,' I continued, 'you just go ahead and write your little stories with the rest of the kids, and we'll work.'

'Please,' Sarah said. 'My stories will not be "little." They will be tremendous works of great literary worth.' Unable to keep a straight face, she let out a chortle that turned into a cough.

As I pounded my partner's back, Clare glanced back uncertainly at us.

I gave a little wave to assure Clare that no one was choking to death – yet – and she turned her attention back to Kate, who she had been chatting with. Or at least listening to.

Sarah had gotten her breath back and was talking again. 'There's nothing to say you can't participate in the workshops. Or at least some of them.' She snuck a look at Kate. 'If it's all right with Kate, when you're not working.'

'Are you afraid of her?' I was a little surprised. Sarah wasn't afraid of much. 'Her bark is—'

'Her bark is plenty bad,' Sarah interrupted, lowering her voice. 'She's quite capable of tearing anybody in town to shreds with it. Take Harold Byerly. He blames her for his being forced into early retirement and he's probably right.'

Kate's editorials in the *Observer* had been less than forgiving when County Worker Harold left his snowplow for a bathroom break and said plow went rogue.

'But that's what I don't get – why is Harold here? And Gloria, too. The *Observer*'s coverage wasn't exactly sensitive when her husband was killed in that hunting accident.'

Gloria Goddard and her late husband's pharmacy had shared the same strip mall as Uncommon Grounds until we moved to the train depot.

'You think?' Sarah asked. 'Kate insinuated Hank was drunk and not where he should have been.'

'Which may have been the case,' I pointed out. 'Deer hunting and alcohol are not mutually exclusive up here.'

'Which is what Kate's editorial was campaigning against,' Sarah said. 'And I don't disagree that drunks toting rifles in the woods is a bad idea. It was just that she used Hank as an illustration. It didn't go down well in the community.'

'People loved Goddard's Pharmacy and Hank and Gloria,' I said. 'And so, I ask again, why would Harold and Gloria want to come this weekend? I doubt it's because Kate asked them nicely.'

'People think twice before saying no to Kate,' Sarah said. 'They're afraid of her.'

I would say 'not me,' but I was nearly four hundred miles north of where I wanted to be, so I couldn't talk.

'But I'm thinking Harold is here because he's bored,' Sarah continued. 'He just moved into Brookhills Manor, and I'm not sure senior living is what he thought it might be.'

'And Gloria?'

'She's fully recovered from her stroke, so she's been stepping out lately, I hear.' Sarah's expression told me she was leaving something unsaid.

'Are you insinuating there's something going on between the two of them?' I asked, glancing back toward the van where the rest of our party, including Harold and Gloria, were sorting out their luggage.

Brookhills Writers had moved their monthly meeting to our coffee shop about six months ago, having outgrown the cramped conference room in the *Observer*'s offices. And Harold Byerly had even more recently joined the group, always choosing to sit in the chair next to Gloria, if it was available. 'And now she's saving it for him,' I mused aloud.

'Her virginity, you mean?' Sarah's face was screwed up. 'I think that maiden voyage sailed years ago. Or at least I hope it has. Gloria and Hank were married for like four decades. That's a long time not to have sexual—'

'No, not her virginity,' I said irritably. 'Gloria saves a chair at the writers' meetings for Harold.'

'Probably prefers sitting next to him rather than a poet or memoirist.' Sarah grimaced. 'They tend to be either too introspective or too self-involved.'

Sounded like the perfect person to sit next to. Maybe they wouldn't talk. 'That's not the same thing?'

'No way. The former thinks you'll be interested in how they feel, the latter in what they've achieved.'

'And they're both wrong?'

'If they're sitting next to me, they are,' she said. 'Which is why I sit on Gloria's other side.'

Three writers sat at each of our tables, so that kept them all safe from their comrades apparently. 'But back to my question: are Gloria and Harold dating?'

'And why shouldn't they?' Sarah asked. 'Harold is maybe ten years younger than Gloria, but women outlive men by five years anyway, so this just evens the odds a bit.'

There was a perverse logic in that. 'Is that why they're here then? A rendezvous away from the prying eyes of the rest of Brookhills Manor?' The senior living facility was just a block away from our coffee shop and provided some of our best customers, at least as long as they remained upright.

'No secret is safe there,' Sarah agreed.

'I'm actually surprised more people from the writers' group aren't here.' Attendance at the meetings usually hovered between fifteen and twenty, about a quarter of them seniors from Brookhills Manor. 'Kate being your fearless leader and all.'

'This weekend was by invitation only. Kate's invitation, naturally, for members who want to write crime novels or short stories.'

'Which is Harold, Gloria and Clare?'

'And me,' Sarah reminded me. 'It's kind of an honor. Kate is the only published author among us and she wanted us at this inaugural retreat.'

'Published author,' I muttered. 'She publishes herself in her own newspaper.'

'You know full well that she wrote for television before that. Even you can't dispute she's a good writer.'

But I could dispute she was a good human being.

'Face it, Maggy,' Sarah continued, 'Kate is what passes for a bigshot in our little town of Brookhills. Better to be on her good side, rather than her bad.'

'I didn't know she had a good side,' I muttered, having been stabbed in the back by Kate on more than one occasion.

The most memorable pre-dated both Uncommon Grounds and my friendship with Sarah. I was working in public relations at First National, which put on the annual Fourth of July fireworks. An hour before the show was slated to start, a severe thunderstorm rolled in, causing me to cancel the show and send a quarter of a million people running for cover. Kate was the news producer at a local television station but had taken it upon herself to interview me on live television. Her take was that I had done something wrong – neglected to throw a virgin into a volcano to appease the weather gods, I guess. Anyway, as she pelted me with questions – why did I cancel the show or, alternatively, why didn't I cancel it earlier and on and on – I finally pointed out that I had been in consultation with her station's own meteorologist when making those very decisions.

That pretty much shut her up and ended the interview, but neither of us had forgotten the encounter.

'Please don't screw this up by being pissy because you and Kate have history,' Sarah pleaded. 'And she's not all bad. She helped us catch the killer at that barista competition a couple years ago, remember?'

'It was three years ago and her film crew taped us catching the killer,' I said dryly. 'Jerome actually had the camera and Kate just scurried after him.'

Jerome Vickers was an intern camera operator at the time. He'd subsequently followed Kate to the *Observer* as a news photographer.

'You've got to relax, Maggy,' Sarah said. 'You might even find yourself enjoying a weekend devoted to crime-writing. With all the bodies you've stumbled over in the last few years, you would be a natural.'

'Corpses do seem to throw themselves at my feet.' I think I blushed. 'But all my writing has been news releases and corporate reports. And not even that since I quit public relations and opened the coffeehouse.'

'That's more professional writing experience than the rest of us have.' Sarah was trying to flatter me. 'And you've been exposed to the dark side. Kate says in order to write a believable villain you have to get into his or her head and you—'

'Can't fathom what kind of anger it takes to actually kill somebody,' I said bluntly. 'And I don't want to.'

'But it's a process, like method acting. You know how you feel when you say good morning to somebody all cheery-like and they don't say it back?'

'Yes. Like I want to kill them, but figuratively.' Which admittedly made me then question my motives and whether I truly cared if they had a good morning.

'Right.' Sarah seemed delighted I was buying into this. 'You just need to channel that feeling.'

'But I would never actually kill anybody,' I said. 'In fact, I smile pleasantly and take their order. I mean, when they finally decide to acknowledge my existence and place it.'

'That's it.' She gave a malevolent grin and draped an arm around my shoulder. 'But when you're writing, you build on that snarkiness. Amplify. Exaggerate. Delve into the darkest reaches of your mind.'

My darkest reaches told me there was a rat lurking there.

'What is it you really want out of this weekend, Sarah? I mean other than Tien and me doing the food service and leaving you to suck up to Kate and enjoy your conference.'

She withdrew her arm, feigning she was wounded. 'Ouch, that's not fair. I'm happy to help. I'll even do breakfast on Sunday.'

Which probably would consist of a granola bar handed to us as we boarded the van for our drive home. 'It's five-thirtyish on Friday evening, so that's not a huge help right now.'

'But there are workshops tonight and all day tomorrow,' Sarah said. 'I don't know what my schedule will be, but I'm happy to pitch in if I have the free time.'

Big of her. 'I can't believe this place doesn't have its own caterer. Didn't you say it's a conference center? At the very least they need basic food service, not to mention some very basic maintenance. Is this mold?'

In addition to the sap, I had detected black stains on the logs of the lodge.

'I told you it's *going* to be a conference center.' Sarah glanced toward both the lobby where Kate stood and the van behind us, presumably to make sure we couldn't be overheard. 'And retreat. Kate's friend Lita inherited the place from her grandparents. It was vacant for a couple of years as the estate went through probate, but now Lita is planning on renovating it. The plan is for Kate to partner with her to turn it into a retreat and convention center. It could be a very lucrative investment.'

'For whom? I sure don't have money to invest in anything but Uncommon Grounds, do you?'

'Not unless the feds find a pot of money Kip Fargo squirreled away.'

When Sarah sold Kingston Realty to kick in with me at Uncommon Grounds, she'd invested the proceeds with Fargo. Unfortunately, Sarah's money turned up missing – along with that of a dozen other investors in Brookhills – when Fargo died under mysterious circumstances about a year ago.

'I'm sorry,' I said, ashamed to have brought it up. Sarah

had every right to dream of investing in something greater than our next espresso machine. Even if she didn't have the money. 'What kind of staff is there up here?'

'Just a caretaker for now, but obviously it'll be expanded when the project goes forward,' Sarah said, warming to her subject. 'The weekend is to see how the facility works as a retreat and how much staff they'll actually need, plus what functional and code changes will have to be made to the building.'

It occurred to me that Sarah's vast knowledge of real estate could bring something other than cash to the project.

I sniffed, getting mostly woodsy smells with a side of mold and mildew. 'Had Kate seen this place before today?'

'I don't think so.'

'It's going to be expensive,' I said. 'Not that I have to tell you that.'

'No, but Lita has money. Inherited, I think, like the lodge. Apparently she's always on the lookout for good investments. Owns a number of commercial properties.'

I looked at her.

'I've never met the woman, but I hear things.' Sarah did have her finger on the pulse of the community. Plus, she was an eavesdropper extraordinaire. It astonished me how openly people talk while sipping a latte or cappuccino at our shop. And there was Sarah behind the counter, listening.

'How do Lita and Kate know each other?' I asked, confident she'd know.

'I heard her tell Jerome that they went to school together.'

See? 'Jerome was at the shop? When? I haven't seen him for months.'

'He came by at the end of our writers' group on Tuesday night to talk to Kate about this weekend. You should have stuck around.'

'Our' writers' group. Once I realized Sarah was 'sticking around' for the full ninety minutes of writers' group each month, I put her on the schedule to close the shop those nights, freeing me up to go home. I hadn't realized, though, that Sarah had gotten so invested in the group. And, seemingly by extension, this writers' retreat.

'So Kate has invited a select few of the writers up here, along with Tien to do the cooking and me to act as sous chef and barista, as guinea pigs?'

'You must get in the mood, Maggy. This is a crime writers' weekend.' Sarah waggled her eyebrows. 'You're more like . . . victims.'

TWO

I grinned, but I was shaking my head. 'And you volunteered us for this. Thanks for that. When do we get to meet the moneyed Lita?'

'Kate said that she would meet us here. And try to be nice, Maggy.'

Sarah Kingston telling me to be 'nice' was akin to Attila the Hun telling Mary Poppins to play nice. 'Of course I'll be nice. Despite hating everything about the woods.'

'Just keep your opinion of the lodge to yourself, OK? And don't alienate Lita or make her think you're an obstructionist.'

'Why should she care what I think?' If Sarah wanted to get involved in this project, that was up to her. But how did that involve me?

'Just for once in your life listen to your mother's advice. Don't—'

'My mother's dead.' I folded my arms. I could be stubborn, too.

'Then listen to your *dead* mother's advice—' She held up a hand as I opened my mouth. 'When she was alive. You said she always said not to burn bridges.'

'She did say that,' I acknowledged, 'though the full form was "don't burn your bridges before you come to them," which was her mish-mosh of "don't burn your bridges" with "don't cross your bridges before you come to them."'

'But both sayings are excellent advice,' Sarah said, nodding. 'Along with my mother's favorite: "Don't cut off your nose to spite your face."'

This blather was meant to distract me. 'Why not?'

'Because you need it to smell,' Sarah snapped. 'But my point is, who knows? Some day we may need Lita. Or Kate. So be *nice*.' This last came from between clenched teeth.

I cocked my head. 'You want me to suck up to the rich woman.'

'Exactly.' Now Sarah folded her own arms.

I shrugged. 'Why didn't you just say that?'

Sarah groaned. 'I think I did.'

I decided to let it lie, given we had the whole miserable weekend ahead of us. I could always torture the truth out of Sarah after I'd met the woman in question.

'Should have brought Amy,' Sarah was muttering. 'She, at least, has a positive attitude. Even now.'

Amy Caprese was our star barista and marketing guru. Rainbow-haired, pierced and, as Sarah said, normally upbeat, Amy had lost her fiancé just three months ago. When the barista heard about the trip, she'd immediately volunteered to stay home and man the shop, probably anxious for the comparative peace of a weekend without us hovering over her.

Besides, with Uncommon Grounds located in an historic train depot that served the commuter train between Brookhills and Milwaukee, Saturday and Sunday were almost alarmingly quiet compared to the madhouse of the work week.

'Amy does have a positive attitude,' I said as something small and winged buzzed by my ear. 'She was positive she didn't want to drive nearly seven hours up here.'

'But that's the beauty of Payne Lodge. Its location is—'

Something in me snapped. 'Pain Lodge? Really?'

Sarah pressed her lips together. 'Payne: P–A–Y–N–E.'

'Fine, but are they going to spell it out for everybody?' I was trying to catch sight of the mosquito or whatever other disease-laden insect had just buzzed me. 'Wouldn't it be better to name it something that doesn't scream S and M or bad slasher movie?'

'Payne is Lita's family name.' Sarah was ignoring my outburst. 'It's what the property has always been called for a century – it's even on the deed.'

'Which you've obviously looked up.' Just what was my partner up to?

'Of course. That's basic research in my field.'

I opened my mouth, but she waved me down. 'Yes, yes. My *former* field. But the Payne family was big stuff up here at one time and Lita is the last of them. I also came up with something else you'll find interesting.'

I folded my arms.

'It involves Kate,' she dangled temptingly.

'Fine. What?' I relented, glancing apprehensively at the darkening sky overhead. Unless the sun set two hours earlier up here than it did in Brookhills, we were in for a storm.

'You sure you want to know?' Sarah teased.

I pulled up the handle on my roller bag and started to push past her.

'Lita is part-owner of the *Observer*,' she said, holding her ground. 'Maybe even sole owner.'

'The *Brookhills Observer*?' I turned as the buzzing started up again. 'I thought Kate owned the *Observer* and this Lita is just a friend.'

'Good and longtime friend, apparently. And a silent partner in the paper.'

'Interesting.' I swatted at my ear. 'Too bad we couldn't have had our little retreat at their cozy little newspaper office instead of a hundred miles from anywhere in bug heaven.'

'I think you're missing the point of a retreat.' Sarah smacked me on the side of the head. 'Got it.'

'Thanks.' Ouch.

'Anyway,' Sarah continued, wiping her hand on her pants, 'look on the bright side.'

'Which side of this multi-faceted weekend is that?'

'If things don't go well, Lita may just sell off the property.'

I felt my eyes narrow. 'And you just happen to be a real estate broker.'

'In my former life, as you constantly remind me. Though, happily, I do keep my license current.'

Of course she does. 'What are you saying now? You want things to go badly this weekend?'

'I'm saying that however the retreat goes, I'll have made Lita's acquaintance. And, if she needed an agent . . .'

She shrugged. 'Contacts. That's how business is done, Maggy.'

'Real estate business,' I said tightly, my heart dropping. Maybe that's what this weekend was about. Sarah was positioning herself to re-open her agency. Maybe even go into commercial real estate with this Lita person.

But what about me? the whiny little voice in my head asked. I couldn't afford to lose Sarah as a partner in Uncommon Grounds. For one thing, she owned the depot where we were located, meaning we didn't have to pay rent. For another . . . well, she was my friend. Pain in the butt or not. 'You're not—'

But Sarah was picking up her duffel. 'Now let's get inside. It's supposed to storm tonight, and God forbid you get wet and have something else to complain about besides the bugs.'

'Here.' An age-spotted hand thrust a packet at me. 'I can't help with the storm, but this should help with the bugs, at least.'

'Thanks, Gloria,' I said, recognizing the hand that fed me the insect repellant towelette. Gloria Goddard must have shuffled up the path from the van as I was busy angsting. 'I didn't think to pack any.'

'That's a good note for me to give Kate,' Sarah said. 'The lodge could provide bug spray in every room.'

'That would be thoughtful,' I said, any intention of being 'nice' about the weekend abandoned at the thought of Sarah deserting me. 'Right there on the counter next to the shampoo, conditioner and bear spray.'

The octogenarian grinned. 'Black bears, which are the only kind they have up here, rarely attack a human being. They are far more likely to cause property damage foraging for food than trouble us. It really is the mosquitos and deer ticks you have to watch out for.'

I held up my hands in defense. 'So I've heard and believe me, I plan to take them very seriously.'

'Plan to?' Sarah repeated. 'You mean the last twenty minutes of paranoia you've subjected me to is you *not* taking them seriously?'

Accustomed to our arguments, Gloria slid by to step into the lodge. 'Wouldn't want these woods to be the end of you, like they were for my Hank.'

Sarah waited until the older woman was out of earshot before asking. 'It was Hank's own hunting partner who shot him, right?'

'Mistook him for a deer, I understand.'

Sarah cocked her head, eyeing Gloria's back. 'You don't suppose that hunting partner was Gloria, do you?'

I was about to say no, but hesitated. 'Honestly, I don't think the shooter was ever publicly named. Gloria has never said either, to my knowledge.'

'Hmm.' Eyes narrowed, she turned to follow Gloria. 'It would make for an interesting twist at the end of the story.'

'It's her story, if she did kill him,' I called after Sarah. 'She'll probably want to write about it herself.'

'Somebody's dead already? But you just got here.' Tien Romano was struggling toward me towing a blue and white molded-plastic cooler, its wheels carving grooves in the gravel walkway.

'I'm sorry. I should have waited to help you with that.'

Tien had two of my favorites – roast chicken with lemon orzo and red wine braised short ribs on gnocchi – planned for the weekend.

'No worries. Harold lifted it out of the van for me.' She released the towing handle and wiped her hand on the thigh of her jeans. 'Now what's this about wanting to kill somebody? I already have dibs on Kate and Sarah for bringing us up here.'

'Gloria.' I grinned. 'Sarah is in search of inspiration for her plot and has decided that Gloria shot her husband while the two of them were deer hunting.'

'In order to inherit the pharmacy that Gloria already owned and was totally sick of?' Tien made a face. 'Not much of a motive.'

Tien's father Luc had owned a market in that same strip mall since Tien was a baby, so she knew Gloria as well as anyone.

'Accident, as ruled by the coroner.' Harold Byerly was

coming up the walk with a canvas bag in one hand and what looked like a women's vintage makeup train case in the other. 'Hank's body was recovered so cause of death was never a mystery. That's not always true with a body found in these north woods, you know. Take ice fishing, for example.'

The Northern Wisconsin winter sport of ice fishing involved a frozen lake, a chiseled hole, and a tent pitched over it so you could fish and drink beer in relative comfort. Not on my bucket list, but the endeavor seemed innocuous enough for the fisherman or -woman, if less so for the fish. And I couldn't believe even they were in much danger after the first six pack.

Tien was frowning. 'There are a lot of ice fishing fatalities?'

'Vastly underreported.' Harold was shaking his head sagely. 'Think about it. Ice cracks and in you go, never to be found.'

'But wouldn't somebody report them missing?' Tien asked.

'Or, if not, wouldn't the body be found after the thaw?' I blinked. 'I wonder if a body would rise back to the surface or if, caught under the ice, it would get eaten by any—'

'Actually, Maggy, I think you'll find this interesting.' Harold set his case on Tien's cooler and unsnapped the latches to lift the cover. 'If you take a look at the statistics I brought for the workshop—'

The lid slammed, nearly catching his hand.

'I'm disappointed in you, Harold,' Kate admonished, having apparently returned to herd stragglers. 'I would have thought your creative prompt would have been more personal than statistics.'

'Creative prompt?' I asked.

'Everyone was to bring a seminal moment from their lives to build a story on.' Kate was watching Harold as she spoke. 'Some time when . . . well, let's say things could have taken a different direction. Hopefully a more catastrophic one that we can build on creatively.'

So this was where Sarah's prodding me to imagine murdering our customers had come from, as well as her imaginative re-working of Hank Goddard's death. She was parroting Kate's 'method.' It made me wonder what creative prompt my partner had brought to show-and-tell.

'Maybe I didn't understand the assignment,' Harold said, rubbing his chin. 'If you can give me more time—'

'Oh, it's quite simple in your case. Your creative prompt would be "snowplow."'

'Snowplow.' Harold's face had gone dark.

'Certainly,' Kate said. 'Use your imagination. What if, for example, you had been more involved in that man's death than you claimed? I want you to take that idea and run with it.' She smiled sweetly. 'Run, I said, not run over.'

'That's not even funny,' I said. Harold's jaw was twitching.

'Not just that, but it's cruel,' Tien added, glancing back at the man.

'Nonsense,' Kate said primly. 'Fiction – and especially crime-writing – is all about creating conflict. Imagining how a situation could possibly get worse, and then making that happen. You can't be timid about it, Harold,' she said, grasping his arm. 'And what better way to desensitize yourself than by looking at your own personal story.'

Combined lesson and torture session apparently over, she released him. 'Now, will you three come inside, please? You're creating a bottleneck.'

'What are you talking about?' I glanced over my shoulder. 'All of your victims are already trapped inside.'

She glared at me and I glared right back.

Since we met, Kate had gone from aforementioned news producer on a local network affiliate to editor of our suburban weekly with a brief stop in public access cable news. I, on the other hand, had jettisoned the corporate world to open a suburban coffeehouse when I divorced my cheating husband.

Both of us had ways of coping with the downward trajectory of our careers. Me, I pretty much didn't give a damn as long as I had my coffee, my wine, my friends, my son, my fiancé Sheriff Jake Pavlik and our two dogs. Oh, and peperoni pizza. I wasn't sure if Kate had anything or anybody in her life besides work and making herself the biggest, baddest fish in our small pond of Brookhills.

'We still have two attendees on their way, plus Lita,' she said, turning. 'So *move*.'

'Wow, she's in rare form, isn't she?' Tien said as Kate went back in, leaving us blessedly alone, if not unscathed. 'Talk about insensitive.'

'Oh, don't worry about me,' Harold said, waving his hand. 'I'm used to Ms Hoity-Toity McNamara.'

Harold might say he was fine, but he had the look of a near drowning victim coming back up for air.

'I told Sarah that I'm kind of surprised you're here,' I told him, 'given the way you feel about Kate.'

'I wasn't thinking so much about her,' he admitted. 'I just have a lot of time on my hands these days and this was a free weekend away with the rest of you. Folks I like.'

I smiled. 'Sarah told me you were all specifically invited to attend. I guess I should have assumed the weekend is free to the participants.' Or victims, as Sarah had put it.

'Absolutely,' he said. 'Believe me, we get enough of Kate lording it over us in our monthly writers' group. We sure as hell wouldn't pay for the pleasure of her company twenty-four seven for two days.'

'So who is paying?' Presumably the use of the lodge was free, but somebody had to pay for the rented van and gas, as well as the food and coffee we had schlepped up. And our hourly wages, of course.

'Sponsor, I'm told.' Harold snapped the latches of his case closed and picked it up. 'Can I give you a hand with that cooler, Tien? I bet there are the makings of your world-famous sticky buns in there.'

Tien didn't commit, I noticed. 'I would love a hand, Harold. Thank you.'

Harold lifted the wheels of the cooler over the threshold as Tien pulled and they disappeared into the lodge.

Alone outside, I eyed the towering gray clouds building overhead. When I'd heard rain was forecast, it hadn't sounded like the worst thing in the world to me. At least we would be inside the lodge where there would be no animals to attack us or bugs to fight off. But now the prospect of being trapped inside with the likes of—

'Close that door!'

—Kate.

'Yeah, Maggy. Were you born in a barn?'

And Sarah.

And whatever they were plotting, terrified me.

I stepped inside and closed the heavy wooden door behind me.

THREE

As I stepped in, I saw a powder room to one side and coat hooks and a closet to the other, forming a narrow-ish entrance hall. The confines of the foyer, though, only made the lofty main room that it spilled into seem all the more spectacular.

The centerpiece of the impressive space was a 360-degree fireplace with a massive fieldstone chimney extending thirty feet to the peak of the timbered ceiling. The interior of the lodge's log walls hadn't been covered over in plasterboard, instead leaving the wood visible and *au naturel*. It made the room a bit dark for my taste, but it did ooze rustic charm right along with the sap. The wide windows' green brocade curtains had been pushed to each side to let in the great outdoors.

In front of the fireplace were two conversational groupings of four burgundy leather chairs each with its own brass-trimmed steamer trunk serving as a coffee table. On the far side of the fireplace were two rustic wooden dining tables and a small café counter and serving area.

Clare had been chatting by the fireplace and now crossed the room to me. 'Isn't this beautiful? I hope it cools down enough with the rain to have a fire.' She nodded toward the firewood already stacked and waiting to be lit. 'Kate says that's cherry wood. I bet it smells lovely.'

'You must be in your element,' I said to the antique shop owner as Tien, having parked her cooler, came to join us. 'Are you going to do some nosing around for antiques while you're up here?'

'Not right up here, since I think the last sign of civilization was twenty miles back, but Kate says we're to stay focused on our writing this weekend anyway.' She grinned, pink tingeing her cheeks. 'But I admit I thought about driving up on my own so I could putter on the way home and find some new things for the shop.' She made a face. 'It's just such a long drive to do alone.'

'I wish you had mentioned that,' Tien said. 'I would have kept you company on the drive. By the way, I saw the mannequin in your window. Are you selling vintage clothing now, too?'

'It's actually the dress form that's vintage – or antique, more precisely, since it's nineteenth century.'

'I noticed the cast iron ball claw feet,' Tien said. 'Amazing.'

I had not noticed the mannequin's feet. I had just been waiting and watching for the battered old thing to don something half as fun as the clothes Clare regularly sported, but that apparently wasn't in the cards.

'That's a great jacket,' I told her now. 'I assume it's vintage? Or antique?'

Clare grinned. 'Vintage is correct. We reserve "antique" for something that's a century old.'

'Whatever it is, it's great.' Tien was fingering the sleeve of Clare's navy and gold brocade jacket.

'Thanks,' Clare said, opening the jacket so we could see the silk lining. 'I do wear a lot of vintage – partly because it's kind of my shtick with the shop and all, and partly because I just love the stuff. This is sixties.'

'And you pair it with jeans and a simple white T-shirt, and it looks smashing,' Tien said, shaking her head. 'I don't know how you do it.'

'It's actually why it looks smashing, as you say, and thank you very much.' She blushed. 'To showcase an old piece I think it's best to put it against a modern backdrop. It's the same philosophy I have in the store.' She seemed to gather herself. 'But enough about work. Isn't it great to get away for the weekend?'

'Except Tien and I are working,' I said. 'Providing sustenance as the rest of you create.'

'Chicken with lemon orzo I think tonight,' Tien said. 'Assuming the caretaker got the things I asked for.'

'You didn't stuff a couple of chickens in there?' I asked, nodding toward the cooler.

'There are only so many things I'm willing to tote seven

hours in an ice chest,' Tien said. 'Raw chickens aren't among them.'

'Roast chicken with lemon orzo,' Clare repeated. 'Is that the one you cook in a Dutch oven?'

'Which I've been assured they have in the kitchen,' Tien said inclining her head. 'I have the orzo, along with the lemons and vegetables with me.'

'So if there's no chicken, we'll have it vegetarian.' Like I said, Clare was always one to look on the bright side.

Me, I wanted my chicken. 'How long does it take?'

'Probably at least two hours in an unfamiliar kitchen.' Tien checked her watch. 'That's a good point, Maggy. I should ask Kate if she'd prefer we just have sandwiches tonight.'

That was not my point. I wanted chicken.

'What else do you have planned, Tien?' Clare asked.

'Short ribs, but those will take even longer so they're tomorrow,' Tien said, checking her watch again. 'I chose homey things that didn't require precise timing because I wasn't sure what our schedule would be or what the kitchen would look like.'

'Maybe we should scout it out?' I suggested, still not willing to give up on the chicken.

'I'm not even sure where it is,' Tien said. 'The caretaker should be here somewhere. I'd prefer he show me around, light the stove and such.'

'Light the stove?' I asked. 'Is it woodburning?'

'No, but apparently it is quite old,' Tien said. 'Gas or propane, I believe.'

I shook my head. 'Thanks for doing this, Tien. Truly.'

'Don't be silly,' she said. 'You're helping me.'

'Helping, yes. But other than my toting the coffee beans, all of the planning has landed squarely on you.'

'No sweat. It's what I do,' Tien said. 'But I will pull you into service doing prep. There will be carrots to peel and leeks to slice.'

'I'm your woman,' I said.

Clare smiled. 'And Sarah, too?'

My partner might do many things this weekend: ingratiate herself with Kate and Lita. Position herself for a property listing. Hell, she might even write. But one thing she wouldn't do was peel carrots.

'Sarah is participating in the writing workshop,' I said, chin-gesturing toward the fireplace where Sarah stood chatting with Kate. As the three of us looked on, Kate checked her watch.

'. . . really surprised when Sarah sat down at our first meeting at your shop,' Clare was saying. 'I didn't realize she wrote. She's quite good, you know.'

I didn't know. 'What exactly does she write?'

'Well, she's read us just a few things, but I think you'd call them mostly psychological suspense,' Clare said. 'Twisty little stories in which things aren't at all what you think they are.'

I imagined Sarah would excel at that, since she was twisty herself. A no-nonsense chain-smoking real estate agent when I met her, she'd chucked it all to serve coffee with me. Happily single and childless for forty-some years, she'd stepped up to adopt her best friend's two children when she was killed. And, simplest example, her two most prized possessions were a 1975 muscle car and a chintz-furnished Victorian house.

Yup, Sarah was a pile of contradictions right down to this weekend she'd railroaded us into. Maybe my best path was to strap myself in for a twisty ride.

'. . . so interesting. She surprises us every couple of years,' Tien was saying. 'A while back she took up tennis and was quite good at that, too.'

'Tennis? Sarah?' Clare was a newcomer to Brookhills but had been there long enough to recognize the incongruity.

'She didn't stick with it long,' I said, 'but she was totally committed, right down to the little white tennis dress. I had never seen her legs before.'

Sarah favored trousers and a baggy jacket, à la Katherine Hepburn, when she wasn't wearing our informal uniform of jeans and an Uncommon Grounds T-shirt at the shop. For this weekend's adventure, though, she had mixed it up by pairing jeans with the baggy jacket.

I shivered as the door creaked back open and a cold wind

swept through. Clare was probably going to have her wish for a blazing fire.

'Cold, Maggy?' she asked now. 'Your—'

'I know,' I said, holding up my hand. 'I'm a fine one to talk about Sarah's bare legs. Believe me, I'll be changing at the first opportunity.'

'I was actually going to say I think your shorts are adorable,' Clare said. 'It was so hot this morning, I thought about wearing shorts, too. Or maybe a sundress.'

'When a day starts off hot this time of year, you almost have to expect storms later,' Tien said, an ominous roll of thunder underscoring her point. 'I bet they get some wild electrical storms up here.'

'And tornadoes.' I was imagining the giant logs of the cabin scattered about like so many pick-up sticks, our bodies strewn among them. Not that I'm a pessimist or anything.

Clare shivered now, too, but more in delicious anticipation than in response to the cold. 'A dark and stormy night,' she said, going to the door to look out before pushing it closed. Could anything be more perfect for a gathering of crime writers?'

Or more cliché?

'You said Sarah writes suspense,' I said. 'What about you, Clare? What are you working on?'

'Something about antiques, I hope,' Tien piped in.

'Absolutely,' Clare said, nodding her head. 'I'm thinking about a caper. You know, the heist of a rare vase or painting. I just . . .' She glanced back at Kate. 'Well, Kate says I'm too nice, that I instinctively want everybody to live happily ever after, which of course is absolute disaster in a crime book.'

She lowered her voice. 'And it's not just me, you know. Kate says none of us infuses enough conflict in our work. That's why she wanted to bring us to such a remote spot. So we'll start thinking . . .' She waved her hands in the air, searching for a word.

'Creepier?' Tien suggested.

'Exactly.' Clare grinned, but sobered suddenly as another roll of thunder sounded, this one considerably closer and twice as loud. 'Oh, dear. As much as I love the idea of storms here, I hope we're not getting them at home. The thunder scares poor Spikey.'

Spike was a big, affable mix of boxer, chow and shepherd. He looked formidable but had been known to be frightened by a ceiling fan. His sister by bond, if not by blood, was Terra, a cattle dog/husky mix who mothered both Spike and a battered stuffed squirrel she insisted on carrying around.

'How are Spike and Terra?' I asked. 'I missed them the last time I stopped into the shop.'

'Oh, they're lovely – just turned two,' Clare said, her face brightening before it darkened again. 'I . . . well, I haven't been bringing them in much lately.'

'They're such a draw, though,' I said. 'Everybody loves them.'

'Not everybody,' Tien muttered.

'Terra scratched a customer the other day,' Clare explained. 'You know how she carries around her squirrel and paws at you to look at it?'

'Absolutely. She's adorable,' I said. 'Somebody got scratched? Did she draw blood?'

'No, but the customer was quite upset.' Clare glanced toward the fireplace, where Harold and Gloria had joined Kate and Sarah. 'Excuse me if I go mingle?'

'Of course.' Tien turned to me as Clare left us. 'What she's not saying is the "customer" was Kate, who threatened to report it.'

'Report what?' I demanded, as if I was defending one of my own canines. 'Terra is just two – nearly a puppy. Puppies do these things.'

'But not in a place of business, according to Kate,' Tien said, and lowered her voice. 'You know how Clare loves those two puppies. Kate's threat gave her a real jolt.'

'Of course it did,' I said. 'I remember when Frank sat on that poodle. The owner threatened to sue me and have Frank taken away.'

Tien suppressed a grin. 'Frank sat on a . . . I assume it was a toy poodle?'

'Miniature, which is bigger, and an annoying miniature at that. You don't see Mocha complaining and Frank sits on her plenty.'

Tien laughed outright now. 'It amazes me how that five pounds of fur manages to lord it over your one-hundred-and-ten-pound sheepdog.'

'Sheer force of chihuahua will.' I was watching Kate holding court with Sarah, Clare, Harold and Gloria. 'It's like Kate has invited everyone she's ever offended this weekend. No wonder they're all thinking murder.'

'Let's be fair,' Tien said. 'Is there anybody in Brookhills that Kate hasn't rubbed the wrong way?'

'You, maybe?' I asked. 'Have you had any run-ins with her?'

'Not me, but my dad and Angela did, when they opened the restaurant.'

After the market closed, Luc and his partner Angela Fiorentine had opened an Italian restaurant in nearby Wauwatosa. Luc's Ristorante had garnered great reviews from critics except, as I recalled now, our hometown rag. I winced. 'Didn't she say the last thing the area needed was another hackneyed Italian restaurant?'

'Called my dad Chef Boyardee,' Tien said, nodding.

'His reaction was perfect, though.' I chuckled. 'Hanging a portrait of Chef Boyardee in the dining room?'

'Yup. And wrote a long letter to the editor saying how proud he was of the comparison, since the real Chef Boyardee, Ettore Boiardi, had done damn well for himself.'

'Worked as an apprentice chef in Italy at ten before coming to the US with his parents in 1914, as I recall from Luc's letter.'

'Where he eventually became head chef at the Plaza Hotel in New York,' Tien recited from memory, 'and then opened his own restaurant. His spaghetti sauce was so popular that he put it in cleaned milk bottles for people to take home. Eventually he partnered with customers who owned a grocery store to can the sauce and market it.'

'And the rest, as they say, is history. That really is

impressive. And I was equally impressed with your dad and how he handled Kate. I wish other people would stop kowtowing to the woman.'

'You mean like coming here when she cricks her finger?' Tien turned to count heads. 'Harold, Gloria, Clare, Sarah, Kate, you and me. Seven . . . is this all of us now?'

'Two more are coming, plus Lita, according to the queen bee.' I surveyed the crowd. 'That will be eight, plus you and me, so ten for us to feed and water.'

'Lita is the woman who owns the lodge?'

'Yes, and there's the caretaker, too, somewhere.' I felt an involuntary shiver, as we heard the wind pick up outside. 'Why does that make me think of Jack Nicholson in *The Shining*?'

'Because he was just so nightmarishly perfect,' Tien said. 'Though I've spoken to this caretaker, and he sounded perfect in an entirely different way.'

'The man offers to get you chickens and you're in love?'

'Not just chickens,' she said with a grin. 'Short ribs, too.'

'Well, that's all right then, I guess.' But I had another question. 'Did you also speak to Lita Payne?'

'No, just the caretaker.'

'She owns the lodge and also the *Observer*, or at least a good hunk of it.'

'Really? Kate always acts like the paper is hers and only hers.'

'That may be true, editorially,' I admitted. 'From what Sarah told me, Lita is a silent partner.'

'Talk about the perfect partner. Hands you a wad of cash and walks away.'

'She didn't walk away entirely. Apparently, Lita is why Kate dragged us up here to the middle of nowhere to test their new concept for a writers' retreat.'

'Not exactly new,' Tien said doubtfully. 'I mean, being off the beaten path is pretty *de rigueur* for a writers' retreat, isn't it?'

'That's true,' I said, chewing on that. 'There have to be at least a dozen so-called retreats in northern Wisconsin. I wonder what they're planning to do to differentiate themselves.'

'Maybe that's what we're here to help them find out,' she said, tilting her head.

'I'm more than happy to give my opinion on anything and everything,' I said. 'Especially the food and beverage guidelines we were sent.'

'They are awfully restrictive,' Tien agreed.

'Unless they're going full-blown health spa, in which case, what are we all doing here?' I gestured toward the rest of our motley crew of ages, sizes and shapes.

'I know.' She ruefully toed her cooler. 'Harold won't be the only one disappointed when there are no sticky buns tomorrow morning.'

No sticky buns? Where was Tien's rebel spirit? 'I'm supposed to serve decaffeinated coffee. Swiss water process, which is the only kind of decaf we serve at Uncommon Grounds anyway.'

'And?'

I lifted an eyebrow. 'And what?'

'You said you're supposed to,' Tien said. 'Does that mean you smuggled in caffeinated coffee?'

'Of course.' I lowered my voice. 'Most of these people are our customers and we've been topping off their tanks for years. The caffeine withdrawal from cutting them off cold turkey would make a morning-after hangover seem like nothing. Which brings me to another substance that's banned here.'

'Alcohol?' Tien guessed.

'You got it,' I said, shaking my head mournfully. 'Even wine, which we all know is medicinal.'

'I'm very sorry for your loss,' Tien said with a grin.

'I'm bent, but not broken,' I said solemnly. 'So we still have three people coming, but don't you think we should check out the kitchen, even without your handsome caretaker?'

'I said he *sounded* perfect, so don't hold me to the handsome part,' Tien said, swiveling her head to pan the room. 'There's a door on each side of this main room, but I'd bet on the one by the café, wouldn't you?'

'Unless the builder was . . . wait, don't move!'

I slapped her hard on the shoulder.

'What in the world?' Tien said in a hurt voice, rubbing where I smacked.

'Mosquito.' I held up my hand to show her the remains as the front door opened.

'Are you sure?' Tien leaned forward to examine it and then backed right off. 'It's the size of a hummingbird.'

'Murderer!'

FOUR

The gasp had come from behind me. 'Hummingbirds carry the souls of the dead.'

A young woman wearing green cotton bib overalls over a white T-shirt stood in the doorway. Her hair was pink and braided with beads, reminding me so much of Amy back home that I smiled automatically.

'You can smile? Really?' Pink mottling rose in her face enroute to her matching hair. 'You killed a hummingbird. That means one poor soul won't make it to heaven.'

Tien and I exchanged looks. 'Because it doesn't have transportation?' I asked.

'That does seem a bit punitive,' Tien added, pursing her lips. 'For the soul, I mean. It's not its fault Maggy killed a hummingbird.'

'I didn't kill a—'

'Excuse me. Don't mean to interrupt.' A man of about thirty with a stubbly beard and a dark close-cropped head of hair had come up behind Pinky. Sliding Tien a smile, he set a floral-patterned duffel down next to our hummingbird lover. 'Anything else I can do for you, ma'am?'

The 'ma'am' meant this wasn't her significant other unless they were given to role-playing. Nor, probably, was it a taxi or rideshare driver, given our remote location.

Perfect, I mouthed to Tien.

'You must be Cabot,' Tien said, holding out her hand. 'I'm Tien. We spoke on the phone.'

'I am, ma'am, and it's a real pleasure to meet you in person.' He shook her hand and then turned to me. 'Cabot Foxx.'

The name sounded fictional, but then we were at a writers' conference and who knew what Kate might have up her sleeve for this inaugural journey. 'I'm Maggy Thorsen. I'm helping Tien with the food service this weekend.'

'Pleasure to meet you,' he said, shaking my hand. 'Can I

show you the kitchen?' he asked Tien. 'It's old, but I think we have everything you need. I did get the chickens – three nice plump roasters – along with those short ribs you asked for. Hope on the bone is all right. We don't do much boneless this or that up here.'

'Absolutely,' Tien said, going to reclaim the tow handle of the cooler. 'The meat is always more flavorful when it's cooked on the bone.'

'Let me get that,' he said, taking the cooler from her. 'We'll just circle around the fireplace there and go in that door just past the café.'

Tien threw a smile at me over her shoulder as they started away. 'Will you be eating with us, Cabot?' I heard her ask. 'The headcount didn't specify, and we wouldn't want you to go hungry.'

'That's very kind. I would normally just make myself a sandwich back at my cabin, but if you're sure it's no extra trouble—'

'No. No trouble at all,' Tien said, touching his arm as they skirted the tables toward the café and kitchen. 'We certainly wouldn't want you to starve. And what about Lita Payne? Will she—'

'On her way. The storm that's on our doorstep here is slowing her down, but she'll arrive tonight. Whether that'll be by dinner, I can't say, but she—'

The sobbing of the young woman next to me kept me from hearing anything further as Tien and Cabot disappeared through the swinging door into the kitchen.

Annoyed, I whirled on her. 'Oh, for God's sake. I didn't kill a hummingbird. I killed a mosquito.' I held up my hand, which still had the carcass pasted to it. 'Tien said it was the *size of* a hummingbird.'

The bird-lover leaned in to look at the contents of my hand and then sniffed. 'Well, it's not. That's much smaller than even the calliope hummingbird and it's the tiniest bird in North America.'

I regarded my hand. 'It looked bigger before I squished it,' I admitted. 'But Tien was being funny.'

'Well, I don't think the whole thing is remotely funny,'

Pinky said, thrusting out her bottom lip. 'Hummingbirds are on the list of federally protected migratory birds.'

Was she threatening to call the feds on me?

'Yes, but I didn't kill one. I promise.' I crossed my heart.

'Well, that's certainly a relief.' A bespectacled young man now popped up behind her. 'No souls have been killed in the making of this weekend.'

He gave me a lopsided grin. 'Yet.'

'Jerome,' I said delightedly and awkwardly side-stepped Pinky to hug him. 'Sarah said you were at the shop on Tuesday. I was so sorry to have missed you, but now you're here.' I stepped back and surveyed him. 'Still working for Kate, I see.'

'As a freelancer – the *Observer* doesn't need a full-time photographer. Besides, I prefer videography. I've also been dabbling in cinematography.'

I closed one eye to regard him. 'I should probably know what the difference is.'

'Most people don't,' he assured me. 'Videography is more making a record of what's happening at that moment. Cinematography is using all the elements – light, perspective, setting, lens choice – to tell a story.'

'Film-making, then.'

He grinned. 'In its finest form, yes. But I'm not there yet.'

'He will be,' Pinky said, taking his arm possessively, as a flash of lightning lit the room.

'Is it getting bad out there?' I craned my neck to look out the window, but all I could see were black shapes – trees and bushes – bent by the wind.

'The wind really picked up the last few miles. The rain can't be far behind.'

'I thought those trees were going to topple right over on us,' the girl said, clutching his arm even tighter. 'And the sky got so dark suddenly. I can't tell you how relieved I was to see the lights of the lodge.'

'No worries,' Jerome said, putting his hand over hers. 'I had it all under control.'

'You didn't want to come up in the van with us?' I asked, though I didn't blame the two twenty-somethings for preferring to drive rather than ride with the forty-and-up crowd.

Jerome made a face. 'I have motion sickness and it's a very long drive on winding country roads.'

'Tell me about it. I don't know which was worse – Sarah's kibitzing or Kate's driving. I thought those last twisty-turny miles into the woods would never end.'

'I don't think I got above fifteen miles an hour,' Jerome admitted. 'But I'm OK as long as I'm driving.'

I turned to the young woman who I had been largely ignoring. 'The last time I saw Jerome, he was hanging out of the news helicopter for a shot.'

While I'd first met Jerome at that barista competition three years ago, our latest encounter had been this past April, when my sheepdog Frank had unearthed a human bone in our neighbors' yard and Jerome had been dispatched to cover the story from the air.

'As I recall, you yelled at me to be careful,' Jerome said.

The photographer/videographer/cinematographer had also gone to the same high school as my son Eric, so I tended to be a wee protective of him.

'I didn't think you heard that,' I said, feeling my face get warm. 'But I remember you had one hand on the side of the door and the camera in the other. Gave me the willies.'

'And being closed up inside the helicopter gives *me* the willies,' Jerome said. 'Those things are even worse than buses and vans.'

'Were you actually in mid-air?' Faith asked. 'Weren't you afraid?'

'Nah.' He pulled her to him and gave her a kiss on the nose. 'I'm a tough guy.'

'Good thing you're here then to protect me.' She nestled in closer. 'This place gives me the creeps. I can't imagine what might be prowling about. And then with this storm . . .' She shuddered.

Whether she was genuinely nervous or the 'protect me' act was for Jerome's benefit, I couldn't be sure. But at least I wouldn't be the only weenie at this roast.

'I'm Maggy Thorsen,' I told her. 'And you are . . .?'

'Faith Brey.' She offered her hand.

'I would shake, but . . .' I held up the smooshed mosquito.

'It is big for a mosquito, isn't it?' she said, squinting to take another look.

'But definitely not big enough for a hummingbird,' I said, having learned my lesson. I dug out the repellant towelette Gloria had given me and used it to wipe my hand.

'I'm afraid I haven't made a very good impression at my first writers' retreat,' Faith said. 'Can you forgive me for accusing you of hummingbird homicide?'

That made me laugh. 'I can. Are you a writer then?'

She nodded, blushing. 'A little. But not crime-writing, like the rest of the participants, so I'm here to listen and learn.'

'Faith is being modest, Maggy,' Jerome said, taking her hand. 'She's published. Multiple books.'

'Really?' I said, turning back to the girl. 'Congratulations. Do you write under your own name?' This was a nice way of saying I had never heard of her.

She shrugged a little awkwardly. 'They're inspirational. I try to help people through tough times. You know, like with the' – she wiggled her fingers in a frantic flying motion – 'hummingbirds.'

'Which is why you would be protective of them,' I said. 'Sure glad I didn't actually kill one.'

'Me, too,' she said, letting her guard slip further. 'I would have to kill you.'

'Which would make you fit in with the rest of these psychos after all,' I told her as a gust of wind blew the door behind us wide open, slamming it against the wall with a force that made us jump and nearly toppling a covered easel that had been set up by the fireplace.

'I could have sworn I closed that door tight,' Jerome said, going back to shut it.

'All very theatrical, though I can't see how even Kate could drum up a thunderstorm on cue,' I said. 'But as everybody has been saying, it does go nicely with the murder and mayhem theme of the weekend.'

'I guess so,' Faith said, her eyes wide as she glanced around. 'Is Lita Payne here?'

'Running late, from what I've heard,' I said. 'Do you know her?'

'Only by reputation.' She glanced at Jerome.

Jerome turned to me. 'I told Faith about Lita and how she and Kate were putting together this weekend.'

'I jumped at the chance to meet a woman who supports the arts,' Faith said.

'I hope you won't be disappointed,' her beau said. 'Just because Lita owns a newspaper doesn't mean she's—'

'Oh, but she also has an interest in a publishing company from what I understand,' Faith said, and turned to me, blushing. 'You know, industry gossip. But I'm hoping she might be interested in my new work on loss and grieving.'

'I hope so, too, sweetie,' Jerome said, rubbing her shoulder.

'Thank you, sweetie,' she said, getting up on her tiptoes to kiss his cheek.

Young love. 'And what about you, Jerome?' I asked. 'I assume Kate has you working like she does Tien and me?'

'I'm documenting the weekend.' Jerome stepped further into the main room to locate Kate before he continued. 'Kate is hoping this weekend is such a success that Lita will agree to develop it into an annual event.'

I frowned. 'I understood this was sort of a shakedown cruise. You know, to find out how the facility works as a retreat.'

'You know Kate,' Jerome said, 'always looking two steps ahead.'

Was it wrong that I hoped she tripped over her own feet as a result? 'So you knew that Lita owns the *Observer*?'

'She doesn't get involved editorially, if that's what you're wondering. In fact, I've never even seen her at the paper.'

'She lives in Manhattan.' Faith wrapped her arms over her overalled chest and gave a little shiver. 'Why would she care about Brookhills' suburban weekly?'

The sometimes photographer of that suburban weekly looked a little hurt.

'Sarah said Kate and Lita went to school together,' I said to move along the conversation. 'At Northwestern, I imagine?'

Northwestern University was a highly regarded school north of Chicago, and Kate didn't let the fact that she was a graduate go unnoticed.

Jerome nodded. 'They grew up together somewhere near

Chicago. I got the impression the two families were friends, because Lita went to live with Kate's family after both her parents were killed in a car accident. Kate told me all about it when she filled me in on this project at your shop on Tuesday.' Which is likely when Sarah got her information, as well.

'I think she wanted me to understand how important Lita is to her,' Jerome continued.

It did put the two women's friendship and Lita's investment in the *Observer* in a different light.

'How sad,' Faith said. 'And Lita had nobody else? No other family to take her in?'

'Just her grandparents who lived up here.' Jerome shrugged. 'From what Lita told Kate, they were a bit eccentric.'

'And buried way up here in the boonies,' Faith said and then blushed. 'I mean before they were actually buried.'

'Way up here in the boonies,' I added and got a co-conspiratorial grin from Faith.

Jerome ran his hand over the log wall. 'Eccentric or not, this place is pretty coo—' He pulled his finger away.

'Sap?' I guessed.

'Sliver,' he said, holding it up to show us. 'I—'

'Cabot?' Kate had raised her voice and was glancing around the room like she had misplaced something important. 'Is Cabot Foxx here somewhere?'

The man in question stuck his head out of the kitchen. 'I am.'

She waved him over to stand next to her and the easel.

As he moved to the center of the room, Tien also emerged from the kitchen looking a little flushed.

A shadow seemed to cross Kate's face. 'Still nothing from Lita?' I heard her whisper to the caretaker.

'She just called. Says it's slow-going with the rain, but she hopes to be here around seven thirty.'

Kate checked her watch fretfully. 'It's just after six.'

'She did say you could get started without her,' Cabot offered.

'But she wrote the syllabus.' She eyed him. 'I don't suppose she sent her materials ahead?'

'There is a box that arrived earlier this week,' Cabot said, cocking his head. 'I put it in Lita's room. Maybe the syllabus is in there?'

'If she had driven up yesterday like she said she was going to,' Kate said testily, 'she wouldn't be fighting this storm *and* we would have the syllabus.'

'I know,' Cabot said. 'And I'm sure she regrets that, too, now. Which—'

'Is why she called you here, rather than calling me on my cell,' Kate said. 'She knew I would give her hell.'

He seemed to suppress a smile. 'I do work for her.'

'I suppose I do, too, after a fashion.' She sighed and clapped her hands. 'Can I have your attention everybody?'

Since, like me, the other people in the room were already actively eavesdropping on their conversation, it didn't take much.

Kate cleared her throat. 'First of all, thank you one and all for making the trek up here and welcome. For those of you who haven't had the pleasure of meeting him yet' – she threw the caretaker an appreciative look – 'this is Cabot Foxx. Cabot manages the physical facility here for our host and my lifelong friend, Lita Payne—'

'The woman who puts the Payne in Payne Lodge,' a low voice murmured behind me.

I choked down a laugh and turned to see Faith Brey. She clapped a hand over her mouth. 'Sorry.'

'Don't be,' I told her in a low voice. 'I've been making S and M jokes since I heard we were at Payne Lodge.'

'Don't encourage Faith, Maggy,' Jerome said with a grin. 'She comes off all wholesome and sweet, but there's a wicked streak hidden down deep.' The look he gave her indicated he wasn't the least bit sorry about that.

'. . . has spent her life nurturing the arts and particularly the written word. Lita has been delayed by the storm that's blowing in, but she didn't want us to waste one moment of creativity in marking the first of what we hope will be an annual event.' She swept her hand toward the easel.

Taking his cue, Cabot snapped the cloth smartly off the easel, revealing a logo that read *Payne Lodge Writes*. The L in lodge was a stylized quill pen.

'Pithy,' I muttered to myself. 'Bet Kate's already trademarked it.'

'She has.' Sarah had sidled up to me. 'Though I still think I deserve some credit.'

'You came up with it?' I indicated the sign.

'I came up with a variation,' she said, cocking her head to squint at it. 'One which was better – cleaner – in my opinion.'

'And that was?'

'Leave out the "w."'

I was trying to understand. 'So that would make it . . . Payne,' I made an 'r' in the air. 'Rites?'

'So much better for a crime writers' conference, don't you agree?' She was nodding her head. '"Rites" just screams murder.'

'And Satanic rituals. Yet it doesn't even whisper creative *writing* conference.'

'The quill pen would get the point across just fine.' Sarah folded her arms.

'Right,' I said, as Kate glanced our way.

I held up a hand in apology and she went on. 'I know we're all anxious to get started, so Cabot will make sure your luggage gets to your rooms.'

Faith raised her hand. 'Are our rooms here in this building or do we need to go back outside?'

Cabot smiled. 'Happily, they're right down that hall.' He pointed to the door on the opposite side of the fireplace from the café and kitchen. 'We'll be snug and warm inside, regardless of how the storm tries to blow our house down.'

'What is the latest forecast?' Harold asked, as a *yip, yip, yip* started up outside.

'What's that?' Tien asked uneasily.

'No worries, just coyotes wanting to hunt,' Cabot said, as a high-pitched scream interrupted the yipping.

I cringed.

'As for the weather,' Cabot continued, 'they've just updated the thunderstorm watch to a severe thunderstorm warning through noon tomorrow. High winds, as we're already seeing, plus heavy rain and possibly hail. That shouldn't affect us beyond maybe losing power, so long as we stay inside.

Unfortunately Lita is driving up from Minneapolis, which is not only the closest major airport but also southwest of us – the direction this monster storm is blowing in from.'

That set the group chattering.

'Monster storm,' Clare repeated.

Gloria was tut-tutting. 'That poor woman has had to fight the thing the entire way here.'

'Power?' was Sarah's concern.

Kate raised her voice, trying to put a good face on it. 'The weather has slowed Lita down slightly – that's no surprise. But she assures us she will be here tonight.'

'Don't see how she'll make it at all,' Harold said slowly, hooking his thumbs in his belt. 'The roads up here flood regularly and then there are rock and mudslides and fallen trees.' Until recently the man had driven trucks and snowplows for the public works division of Brookhills County, so maybe he knew a lot about roads. Or maybe he was just being a guy. Or a pessimist.

The big front window rattled, and as I turned to look, the glass heaved, almost as if the lodge was breathing. A shiver went up my spine. What was worse? Being stuck in this decaying log cabin with Kate and company during a 'monster' storm? Or sitting in a car. Alone.

'I'm sure Lita will be careful and pull over to wait out the storm if need be.' Kate's face said that was the last thing she wanted her friend to do. She cleared her throat. 'In the meantime, as Cabot says, we'll be warm and safe here.'

A howl emanated from the chimney, exploding into the room and making Kate jump.

'*That*,' Cabot said, grinning, 'was just the wind. And don't you all worry about Lita, she'll make it up here just fine. And when she does, she'll find you all busy at work, I bet.'

'Absolutely.' Kate shoved a strand of auburn hair resolutely behind one ear. 'Isn't that right?'

She got a half-hearted 'Right' from the group.

'What was that?' Hand cupped to ear.

'Right!' I was not a fan of this cajoling, team-building crap. And, in fact, I wasn't actually part of the team at all. I was merely the hired help. But I did know Kate and she wouldn't get off her soapbox until she got the level of enthusiasm she deemed appropriate.

Besides, I did feel some semblance of sympathy. Her partner in fictional crime was nowhere to be found, yet Kate was trapped in the woman's lodge with a testy bunch of writers as a storm raged and coyotes prowled outside our door.

And, if all that weren't bad enough, she planned to serve decaf in the morning. Luckily for Kate, I had her back on that one.

'Now as I said,' she continued, raising her voice even further to be heard over the wind and rain now pelting the windows, 'Cabot will take your luggage to the rooms you'll be sharing. In the meantime, let's pull these armchairs—'

Gloria had her hand up this time. 'You didn't say that, actually.'

'I didn't say what, actually?' Kate seemed at a loss.

'That we would be sharing rooms. I have insomnia, so that won't be convenient.'

'I'm afraid there are only so many rooms, Gloria,' Kate said.

Gloria folded her arms. 'Well, then I had better not get a snorer, or I won't be able to sleep.'

'I thought she didn't sleep anyway,' I heard Faith say to Jerome.

'As I understand it,' Kate said, 'there are five guest rooms in the main lodge and two separate guest cabins. I doubt anyone wants to go out into the storm, do we?' An ominous growl of thunder seemed to challenge anybody who might.

'You sure wouldn't want to stay anyway, once you got out there.' Cabot bent to snag a duffel. 'Those two cabins haven't been touched since the seventies. You'll be much more comfortable in here, believe me.'

A general grumbling followed the caretaker as he left the room with a load of luggage. Kate picked up the fireplace poker to tap on the fieldstone. 'Everyone, please? Your attention again?'

All eyes returned to Kate, which was the way she preferred it. 'Anyway, as I was saying, I had hoped this room would be set for us, but I'm sure we can create our own cozy work circle.'

We all looked at her.

'The chairs.' She waved her hand vaguely toward the fireplace and the big burgundy chairs. 'Each of you pick one and move it to make one cozy circle so we can get started.'

'They each must weigh like two hundred pounds,' Gloria said, giving the nearest one a shove that went nowhere.

'We don't have to move them all,' Harold said. 'We can just take these two' – he nodded to the chairs from each of the four-chair seating areas that backed up to each other – 'and tug them out a ways to form one big circle.'

'Good idea,' Jerome said, going to help him move first one chair and then the other.

'Should we push the trunks together, so they form one big table in the middle?' Clare asked as the two men stood back.

'We could.' Jerome gave the second chair a positional tweak and then turned to give the pseudo-coffee table a shove.

'Uh-oh.' Clare cringed as the metal trim of the old trunk seemed to catch on the plank floor, scraping. 'You two had better lift instead of—'

'Oh, just leave them,' Kate snapped impatiently as Harold moved to help.

'Fine by me,' Harold said, holding up his hands as he backed away. 'I'm going to have a quick cigarette on the porch before the storm gets any worse.'

'There's no smoking on the Payne Lodge grounds,' Kate warned as Harold moved to the door. 'Cabot will tell you that Mr and Mrs Payne didn't smoke or eat processed food and lived well into their nineties, self-sufficient to the end.'

'This was Lita's grandparents?' I asked, doing the math. Kate – and therefore Lita, I presumed – was in her mid-forties.

'Yes,' Kate said. 'And before Lita gets here, I should add that alcohol is also on the verboten list. Her parents were killed in a drunk-driving accident.'

'Who was drinking?' Gloria asked, tilting her head.

'The other driver, I'm sure,' Clare said, seeming uncomfortable at the older woman's direct question. 'Not that it's our business.'

'That's never stopped Kate before,' Gloria said pointedly, apparently still smarting from Kate's insinuations that Hank was drunk when he was killed in the hunting accident.

'True,' Harold said, cracking the door open. 'A personal incident like this would make a perfect creative prompt. You know, to show us how it's done?'

'You mean explore what if it was Lita's mother or father who was drunk?' Sarah asked. 'That would be an interesting starting place. And did he or she mean to—'

'It was her father, OK?' Kate snapped, and then to Harold, 'Will you *please* close that door.'

'Fine.' The former snowplow driver tried to slam it, but the wind howling through the opening defeated the grand gesture, so he had to go back and sheepishly shove the thing closed, hard.

'Thank you,' Kate said, rubbing her forearms against the cold as she calmed herself. A deep breath. 'They went out for dinner on their twentieth anniversary and shared a couple of bottles of wine. Her father nodded off on the drive home and their car veered into the path of a semi-trailer. Lita was fourteen and staying overnight at my house. She didn't find out her parents were dead until our guidance counselor called her into his office at school the next morning.'

The room was silent, except for the wind and rain outside buffeting the trees against the lodge walls.

'I'd appreciate it if you didn't mention it to Lita,' Kate continued. 'But I can't stop you.' Another breath, and she lifted her head. '*Now*, doesn't a fire sound lovely once Cabot finishes with the bags?'

It does, I thought, as everybody clambered to try to lighten the mood.

But what really sounded lovely right now was to be at home with – apologies to Lita – a moderately-sized glass of red wine in my hand and a slice of highly processed peperoni pizza on my plate. And most importantly, a sheepdog, a chihuahua and a sheriff on the couch next to me.

With a sudden pang, I realized I desperately wanted to go home. The feeling brought me back to summer camp when I was eight.

But when I was eight, I didn't have a cell phone to call home. The thought sent me scrabbling for mine.

'I think coffee is in order, too,' Kate continued. 'Decaf, naturally, courtesy of our sponsor this weekend, Uncommon Grounds.'

Sponsor? But I was busy digging in my purse for my phone and gasped when I came up with it. 'No bars?'

FIVE

At my two agonized words, hands dove into pockets and purses.

But Kate McNamara was too busy wagging her head at me to notice. 'You're looking for a bar, Maggy, really? After what I just told you?'

'Bars, not bar,' Gloria said between clenched teeth. 'She means there's no cellular service.' She held up her phone.

'Any rain, the cell towers drop out,' Cabot said, returning to the main room to turn on the lights. 'Even at the best of times, the service is spotty up here.'

'And Internet?' I asked.

'Nope.' As handsome as he was, I was starting to wish Cabot would stay away. Seemed like every time he stepped in the room, there was more bad news. Torrential rain, raging wind, marauding animals and a junk food, booze and Internet ban. What was left to plague us? The approaching storm could tick hail off the list, and I was willing to bet there were already plenty of frogs, flies, lice and locusts up here.

Tien, too, was having a hard time believing this latest blow. 'You mean no wireless, right? Surely the lodge has a wired connection – ethernet.'

Kate glanced at Cabot uncertainly, and I thought I saw a touch of fear in the journalist's eyes.

'I'm afraid not,' he said regretfully. 'But you all will be busy anyway, right? Writing and such?'

Kate, now cut off from her own chosen vice, was less perky. 'Oh,' she said, her voice cracking a little. 'Yes, of course we will.'

'I think the iron maiden is going to cry,' Sarah whispered in my ear.

'It is unnerving to be totally out of contact, isn't it?' Tien said. 'I mean, the apocalypse could be happening out there for all we knew.'

'Somebody's been watching too many disaster movies,' Kate said.

Personally, I loved disaster movies. 'There is a phone in the lodge, though, right? And radio and television, of course.'

'There's a weather radio for sure,' Cabot said. 'Television, no.'

Oh, God. We'd died and gone to hell. Not that we'd ever know it, of course.

Throwing a concerned glance at Kate, Jerome spoke up. 'Not to worry. It won't be for long and we can still use our phones. We'll need plenty of photos to post on the website and online.'

'And how exactly do you propose we post them?' Gloria demanded, visibly upset. At Brookhills Manor, free Wi-Fi was right up there on the list of basic human needs with food, water, shelter and air conditioning.

'Cell service improves as you head south toward Spooner,' Cabot offered. 'You can do it Sunday on the way home.'

Kate's face brightened a smidge. 'I'm doing a feature for the *Observer*, and you'll all certainly want to be part of that. Plus, Jerome will be taking video we hope to place on local news.'

'Local news?' Faith made a face.

'You realize it *is* my job you're talking about,' Jerome told her, finally seeming to lose patience with his date.

'Your job is content – photos, videos,' Faith said, turning on him. 'I'm talking about the delivery system. It just surprises me that you're still talking about newspapers and broadcast news programs instead of digital.'

'She's right.' Gloria was nodding now. 'I get my news from the phone and' – she held hers up – 'this thing is as useless as a brick right now.'

'Fine.' Kate's face was as stony as that brick Gloria was talking about. 'Count me in as a dinosaur. But images and the written word are still important, regardless of the way they're delivered, as Faith puts it.' She glared at the girl. 'We are writers, after all.'

Faith just rolled her eyes.

Kate clapped her hands again to get our attention, as if we weren't already stuck with her. 'Now I think there may have been confusion over what I meant when I asked you to bring creative prompts from your own lives.'

Clare hesitatingly raised her hand. 'I brought my uncle's obituary. I thought his life might—'

'No, no – we want something more personal,' Kate said. 'I've already spoken to Harold about his and, as insensitive as his suggestion that we use Lita's parents' accident as one was, he was right. As was Sarah, if also insensitive.'

I glanced over at my partner and saw a smile that didn't waver.

'Insensitive because it struck too close to home for you,' my partner told her. 'If you want us to probe our own wounds, then you have to be willing to probe yours.'

I think my mouth must have dropped open. 'Well said.'

Kate ducked her head before giving a little nod. 'Fair enough. Before we convene formally, let's just make sure we're all on the right track and then Cabot can get this fire started after he's done with the bags. Maggy, we can still use that coffee.'

To Cabot's credit, he hopped to. I stayed put.

'Now Harold,' she continued, 'we've already spoken about your prompt, "snowplow."'

Gloria gave a harrumph.

Kate ignored it. 'I want you to probe the possibilities had you truly wanted to kill the man that your plow flattened,' she told Harold. 'How you would have done it and also, how you would have covered up the deed. Or what if things had gone awry.' She chuckled. 'Even more awry than they did.'

Yes, Kate was back on form. Mean.

'And Clare, when your dog attacked me—'

Clare opened her mouth to protest, but Kate kept going.

'Imagine what would have happened if I reported him—'

'Her,' Clare said sullenly.

'And what if he was put down and you decided to take vengeance on me?' She smiled, throwing out her hands, palm up. 'Now wouldn't that make a wonderful plot?'

Clare looked like she was going to throw up.

'Or Gloria—'

Gloria's head jerked up.

'Your husband Hank was accidentally shot by his hunting partner. But what if that hunting partner was having an affair with you, and you had both plotted to get rid of him?'

'That's actually better than mine,' Sarah leaned in close to whisper.

'Or Sarah.' Kate wasn't letting anyone off. 'You kindly adopted the children of your best friend Patricia, when she was killed at Maggy's coffee shop the morning it opened. What if you killed Patricia to do just that? Steal her children. You would need to make them younger, of course. Nobody steals teenagers, do they?'

'More likely to give them away,' Cabot opined, crossing through the room to pick up another bag.

'But I think it could certainly work with a baby or toddler, or maybe one of each,' Kate continued. 'You know, you being a lonely spinster and all.'

'Spinster?' Sarah sputtered, starting forward.

I grabbed her arm. 'It's just like you said. Not so much fun speculating when it's your life,' I whispered in her ear.

'Kate is—'

'A bitch, yes,' I said, nodding.

'And Maggy . . .' This was Kate again.

I shook my head. 'I'm not part of the workshop.'

'Oh, but I just want to illustrate my point and your life is so rife with possibilities,' Kate said. 'For example, you were suspected in Patricia's death, weren't you?'

She knew damn well that I was. In fact, that was when I met Pavlik. 'But—'

'What if you were in on Sarah's plot because you two were lesbian lovers?'

Sarah took a step away from me.

'Now, I'll leave you all to think about what I've said while I gather some papers and prepare my thoughts for this first session,' Kate said, turning toward the guest room corridor. 'We'll convene here in fifteen. With coffee, I hope, Maggy?'

This last was tossed over her shoulder as the hall door closed behind her.

'Creative prompts,' Faith repeated in a fair imitation of Kate.

Gloria twittered and joined in. '"I must prepare my thoughts before we convene."'

'I don't know how you can laugh,' Faith told the older woman. 'I would be "prompted" to kill her.'

'Faith, I told you—' Jerome started, but she shut him down with a look.

Apparently I wasn't the only one told to be nice this weekend.

'I'm just angry and so should everyone here be,' she snapped at him. 'No Internet, seriously? And Mom's not letting us sleep together? What are we, five years old?'

'You wanted me to ask Kate if you could come,' he reminded her, as Gloria wisely moved away. 'You insisted, in fact. And now you're complaining.'

'I wanted to come because Lita is going to be here. Besides, I wasn't going to let you spend the weekend with the old cow. She acts like she owns you.'

I didn't necessarily like hearing somebody my age called an old cow, but in Kate's case I would let it pass.

Jerome was pulling at the collar of his golf shirt. 'I've told you. I was an unpaid intern at the television station where Kate worked as a producer the summer after high school. Kate was my mentor, nothing else.' He glanced toward me and away again. 'Whatever else you might have heard.'

'I didn't *hear* anything,' Faith told him. 'But there are photos of you together online.'

'We worked together,' Jerome protested.

'She had her arm around you.'

'Oh, for God's sake. Maggy hugged me when she saw me.' Jerome swept his hand toward me. 'Do you think we're having an affair, too?'

'Maggy hugs you like a mom.' Faith wrinkled her nose. 'With Kate, it's something else. Something more . . . predatory.'

I wanted to say the young woman was crazy – the whole hummingbird debacle and all – but rumors about the two had been rampant around the television station when Jerome interned there, and Kate hadn't done anything to discourage them. It was almost like she wanted people to think she was this slinky cougar, trailing her young videographer.

Probably an act, but at the time I reminded Kate that Jerome was barely eighteen and told her to knock it off if it was true. Not, I suppose, that it was any of my business. Jerome was legally an adult.

But Faith was right. I'm a mom. And the episode gave Kate and me one more reason to dislike and distrust each other.

'. . . just my employer,' Jerome was saying. 'Nothing else.'

'You honestly believe that,' Faith said, storming away from Jerome. 'You're hopeless, you know that?'

Jerome and I watched as Faith set her sights on Cabot Foxx, who was in conversation with Tien. As she took her leave, flashing a smile at him over her shoulder, Faith moved in, chatting animatedly and touching the caretaker's arm.

'Oldest trick in the book,' Sarah observed, joining us.

'Yeah, well, it's not going to work,' Jerome said, skirting the fireplace to flop into a chair.

'By old trick, you mean manipulation?' I said, turning to my partner. 'It's a time-honored tradition between partners – but you should know all about that.'

'I didn't kill Patricia,' she said, holding up her hands.

I slapped them down. 'Don't be ridiculous. Kate is pushing all our buttons this weekend. Now what's this about Uncommon Grounds sponsoring the weekend? Please don't tell me we're paying for everybody to be here.'

'I was hoping you missed that,' Sarah said sheepishly, 'in the commotion about cell service.'

'Well, I didn't,' I said, pausing to listen. 'Is it quieting down out there?'

As if Mother Nature had heard me, there was a whoosh and the wind picked back up, slamming a tree trunk against the lodge perilously close to the window a few feet from where we were standing.

'Don't suppose the windows are tempered,' Sarah said. 'Though they could be, I suppose. They started requiring safety glass in homes back in 1977.'

'Assuming somebody who cared about building code built this place,' I said, edging away from the window. 'And don't change the subject.'

'I believe you'll find you're the one who changed the subject.' She put a hand up to her ear. 'Hark, the storm is gone. Oh, wait – maybe not.'

I just looked at her.

'Fine,' Sarah said, dropping her hand. 'Yes, we're sponsoring it, but thanks to Lita there really is no cost other than the food and drink. Which we're providing *gratis*.'

This last was barely audible as the wind rose, making a whistling sound through the trees.

'We're not getting *paid*?' I demanded. 'You told me this was a job. I told Tien this was a job. We're honor-bound to pay her, at least. And her expenses.'

'I'm sure that—'

'You are not!' I had raised my voice and Jerome, still alone in his chair, turned to look. 'You are not sure of anything,' I said, lowering the volume. 'And neither am I. Why are we here? And why, especially, are Tien and I paying for the pleasure of being here? If you want to invest with Kate and Lita, do it. Just leave me out of it.'

'I'm broke. I couldn't invest even if I wanted to.' She gestured for me to move farther away from the group.

I slid the brocade curtain closed, like the worn fabric was going to save us from flying glass. 'Do you want to invest?' I asked, ashamed of myself. Maybe this *was* her dream. 'I mean, you have your real estate and building expertise. That would be invaluable to a project like this.'

'It would,' she said, 'but I'm not interested in going into business with Kate, of all people.'

'Then, why?'

'Lita.'

'You want to go into business with Lita and ace out Kate?'

'I was hoping to feel out Lita. See if she might be interested in investing in . . .'

I didn't hear the last as it was swallowed by the wind. 'What?'

'Uncommon Grounds.'

I took a step back. Two steps back. 'I don't want an outside investor. We don't need an outside investor.' Did we? The thought made me sick to my stomach.

'Listen, Maggy,' Sarah said earnestly. 'From what Kate has told me, Lita is the perfect partner. Never kibitzes, just lets her money ride.'

'Until she takes it off the table.' I had a horrible thought. 'You told Kate we were having money troubles? Even I didn't know we were having money troubles.'

'You aren't yet,' she said. 'Uncommon Grounds isn't yet.'

I was watching her eyes, which hadn't left the floor. 'But you are.'

'I have the house and the kids. College is looming for Sam and Courtney is not too far behind. We pay ourselves barely anything.'

'Less than we pay Amy,' I admitted. The only reason I'd been able to afford college tuition and board for Eric was that I shared the expense with my ex-husband, Ted. I'd bought the small house I lived in from our divorce settlement. And now Pavlik and I had combined resources.

Sarah was doing everything on her own. 'How can I help?' I asked, putting my hand on her shoulder. 'I don't want to lose you as a partner.'

'Same.' Sarah let out a sigh. 'God, I'm so glad I finally told you.'

'It takes a weight off, I'm sure.'

'About a hundred and thirty pounds,' Sarah said, cracking a small grin. 'You have been on my back this whole trip.'

'This whole trip is less than twelve hours old so far,' I pointed out. 'And I'll have you know I weigh one twenty-seven as of this morning.'

I was quiet for a second and then added, 'I'm really frightened of bringing in an outsider. Even a silent one.'

'I get it,' Sarah said. 'But an infusion of money would allow us to pay ourselves a living wage. We could also pay rent.'

'Rent?' I repeated, surprised. 'But you own the building. Are you thinking of selling it?'

'It crossed my mind, but I'd prefer that Uncommon Grounds pay rent for the space if we can swing it.'

'Oh,' I said, thinking about it. 'That's only fair, really. Your contribution to the business – the building itself – is much greater than mine. I'm so sorry.'

Sarah grinned a little sheepishly. 'That was my buy-in. I knew nothing about coffee, but at least I could offer you the space. But now—'

'You're valuable in so many ways,' I said, forcing a hug on her. My partner was not a hugger.

She submitted and stepped back. 'So we'll see what kind of vibes we get off Lita and go from there?'

'Absolutely,' I said. 'And Uncommon Grounds will pay rent. An expense for the business and income for you.'

'Sorry about the sponsorship,' she said ruefully. 'It's not like we have the money.'

'You were buying your way in. Again.' I toed my bag, which was still sitting where I'd left it, Cabot apparently having other things on his mind. 'That's five pounds of organic single-origin beans in there.'

Sarah sniffed. 'I didn't tell you to bring the good stuff.'

'It's at the end of its shelf life.'

'Good girl.' Sarah slid the curtain aside and peeked out the window. 'Still dark and stormy, but no sign of our pigeon yet.'

You just had to love Sarah. Otherwise you'd kill her.

I choose love. 'I suppose I should start making espresso,' I said, 'since I pretty much know what everybody drinks. You can drink them during this first writing session. I assume madam would like dinner ready afterwards?'

'Not sure, but I can go ask her,' Sarah offered.

'You're not afraid of bearding the lion in her den as she' – I swept the back of my right hand dramatically across my forehead – 'prepares?'

'I'll take my chances.' She tossed me a salute and started for the hallway only to stop, glancing around. 'Do I hear a phone?'

'I thought there was no cell service.' Clare was looking around, too.

'There's the landline,' Cabot said. 'Old school as that may be.'

'But also completely necessary up here.' Sarah was still trying to locate the ringing. 'Want me to get it? Wherever it is?'

'Here,' Cabot said, going to the café and reaching behind the counter to pick up the wireless handset. 'Payne Lodge. Lita? I can't quite . . . you're cutting out.'

He listened for a second and then clicked off and returned the handset to its stand with an apologetic grin. 'There's one section about three or four miles south of here that's not quite dead – you can get a signal of sorts. If that's where she called from, she should be here soon.'

'Unless she slid into a ditch and that's why she's calling,' Harold offered. 'I mean, assuming that happened in your nearly dead zone and she's stuck there.'

'That's possible, too, I guess.' Cabot ran a worried hand over his chin stubble. 'But she didn't sound distressed, I mean from what I could make out. More irritated than anything. And weary.'

'Her blood sugar is probably low,' Gloria said. 'I could use a little something about now, too.'

Tien chose that moment to pop her head out of the kitchen. 'Did I hear somebody's hungry? How about I get soup and grilled cheese sandwiches going?'

The offer was greeted with the first genuine enthusiasm I had heard.

'But Kate wanted to start the first writing session,' Clare said. 'Maybe when she comes back—'

'What? You can't eat and write?' Harold asked. 'I've made it an art form and I sure can't face her so-called creative prompts on an empty stomach.'

'Me neither,' Gloria muttered.

'Guess I don't have to go ask Kate then,' Sarah said, seeming grateful for the reprieve.

'So you dodged a bullet,' I said to her. 'You didn't say if you . . . confided in Kate.'

'About?' Gloria asked, her head swiveling between us as she passed by heading in the direction of the front door.

'You're not going outside, are you?' Sarah asked her, simultaneously giving me a headshake.

'Toilet.' Gloria upped her gear, her determination to get to the powder room apparently outweighing her need to know. The door slammed behind her.

I turned back to Sarah, unsure if the headshake was a warning not to talk in front of Gloria or that she really hadn't told Kate about her money woes.

I was hoping the latter. Faith's assessment of Kate as 'predatory' was not far off the mark, even if it didn't apply to her relationship with Jerome. Sensing weakness, the newswoman would go in for the kill and I couldn't believe Sarah wouldn't know that.

Besides, the thought of my friend and partner confiding to Kate before me was galling.

Sarah punched me in the arm and grinned, like she could read my thoughts.

'Great.' Cabot seemed glad people were smiling again. 'I'll just get this fire going before Kate lights into me.'

Grinning at his joke, Cabot chose a long match from a cup and struck it on the fieldstone hearth. As he bent to light the kindling, a gust of wind blew down the chimney, howling like the proverbial banshee.

A communal gasp sounded from the rest of us as Cabot backed off good-naturedly. 'Guess we know the flue is open.'

He was trying to be reassuring, but I thought I saw unease in the caretaker's eyes as he relit the match and leaned back in. As the match touched a crumbled wad of newspaper under the kindling, there was a deafening crash and a white-hot flash enveloped the room, catching everyone freeze-framed where they stood.

Gloria sticking her head out of the bathroom, mouth open. Tien still in the doorway of the kitchen. Sarah next to me. Cabot and the match, still frozen in place at the fire.

The hair on the back of my neck was standing up. 'Was that a lightning strike?' I heard myself whisper.

'Damn.' Cabot seemed stunned as he stepped back to look up at the chimney, thumbing his phone for the flashlight app. 'Talk about your act of God. It almost sounded like it—'

Another crack and I felt more than heard something heavy give way overhead.

'Go!' Cabot yelled, pushing me into Sarah.

We both staggered back, grasping at each other to stay upright as the roof seemed to collapse and the lights flickered out, leaving us all in complete darkness.

SIX

'Anybody hurt?' Jerome's voice called.

'What fell?' a woman's voice asked. Sounded like Tien.

'A fieldstone from the chimney.' Sarah was playing her phone's flashlight over the granite face of a soccer-ball sized rock.

'The place is built like a bunker.' Cabot's face was just barely illuminated by Sarah's phone as he leaned over to examine the rock. 'Entire logs for the exterior walls, three inches of solid wood for even the interior doors and full, uncut fieldstones for the chimney.'

Full fieldstones that could fully kill you when they fell from a distance of thirty feet as this one had. I hoped the logs and solid doors would stay where they were.

Other mobile phone flashlights were clicking on, and I could see Cabot cross to the closet by the door. Searching the shelves, he emerged with a large flashlight, not unlike what the police use. It had to be a foot long and God knows how many lumens brighter than our phones. Turning, he played it over the part of the ceiling that met the chimney.

'There,' the caretaker said, holding the light still so the beam illuminated a black hole in the timbered ceiling just to the front side of the chimney. 'The lightning must have hit and knocked that rock there out of the top row.' I could just make out a black space where a fieldstone should have been.

'Hopefully none of the others are loose, too,' I said, taking another step back. My heart was still racing and the ever-increasing sound of the wind outside wasn't helping to calm me down.

'The rest of the chimney should be structurally safe.' Cabot seemed to be reassuring himself as much as he was me. 'The strike looks to have been to the roof, not—'

'But is the roof structurally safe?' Tien asked, wrapping her arms across her chest.

'I can go take a look outside,' Cabot offered, moving to the door. 'I'm not sure I can see anything in the dark, but—'

The front door flew open, nearly hitting the caretaker as the wind took the heavy wooden door again and slammed it hard against the foyer wall. Cabot hadn't been kidding about this place being built like a fortress.

'Tain't a fit night out for man nor beast,' a voice called.

'Lita.' Relief was evident in Cabot's voice, and I couldn't blame him. Who would want to be left alone with Kate and the rest of us in this storm, especially without parental supervision?

A figure in a Burberry checked rain jacket stepped in, dropping her bags by the door. 'I can't believe I made it.'

'You're soaked.' Cabot craned his neck to look outside before shoving the door closed behind her. 'Where's your car?'

'There's a tree across the entrance to the driveway, so I had to leave it on the other side and walk up.' She turned to us. 'Happily, it's a rental.'

She pushed back her hood to reveal a pleasant, no-nonsense face with blonde, short-cropped hair and freckles. 'It was a spectacular walk up. I'm trying to see my way on the gravel, the trees on each side of the driveway whipping and the rain pelting down. And then, I suddenly see this beam of light in the sky pointing me here.' She ran a hand through her hair. 'I couldn't decide if Kate was sending me the bat signal or if there had been a virgin birth.'

'Nothing as exciting as either,' Cabot said. 'Lightning struck the building so I'm afraid we have a hole in the roof and a big rock out of the chimney. What you saw was me shining my flashlight up through the hole.' He demonstrated with his flashlight.

'Oh dear,' Lita said, following the beam of light. 'The rain is already coming down hard and the worst of it is yet to arrive. Is it raining in?'

'A bit.' I'd moved back toward the fireplace while Cabot and Lita were talking and now a drip struck the top of my head.

'I was going out to see what I can do—' Cabot started for the door.

'Well, you're certainly not going on the roof in this weather,' Lita said, stripping off her jacket and going to the front closet to hang it up. She was wearing a chic linen jumpsuit that managed to look good even paired with yellow rubber rain-boots. She slipped out of the boots, too, and set them by the door. 'A little water damage is nothing compared with having to scrape you off the ground when you fall.'

'We could use a bucket,' I suggested, sliding sideways and away from what had gone from a single drip to a small, but steady stream.

'I'll go get one in the storeroom. In the meantime, there are towels in the powder room,' Cabot said. 'Lita, I don't know how many of these people you know, but—'

'Many by reputation, at least.' She stuck out her hand to me. 'You must be Maggy Thorsen and somewhere here is Sarah . . .'

'Kingston,' Sarah said, moving in to shake the woman's hand. 'I'm glad to meet you. Kate speaks so highly of you.'

'And where is my partner-in-crime?' Lita asked, squinting to see the group gathered. 'I assume we lost power at the time of the lightning strike?'

'I'm afraid so,' Cabot said, flipping the wall switch by the door that controlled the room's track lighting on and off. 'I'll check the fuse box when I get the bucket.'

'Bring some lanterns, too?' Lita suggested. 'Do we have gas for the generator?'

'For a while, if I can get the thing started,' Cabot said, pulling a jacket from a hook by the door. 'It's probably best to light the fire for heat and just use the generator for lights.'

'Will it have enough juice for the refrigerator and maybe freezer, too?' Tien asked, nodding toward the kitchen.

'Should have,' the caretaker told her with a smile. 'They're on the same circuit with our main lights.'

Lita's own smile flickered. 'Not an auspicious start for Payne Lodge, I'm afraid. I hope you can all forgive us.'

'Don't be silly. The weather certainly isn't your fault,' Sarah assured her.

Sarah sucking up was a beautiful thing to behold. And rare. I tried to catch her eye, but she studiously avoided my gaze.

'Besides,' Cabot was saying as he went to open the door, 'this happens up here. Part of the Northwoods experience.'

'Can I give you a hand, Cabot?' Jerome's voice asked from just outside our circle of phone lights.

'I would appreciate that,' Cabot said, opening the closet to hand him a slicker. 'You'll need this.'

As Jerome put the raincoat on, Cabot turned to Lita and held up his big flashlight. 'You want to keep this inside here with you all?'

Lita shook her head. 'You'll need it out there. Besides, it appears we have plenty of mobile phones to light our way in here.'

Jerome properly attired, the two men stepped out into the rainstorm. Lita shoved the door shut behind them and then turned ruefully. 'Speaking of mobile phones, I hope Kate or Cabot broke the sad news about the abysmal cell service and lack of Internet up here? I'm hoping to change that, but for now I'm afraid we're stuck with both that and this awful storm.'

'Oh, nonsense,' Clare's voice said from behind a cell phone that nearly blinded me.

As Lita put up her hand to shield her eyes, Clare lowered the phone. 'Oops, sorry. I was just saying earlier that a dark and stormy night was just what we needed to get our crime-writing creative juices going. I'm Clare Twohig, by the way.'

'The antique shop owner, of course,' Lita said. 'Delighted to meet you.'

I had to hand it to the woman, she had done her homework. But if we were simply guinea pigs, why bother to get to know who we were? I just hoped she and Kate weren't looking for the same thing from this weekend that Sarah was – investors.

Or maybe Lita was just that kind of person. Personable.

'This is Tien Romano,' Sarah said, gesturing for Tien to abandon her post by the kitchen door and join us. 'She's a fabulous baker and chef, who provides the food and baked goods we serve at Uncommon Grounds.'

'So good of you to come and help us out this weekend,' Lita said, pumping her hand.

'Tien also caters out of our commercial kitchen when we're not using it,' I pointed out. 'The rent provides another revenue stream for the business and there's the added bonus of having our signature sticky buns literally hot out of the oven.'

Sarah gave me an approving look.

Tien chuckled. 'I also fill in as occasional barista.'

'Excellent business plan,' Lita said approvingly.

I thought Sarah was going to high-five me.

'Have you met Gloria Goddard?' Clare asked as Gloria crossed to us. 'And is Harold here somewhere?'

'In the bathroom,' Gloria said, hitching a thumb in that direction. 'He may be a while.'

'Well, it's a pleasure to meet you, Gloria. I understand you and your husband own a pharmacy. Such an accomplished group this is.'

Lita was an even better sucker-upper than Sarah.

'Owned,' Gloria corrected. 'I'm retired and my husband is dead.'

'Oh, I'm sorry. I thought that you and Harold—'

'He's my boy toy,' Gloria explained. 'He—'

'Who's your boy toy?'

At the sound of Harold's voice, Gloria clutched her heart. 'Geez, Harold. You can't sneak up on a person like that. I thought you were in the bathroom.'

'I was,' he said. 'This place is a marvel. Built so solid there's no worries anybody'll hear you, even when you flush.'

Lovely.

'Could use a fan in there, though.' He turned to Lita and extended his hand. 'Excuse the wet, but it's proof I washed my hands, isn't it?'

The towels. I should probably slip into the bathroom to get them now, before Harold made another excursion.

'Indeed,' Lita was saying, her smile having slipped only a smidge. 'Pleased to meet you, Harold.'

'Lita Payne?' a small voice asked.

I couldn't see Faith's face, but she sounded nervous and nothing like the self-confident, assertive woman who had been arguing with Jerome earlier.

'I'm Faith. Faith Brey.' She seemed to be waiting for some

response from the older woman. 'I texted you?' she added after a moment.

'Of course. Delightful to meet you in person, Faith.' Lita didn't sound all that delighted, making me think Faith had already been badgering her about the book.

'Cabot seems to think the fireplace is usable,' Lita said, turning away from the girl. 'Do you suppose we can get it going?'

'Sure,' Sarah said. 'If it draws properly with a hole in the roof.'

'There certainly is a hole.' Jerome was clattering his way back inside with three old-style lanterns dangling from one hand and a gas can and a bucket in the other. 'We could see your lights shining through from outside. But it's only the very top of the chimney that's damaged, so the fireplace should be operable. Cabot is working on the generator as we speak.'

I went to take the bucket from him, eyeing up the lanterns. 'I was hoping for something with batteries in them.'

'Sorry,' he said, then nodded toward the fireplace. 'You had better put down that bucket.'

I turned back to find what was now a good-sized puddle on the wooden floor. I set down the bucket to catch the direct drips and then went to the powder room, pulling open the heavy door to find a simple toilet and pedestal sink. I didn't see a linen cabinet, so I poached the two towels from the rack over the toilet.

'Here,' I said, tossing them to Sarah. 'I'll lift the bucket; you mop the floor.'

Glancing back at Faith, who was taking another run at Lita, my partner seemed about to argue.

'Or vice versa,' I offered. 'And look at it this way – you can be the guest who's *not* hounding Lita. Or at least hounding her less than Faith.'

'Good point.' She lifted the bucket with one finger, and I got down on my hands and knees. Bare knees, I might point out.

'Cabot said to fill these for light,' Jerome was saying as I stood back up. He was setting the lanterns down carefully on the trunk-style coffee tables.

'But isn't kerosene dangerous indoors?' I asked.

'Yes, but this apparently is paraffin oil.' Jerome held up the container. 'Cabot says it's perfectly safe to burn indoors.'

Sure, if you didn't set something else – like the wood that the whole place was built with – on fire. OK, maybe Harold wasn't the only pessimist among us.

'If you have matches, I can re-light the pilot on the stove,' Tien offered. 'Make us some hot chocolate.'

Jerome dug in his pocket and came up with two books of matches. He passed one to Tien. 'I'll light the fireplace and get some heat in here. It's getting cold.'

I would try to get into the pioneer spirit later, but for now I was freezing my literal butt off. 'I'm going to take my bag back and change into something warmer. Then I'll be back to help.'

'Wait.' Jerome filled a lantern and lit it before handing it to me. 'Just keep it right side up and you'll be fine,' he said with a grin.

'Will do.' I started for the door to the guest room corridor.

'Hold up,' Sarah's voice said from behind me. 'I'm coming with you.'

I stopped short and she ran into me. 'Can you back off just a little?'

'I can't be more up your butt than those shorts are,' Sarah said, still on my heels.

'Back off,' I snapped, turning on her. 'If I didn't know better, I'd think you're afraid of the dark.'

'You do have the lantern,' she said, not giving way. Then: 'Lita seems nice, don't you think? She'd make a great silent partner.'

'I hope you don't mind if I suspend judgement,' I said, turning away. 'At least until we're *not* stuck in the woods miles from civilization with no electricity, a raging storm over our heads where the roof should be, a fallen tree blocking our only means of escape and – oh, yeah – no means of calling out for help.'

'I think you're exaggerating.' She reached in front of me to pull open the door of the guest wing.

'Only about the roof,' I said, rolling my bag through. 'And

I haven't even mentioned having the pleasure of Kate's company.'

'Not in the last twenty minutes, you haven't,' Sarah said, letting the door close behind us. 'But I'll agree that this place is a little creepy, if you'll admit that Lita is great. And maybe because Lita has her own sad history, she'll be more sensitive. Rein Kate in.'

'You mean so she doesn't continue to dig out our dirty laundry and make us play with it?' I asked.

'Weirdly put, but yes,' Sarah said. 'I get what Kate is going for creatively—'

'I swear if I hear the word creative again, I'm going to smack you,' I said, turning on her. 'No matter who says it. *You* will be smacked. By me.'

She held up her hands. 'Like I was going to say, the way Kate is going about this is really kind of . . . mean.'

'You think?' I asked sarcastically, turning one of Sarah's own favorite expressions back on her. 'She brought people up here who don't like her in the first place and now she's rubbing salt into their woods.'

'Wounds.'

'Yes, that.' Not that I was obsessed with the woods or anything. 'Are you sure that Kate and Lita aren't looking for investors in House of Payne, or whatever the hell this is? Lita seems awfully well briefed on all of us.'

'If they're looking for cash from this group, they're barking up the wrong tree,' Sarah said. 'Clare, Tien, you and me – we're all struggling small business owners. Harold and Gloria are senior citizens living out their last days on their pensions.'

'Wow,' I said, starting down the hall again. 'Way to marginalize an entire demographic.'

'Thing is,' Sarah continued, 'Lita's loaded – last Payne in a line of wealthy Paynes.'

'Or why else would you be courting her?' I said logically.

'Exactly.' Sarah glanced around. 'We should let Kate know that Lita made it here, but I'm not sure what room she's in.'

'Check the names on the doors.' We were about halfway down the hall, so I took my own advice, struggling to balance the lamp as I pulled out my phone to read the sticky note posted on the nearest door.

'You do know you have a lighted lantern in your other hand.'

Oh, yeah. I pocketed the phone and lifted the lantern.

'How's that for luck.' I squinted. 'It says Maggy – spelled with an "ie," can you believe it? Like Kate doesn't know how to spell my name.'

My partner leaned over my shoulder to see. 'And Sarah, without the "h." At least she's consistently careless.'

Or thoughtless.

'I bet Cabot did the names,' I said, rethinking it. After all, Kate had just arrived with us. 'She could have provided him with a list with the correct spellings, though.'

'True.' Sarah's tone brightened. 'At least we're rooming together.'

I frowned. 'It would make a lot more sense for Tien and me to share. I mean, we'll be getting up early to do breakfast and probably staying up late to clean up.'

'Don't worry, you won't disturb me,' she said, pulling open the door and holding her light to see inside. 'Yup, my bag is here.'

'And now so is mine,' I said, wheeling my suitcase past her. 'Apparently the help has to tote their own luggage.'

'I saw Cabot take Tien's,' Sarah told me.

'She's young. And single. And beautiful.'

'You're . . .' she hesitated, '. . . single. Until you marry Pavlik.'

'Thanks.' I was surveying the small, sparsely furnished room. Two single beds and a dresser, with an iron pipe rack for hanging clothes.

'I'm more afraid of you disturbing me,' I said, going to claim the bed nearest the window and then making a quick U-turn when I heard the wind whistling through the window frame. 'You snore.'

'I do not.' Sarah swung her duffel bag onto the bed I had detoured toward and grinned at me. 'Dibs.'

'You do snore. And there's a draft coming in that window,' I said, pointing. 'I'll freeze sleeping there.'

'Well, if you would put on some clothes,' Sarah said, nodding toward my legs, yet again.

'Fine.' I laid my wheelie bag flat and unzipped it, pulling out a pair of sweatpants. I slipped out of my shorts and into them, followed by a hooded sweatshirt and held out both arms. 'Happy? I'm still cold.'

'These old double-hung windows don't always seal tight,' Sarah said, coming over. 'See? The wind is coming through between the top and bottom sash. Just make sure they're secure.' She flipped the aged sash lock open and then pushed it back closed again, fighting against layers of old paint. 'That's better.'

'No, it's not. You've made it worse.' I shaded my eyes to try to see out the window, but all I could make out were dark shapes bending and swaying. 'The wind is picking up again.'

'I didn't think it died down in the first place,' Sarah said. 'And don't get too close to that window. I'm pretty certain now that none of this glass is tempered. A good gust of wind could shatter it into shards.'

I stepped back. 'And yet you're just fine with me sleeping in a bed that's practically beneath the guillotine glass window.'

'We'll move the bed a smidge,' Sarah said, sliding a dresser drawer open to investigate. 'And don't worry about the draft, we'll just ask Cabot for duct tape and seal that opening right up.'

Seeing no reason to stay to argue the point, I pushed open the door to the hallway. 'I'll see you back out— Oops.' A figure dodged around the open door. 'Sorry,' I called as they evaporated into the darkness at the end of the hall. 'Rude,' I said, when the person didn't answer. 'Probably Kate.'

'You should have told her Lita is here. Besides, who really is the rude one?' Sarah was, again tagging after me. 'You nearly hit the woman with a door.'

'I just expect simple civility, politeness,' I said. 'Even from Kate. If I apologize for nearly hitting her with a door, I expect her to say thank you.'

'You want her to thank you for apologizing for nearly hitting her with a door.'

'Exactly. Or at least to respond with a "no problem" or "I'm fine." I mean, it's not my fault she was walking past.'

'In a hallway.'

'Stop it.' I retrieved the lantern I'd set on the floor as I changed clothes and stepped out. 'You're going to stay in that?'

'Why not? I'm dressed appropriately for a weekend Up North.' Coming to join me, she looked down the hall. 'Let's check out who is where. You said Kate went down this way?'

'I didn't say, but she did.' As I trailed her down the hall, the building – full logs and three-inch doors and all, gave a shudder. 'Told you the wind had picked up.'

Sarah opened the door straight ahead, at the very end of the hall. 'Bathroom – that's handy to know. I was afraid we were going to have to use the one in the front hall.'

'That's a half bath,' I said. 'No tub or shower.' Or towels now.

'So you see my point.' She was checking the tag on the closed door to the right of the bathroom, just one down from ours. 'This is the one. Hey, Kate?'

No answer, but there was a thud inside the room.

'Knock,' I suggested, but instead, my partner was already trying the doorknob.

'Mind?' The door slammed back closed, nearly taking Sarah's hand off and the lock snapped. 'I'm changing.'

'We just wanted to let you know that Lita is here,' I told her.

A grunt was all I got for my pains.

'Bitch,' I muttered under my breath as I turned away.

Sarah was grinning. 'Let's see who's rooming across from her.'

'I swear you like this kind of dormitory of death stuff.' I held up the lantern to the sticky note on the door. 'Gloria and Faith.'

Just up from them and directly across from our room was the one earmarked for Tien and Clare. Harold and Jerome were the last door on the right, just this side of the door to the main lobby.

But Sarah was busy checking out the door across from the men. 'Can you hold up the lamp so I can see?'

'I don't see a sticky note,' I said, obliging.

'I think I noticed . . .' she was squinting, '. . . yes, this brass plaque says private. I'm betting this is Lita's room.' Her hand was already on the doorknob.

'And marked private,' I said. 'If you want to impress her, maybe ransacking her room isn't the way to do it.'

'I'm not ransacking, I'm snooping.' She went to the main doorway and cracked it open. 'No worries, Lita is still out there talking.'

Letting that door close, she tapped perfunctorily on the one marked private and then pulled it open. 'Besides, if she caught us, I would just say we were looking for our room and didn't see the plaque. It's quite tarnished.' She gave it a rub as she stepped in.

The benefit of having the lights go out, I guessed. An alibi. Even as I had that thought, my lantern flickered.

'Is that a TV?' I heard Sarah say from inside the room.

'I don't see how that can be if there's no Internet. But maybe Lita has a DVD or Blu-Ray player.' The thought momentarily brightened my mood, until I remembered there was no power. 'Damn,' I said, giving my lantern a shake.

It went out in retaliation.

I groaned and stuck my head into the dark room. 'My lantern went out.'

'It's OK. I have my . . .' A thud. 'Ouch!'

From the light of Sarah's phone, I could see the room was a little bigger than ours, with one queen-sized bed rather than the two twin-sized and a chair along a wall of bookshelves. What I couldn't see, though, was Sarah. Nor a TV on the dresser, the big liar. 'Where are you?'

'Down here.' Her voice sounded oddly muffled.

'Did you trip? That's what you get for snooping in the dark.' I skirted the area where I thought I might accidentally tread on my partner and set the unlit lantern on the dresser, pulling out my phone for light.

'This dresser scarf is nice,' I said, holding up the phone as I ran my hand over a white linen runner embroidered in daisies. 'My grandma had one simi—'

'Fascinating,' Sarah's voice said. 'But—'

'Oh, that's a shame. Something must have been spilled.' I touched a dark-tinged daisy on the corner and my finger came away tacky. Hmm. 'I don't suppose you hit your head on the dresser?'

'Oh . . . my . . . God.'

'I'm just asking,' I said. 'Because there's—'

'Kate?' My partner was the type of person who would normally pop up after a trip or fall and deny anything had happened. But she was still down for the count. And thought I was Kate.

'I'm Maggy,' I corrected, getting down on the floor next to her and turning my phone so it would illuminate me. 'How many fingers am I holding up?'

The normal Sarah would throw me a finger of her own in reply, but now she pushed herself away from me and struggled to her feet.

That was when I realized there was still a shadowed shape on the floor beside me and jumped up myself.

Kate McNamara was staring up at me, my phone's light reflecting in her lifeless eyes. Around her head was a halo of blood.

SEVEN

I felt for a pulse. 'Kate's dead.'

'Was it the unblinking stare that gave it away? Or maybe all the blood?' Sarah was anxiously wiping her hands on her already blood-soaked jacket and jeans.

'You fell in her blood,' I told her. 'If I were you, I would just stand still and . . . air dry.'

'Easy for you to say.' She looked like she was going to be sick. 'Can you get me a towel or—'

'Hello?' Clare stuck her head in, holding another lantern. 'Do you know what room Kate is in? Lita would like to get started and Jerome lit the fireplace.' She made a face. 'No power yet. Cabot is apparently having trouble with the generator.'

'There's been an accident.' Placing myself between Kate's body and Clare's gaze, I managed to slide my hand up and over Kate's face to close her eyelids. 'It seems that Kate fell and hit her head on the dresser.'

Sarah's eyes narrowed as she glanced at me and then the body behind me and back again.

'Is everything OK?' Gloria pushed into the room, wearing a burgundy velour tracksuit and fuzzy slippers. 'Is that blood?' she asked Sarah. 'Who did you kill?'

Sarah held up both hands. 'She was dead when I fell on her.'

'You fell on—' Gloria started to say as Lita appeared behind her.

'Now I know you're still finding your way around,' she said, 'but this is my private room.'

I moved sideways, so she could see the body on the floor.

Lita's hand flew to her mouth. 'Oh, my God. Katy?'

Pushing past Gloria, her knees seemed to give out and she hit the floor, crawling to reach her friend.

I put my hand out to stop her as she went to pull Kate into her arms. 'I'm sorry, Lita, but you mustn't touch her.'

'But we have to help her. We have to stop the bleeding.'

'I'm afraid there's nothing we can do,' I said. 'She's—'

'Can I help?' Faith had found her way to the room along with Jerome. 'I have a little medical training.'

I moved away so she could reach Kate's side. Lita stayed right where she was.

Faith checked first Kate's wrist and then her carotid for a pulse. Her expression seemed just this side of panic as she looked up to Jerome. 'Do we have a real flashlight?'

'Cabot has the big one,' Jerome said. 'Use my phone.'

Faith took it and lifted Kate's eyelids, checking for pupil reaction. Then she stood up. 'She's dead,' she said, meeting Jerome's eyes. 'Dead for real.'

She fell into his arms and started to sob.

Sarah caught my eye, but I frowned and gave a warning shake of my head.

'Where is everybody?' Cabot's voice called. Behind him, I thought I glimpsed Tien and Harold before his flashlight blinded me. 'Sorry I haven't gotten the generator started yet. It—'

'There's been an accident,' I interrupted. 'We need to call nine-one-one.'

'But there's no service.' His flashlight was trained on Kate and Lita on the floor.

'Use the landline,' I said. Then to Clare, I added, 'Could I use your lantern? Mine died.'

Clare handed it to me, but Cabot was still standing there. 'But there's no electricity.'

'You said you have a landline, and it can't be VoIP,' I reasoned, 'because that requires the Internet. Which you don't have here, right?'

'No. Yes.' He took a deep breath. 'But I don't understand. What's happened?'

'Kate is dead,' Lita snapped, without turning. 'She hit her head or something. Go call for help, for God's sake, Cabot. Call now.'

'Yes, yes, of course.' Cabot stood a second more staring and then, seeming to gather himself, went out into the lobby, an avalanche of questions from Harold and Tien following him.

'Accident?' Sarah whispered in my ear. 'You did notice her eyes, right?'

'I did,' I whispered, as the volume of chatter increased. Jerome and Faith were huddled by the bookshelves, while Clare had gone to join Harold and Tien in the hall. 'That's why I closed them. This is a group of wannabe mystery writers. Identifying petechial hemorrhaging due to asphyxiation is Murder Mystery 101.'

'Maybe in a book, but you think they would have the presence of mind to realize it in real life?'

I just shrugged.

'Fine, we'll keep it quiet for now.' She was still holding her hands out from her body like a scarecrow, but gave a nearby cardboard box a shove with her foot. I assumed it was the supplies Lita had sent ahead. 'But for you and me, our working theory is that somebody hit Kate and then strangled or suffocated her when she was down?'

'I think it's more likely than Kate accidentally smashing her own head and somebody wandering in opportunistically to finish the job. And speaking of "somebody" – somebody also passed us in the hall,' I reminded her. 'And then presumably locked herself in Kate's room, pretending to be her.'

'The killer?'

'Who else?' I asked.

'There's a lot of blood,' Sarah said, seeming to remember she was covered in it. 'Kate must have been alive for a while after she was hit, since Murder Mystery 101 also tells us that a corpse doesn't bleed.'

'Scalp wounds bleed profusely by nature. She could have lost that amount of blood' – I nodded to the floor and then, as an afterthought, to Sarah – 'in minutes, not hours.'

'She wasn't gone hours,' Sarah said. 'Maybe, what? Twenty minutes?'

'She said she'd be back in fifteen, but it's been more like forty-five, I think.' I was looking at the queen-sized bed, which I could now make out as covered in a white and yellow duvet and matching pillow shams. 'I didn't see any strangulation marks on her neck, so I'm thinking suffocation.'

'Whatever they used to suffocate her would be bloody.' Sarah held up both hands to illustrate.

'Yes, it would.' We moved casually toward the bed so as not to attract attention. We needn't have worried. The others were too busy speculating to notice what we were doing.

There were no signs of blood on the headboard or duvet. I flipped the pillow shams. 'Nothing.'

'He or she would have had enough time to pull the pillow out of the sham and slip it back in after they used it to suffocate her,' Sarah pointed out.

'That would be one cool customer,' I said, going to hand one pillow to Sarah to check, but then realizing she couldn't touch them. Hell, even I shouldn't be touching them. 'And remember when you're talking about "he or she" that most everybody here is a friend.'

'Of ours, but not necessarily of Kate's,' Sarah said. 'You don't like her, for one.'

'Hey,' I said, 'I'm not the one who is covered in her blood.'

Sarah ignored that. 'My point is that Kate was taking potshots at everybody, including you, just before she was killed. You know, saying that you and I killed Patricia—'

'I was a little disappointed at her lack of imagination, actually. She could have come up with at least another one or two potential murder victims for me.' I shrugged. 'But I don't take it personally.'

'That's because you're you,' Sarah said. 'Most people panic when they're accused of something horrible.'

'And kill their accuser?' I thought about that. 'I guess it's possible this started as a heated argument.'

'Right,' she said. 'Maybe a little pushing and then Kate falls and there's blood everywhere. Like I said, the person panics.'

'And puts a pillow over her face rather than calling for help?'

'This was Kate, remember? Kate who threatens puppies and people's livelihoods.'

'Who accuses an eighty-year-old woman of plotting to murder her husband,' I mused. 'Are you suggesting that Kate got a little too close to the truth, somehow, with her creative prompts crap?'

'Not really. Maybe.' Sarah glanced uncomfortably at our friends – the ones we were accusing of murder – before continuing. 'I think it's more likely that there was this argument and fall and the—'

'The panic, as you say.' I rubbed my forehead. 'We've been assuming Kate was knocked unconscious, but maybe not. Maybe she was still conscious, talking and threatening the person. Saying she's going to scream. Call the police. That they're going to go to jail for the rest of their lives.'

'These are nice, normal, everyday people,' Sarah said. 'And they know Kate, and how ruthless she can be. What a weapon the newspaper is. They would be terrified.'

She was right. 'So he or she shut her up.'

Sarah nodded.

We were both silent for a moment, contemplating what this could mean. I took a deep breath. 'The police will solve this. We don't need to be involved.'

'The police up here, not Pavlik,' Sarah reminded me. She leaned down to see the pillow I had just pulled out of the sham. 'No blood on that one.'

'Nope,' I said, going to pull out the next one. No blood, again. 'That first one I checked had a pillowcase, right?'

'Yes,' Sarah said. 'This one doesn't?'

'No.' I set down the pillow. 'So they smothered her and stripped off the pillowcase? What did they do with it?' I glanced around the room.

'Drawer?' she said, pointing to the dresser. 'Or under the bed.'

'But the idea would be to get rid of it. Otherwise, why not just stuff the pillow, complete with bloody pillowcase, back into the sham?'

'Because they thought it might bleed through before they had time to come back and dispose of it?'

'Why risk coming back at all?' I asked.

'It's not a risk if we all believe Kate's death is an accident.'

'True.' I thought about that. 'They could have used the window.'

We made a beeline for the single double-hung window that was a twin to the one in our room.

'It's locked,' Sarah said.

'But it would be, wouldn't it? The killer would toss the pillowcase out and then close and lock the window so no one would tip to it.' I pulled the cuff of my sweatshirt over my hand and tried the lock. 'Stuck.'

Using the back of my hand, I felt the windowsill. 'Does this feel damp to you?'

Sarah tried and shrugged. 'Maybe. I can't see a thing outside, though. We'll have to go out there and search.'

'Yes.' I didn't move.

'What?'

'There's something else,' I said, chin-gesturing to where Faith was leaning down to talk with Lita. Jerome was nowhere in sight. 'If Faith has medical training, like she says, she should have seen the hemorrhaging in the eyes. Why didn't she mention it?'

'Maybe she's lying about the medical training. Maybe she just wanted to get up close and personal to a corpse so she could write about it.'

'To be fair, she's not a mystery writer. She does inspirational stuff. Signs of murder may not be familiar to her.'

'Why is she here then?'

'Same as you. Sucking up to Lita, who has an interest in a publishing company as well as the newspaper.'

'Really?' Sarah said, turning to look at the two women. 'That looks more like arguing than sucking up.'

As we watched, Lita waved Faith away, seemingly in tears.

'Faith?' I beckoned for her to join us at the window. 'How is Lita doing?'

'Upset. I guess they've known each other for a long time. I was telling her about my new book and how it might help her, but she wasn't ready.' She shrugged.

Pitching your book on grief and loss to a publisher who had suffered loss mere minutes earlier wasn't a good look.

'Where did you get your medical training?' Sarah wasn't one to beat about the bush.

'I was a midwife,' Faith said, frowning. 'Why? Think you can do better?'

'I . . . um, no.'

I had to appreciate somebody who could shut my partner up. 'Did you notice anything about Kate's eyes, Faith?'

'You mean the petechial hemorrhaging?' she asked, meeting my own eyes. 'Yes. But as you pointed out' – she glared at Sarah – 'I'm not a medical expert.'

'Did you say anything to Lita?' I asked.

'I didn't think my uninformed speculation that her friend might have been asphyxiated would be comforting somehow.'

'But you didn't say anything to us either,' I said.

'Listen, Maggy,' she said, 'according to Jerome, you have a reputation for playing detective. I didn't want to get you started.'

'Get me started?' Now I was the one who was offended.

Faith glanced around to make sure she couldn't be heard. 'You writer types may get off on the idea of being trapped here with a murderer and ultimately solving the crime, but I'm pretty sure it's not as much fun in real life as it seems in fiction.'

Sarah eyed her. 'You do know that pretending nothing happened doesn't mean that nothing happened.'

Faith just stared at her.

'What Sarah means—'

'I know what Sarah means,' Faith interrupted. 'But I'm not playing your game. I'm playing my game. And in mine, Kate fell and hit her head. End of story.'

'And if we all clap hard enough Tinkerbell will live,' Sarah muttered.

'You laugh,' Faith said, eyes narrowing, 'but there is power in belief.'

'Faith,' I said.

'Yes?' She turned to me.

'No, I meant faith, lower case, as in having faith. Belief.'

'Oh, yes.' But something outside the window had caught her attention. 'Is that Cabot out there in the rain?'

'I asked him to call nine-one-one,' I said, turning. 'What—'

Sure enough, our caretaker was outside holding a lighted

cell phone up over his head, presumably trying to get a signal.

Sarah sighed. 'I assume this means the landline isn't working.'

I peered at the faintly lit figure. 'Does he have something hanging out of his jacket pocket?' Knocking on the window, I waved for him to come inside. 'Cabot, come in! Bring that.'

'What?' Cabot's hand was to his ear.

'The pillowcase,' I yelled.

'A pillowcase?' Faith repeated, her head twisting toward the pillows on the bed. 'What would a . . . ohhhhh.'

'Oh is right,' Sarah said. 'Clap, Tinkerbell, clap.'

'It's the kids who clap, not Tinkerbell,' I told her.

'Shuddup,' she told me.

EIGHT

'I sure hope I didn't destroy any evidence,' Cabot said, rubbing his head with a towel as he sat down. 'That pillowcase was soaked, and I just picked it up, figuring it had fallen out of the clothes basket earlier when I brought the clean sheets around to change the beds.'

Sarah had gone to shower and change, but the rest of us had drifted in to take the big chairs by the fireplace, which so far hadn't smoked us out or fallen on us. A lighted lantern was on each of the two steamer chests, the wind from the hole above us making the flames periodically dance and stutter. The bucket was still in place on the floor next to the hearth, the two wet towels from the half-bath wadded around to catch splatters.

'It was the rain that destroyed any evidence,' I assured the caretaker. 'I assume the fact you were trying to get a cell signal out there means the landline doesn't work.'

'It has a cordless handset, which means it needs electrical power to send the signal to the base.' He turned to Lita. 'We need to get an old-fashioned rotary-dial phone for just these kinds of emergencies. They don't need to be plugged into electrical.'

'Hopefully there will never be another one quite like this,' Lita said wearily. 'Is there any other way to get help?'

'I'm afraid not in this storm,' Cabot said. 'But I'll go back out and work on the generator, see if we can get us some juice. Meantime, I would feel a whole lot better if we could . . . well, make Kate more comfortable, be more respectful.'

'We can't move the body,' I told him. 'I had Jerome take photos, but with . . .' I hesitated about how to continue, '. . . an unattended death, the police will want the scene as untouched as possible.' Difficult, since nearly all eleven of us – now down to ten of us living – had been in the room.

'Are you some kind of law enforcement?' Cabot asked.

'No, she's marrying a sheriff and stumbles over bodies on a regular basis.' Sarah was back from her shower and shoved her way onto the chair with me.

'What came first?' the caretaker asked curiously. 'The sheriff or the bodies?'

'They came simultaneously,' Sarah said and grinned.

'Stop being a child.' I dug my elbow into her ribs. 'But technically Sarah is right. The first murder I was exposed to, the first body I ever saw, was my business partner, Patricia. My fiancé was the investigator on the case.'

'She's leaving out that she was a suspect,' Gloria said. 'Though Kate certainly knew all about it.'

'Kate knew about pretty much everything,' Harold muttered.

'I was a suspect for a short time,' I admitted. 'Though it didn't feel so short then.'

'Oh, for God's sake, Maggy,' Tien burst out uncharacteristically. 'This is all your fault.'

Ouch. 'Is not.'

'Is.' This from Sarah. 'Nothing like this ever happened to me until I met you.'

'What in the world are you all talking about?' Lita had been sitting quietly, lost in her own thoughts and seeming oblivious to the conversation around her. 'My oldest friend in the world is dead. I don't think things could get any worse for me.'

'I know how you feel,' Sarah said. 'Maggy's first victim was my best friend.'

'Patricia was not my victim,' I snapped, and turned to Lita. 'She was my friend and partner, and the murderer was . . . well, it's far too complicated to get into now. But I had nothing to do with it.'

I had the soggy pillowcase on my lap in a plastic bag and was examining it through the bag. 'This sure does look like blood. Where exactly did you find it again, Cabot?'

'Caught in the bushes by the side of the house. Like I said, I just snagged it because I thought I had dropped it when I brought up the wash.'

'Brought up the wash from where?' I asked.

'There's a work room that backs up to the guest wing. That's where the washer and dryer are, along with the generator and the lanterns and all. Unfortunately, it doesn't connect to the lodge, so I have to bring the laundry around to the front door.'

'So there's no back door,' I mused, though it pretty much confirmed what Sarah and I had seen on our tour. 'No way somebody could get in without us seeing them come through the main room?'

'Except through a window, like the pillowcase,' Sarah pointed out. 'The one in the room where Kate was killed was locked and stuck, but there may be others that aren't.'

'We didn't check that,' I said, standing. 'And we need to do that right now.'

'Now?' Sarah asked.

'I can check if you want, Maggy,' Jerome offered.

'No need,' I said. 'Sarah and I will take a quick look. Right, Sarah?'

'Right, Maggy,' she said, standing up.

Sarah waited until we were in the guest corridor. 'You don't trust anybody, do you?'

'Nobody but you.' I had one lantern and Sarah had another. 'Should we stick together?'

'Probably. Just because we trust each other, doesn't mean the police up here will trust either of us.'

'Good point,' I said, opening the door to Harold and Jerome's room. 'I guess I'm getting used to being above suspicion as Pavlik's soon-to-be wife.'

'Only soon-to-be when it suits you,' Sarah said, going to the window. 'This one's locked.'

'Check,' I said, looking over her shoulder. 'You mean because we haven't set the date?'

'Yes, but it's no big deal. You two just seem comfortable the way things are.'

'We are,' I said, leading the way to Clare and Tien's room next. 'But I'm sure we'll get married.'

'Eventually.' Sarah held the lantern while I went to the window, being careful not to trip over the women's bags in the center of the room. As in our room and Harold and Jerome's, this room had twin beds.

'Locked,' I confirmed, and then tried it. 'Painted shut.'

'A lot of these are,' she said, moving on to the last room on the left, which was Faith and Gloria. 'But that would make sense. Even when Lita's grandparents were alive, most of these rooms would have been empty.'

'It is a lot of bedrooms for two people,' I said. 'Maybe they hoped they'd have a bunch of kids and it just never happened.'

There were twin beds in Faith and Gloria's room, too, and Faith had staked out her claim on the bed nearest the window by placing her floral bag on it.

'This one is locked, too,' I said, leaning over Faith's bag to get to the window.

Next up was the bathroom at the very end of the hall. I stuck my head in. 'No windows in here.' The toilet was to the right, the bathtub to the left. The sink and medicine cabinet were straight ahead, where you would expect a window to be.

'I wonder which room Lita's grandparents slept in,' I said, leaving the bathroom door ajar.

'I'm betting this one here.' Sarah had her hand on the doorknob to what was to be Kate's room. 'Old folks like to be close to the bathroom.'

I couldn't argue with that. Hell, I liked to be close to the bathroom. 'Why didn't we check this room, first thing?'

'Because we're dunces.' Sarah tried the door. 'It's not locked.'

She turned the knob, and we stepped in. The room was not dissimilar to Lita's. Queen-sized bed and dresser near the window, but where Lita's bookshelves and chair were in the other room was a chest of drawers. Kate's duffel bag sat open next to the bed and the bedspread – an old-style chenille one, in this room – was wrinkled.

'Somebody's been here,' I said.

'We know that,' Sarah said. 'We heard her.'

'Are we sure it was a woman?' I asked. 'She – or he – only said what? Three words?'

'"Mind?" and "I'm changing," as I recall.' She shrugged. 'Through the door it was pretty muffled. Could have been a man imitating a woman, I suppose, but I kind of doubt it.'

'The window is closed,' I said, trying it, 'and locked. But

it's not painted shut like the others, which would make sense if the old folks, as you put it, were using it.'

'Probably why Kate got this one,' Sarah said. 'She's special.'

'And dead, so no need to be jealous,' I said. 'Assuming the person we heard was a woman, did you hear Faith imitate Kate? It was pretty good.'

'"Creative prompts," all hoity-toity. Yeah, she was, but I am, too.'

'You are, but not as good as Faith,' I said. 'Besides, you were with me.'

'I'm just saying anybody can imitate Kate's voice by being loud and snooty.' Sarah beckoned for us to move on. 'You know what you're doing, right?'

'What do you mean?' I glanced around, surprised. 'What am I doing?'

'Faith is the outsider. You always prefer your killers to be people you don't like.'

Well, who doesn't? 'I like Faith.'

'But not as much as you like the rest of us, and we're all grateful for that.' She stopped at our door. 'We don't have to check our room, do we?'

'Probably not, but I guess we might as well while we're here.' I was pulling the door open, then stopped short as a gust of wind and rain hit me. 'What the hell?'

Our window was wide open.

NINE

'But it doesn't make sense that somebody popped in through your window to kill Kate,' Clare said when we reported back. 'Nobody knows her up here.'

'True.' Sarah and I had taken our same seat and now I swiveled towards my partner. 'You just showered, so you must have gone in to get your clothes. I assume the window was closed like it was when we first went in?'

'No, I just left it wide open because I like sleeping cold and wet.'

Actually, it was my bed that was soaked. Not that I had any intention of sleeping there or any place at all the way things were going.

'So why would anybody open the window?'

'Red herring?' Gloria suggested.

'That's what it feels like to me,' I admitted. 'Or like somebody is messing with us.' Or me, in particular. I glanced over at Faith, who was fiddling with her phone.

'But who? And why?' Tien asked.

'I don't know, but Clare is right that an outsider would have no reason to break in and kill Kate, unless she interrupted something.'

'A robbery?' Sarah was searching her pocket for cigarettes, despite giving up smoking three years ago. 'Maybe a local got wind of the event here at the lodge this weekend and thought it would be good pickings.'

'Kate's bag was open,' I said, chewing on that.

'Which reminds me,' Sarah started. 'Were any of you—'

I put my hand on her leg. 'Not now.'

'Not now what?' Tien asked, suspiciously.

'Let's not send everybody to check their rooms now to see if anything has been taken,' I fudged. I thought Sarah was going to bring up the woman in Kate's room impersonating her, and I wanted to keep that to ourselves.

'My bag was zipped closed,' I continued, 'though that doesn't mean somebody didn't go through it.'

Harold was nodding. 'Maybe they were inside Lita's room when Kate came in. They attacked her and then hid somewhere before bailing out your window when we all came back out here.'

'You caught a glimpse of somebody going by in the hall,' Sarah reminded me.

Like I needed reminding. I hadn't wanted to mention the person I almost hit with the door, since I assumed it was the same person who was in Kate's room. Now it was out there, though.

Not that anybody noticed. 'Maybe somebody was hiding in your closet,' Clare suggested.

'No closet in our room,' I said. 'Just a rack for hanging clothes.'

'Oh.'

'What do you think about a local?' I asked Cabot. 'Is there much breaking and entering around here?'

'Not so you would notice. I suppose kids from town might get up to something, but . . .' He lifted his shoulders in a shrug.

Lita stirred. 'There are lots of people who disappear into the woods up here for all sorts of reasons.'

'Living off the grid?' Faith had finally taken an interest, probably because Lita had spoken. 'That is so cool.'

'Some of them are probably city folk, like me, imagining themselves to be stylishly self-sufficient,' Lita continued. 'But there are . . . others.'

'Others?' we chorused.

I, for one, had goosebumps. We had journeyed from annoying bugs and critters in the woods to a violent electrical storm to one of our number being killed. And now there were . . . "others"?

'Oh, I don't mean the living dead or anything,' she said, holding up her hands. 'But I remember my grandfather telling me that there were people who lived deep in the woods who didn't want to be found.'

'I suppose somebody like that might steal.' Clare seemed

creeped out, too, but trying to be charitable. 'Not because of greed, but out of necessity.'

But did they kill?

'Kate was killed in Lita's room,' I said. 'Maybe that's significant.'

'Nobody could have expected her to be there,' Sarah said. 'So—'

'Stop.'

All eyes turned to Lita.

She was holding up both her hands. 'I know you people love to spin your mysteries, but are you saying that some thief or vagrant broke into my room to rob me and hit Kate?'

'I'm afraid it's more complicated than that,' I told our host. 'It appears she hit her head – or was hit – but then we believe somebody suffocated her. There are petechial hemorrhages in her eyes – tiny red pinpoint ruptures that usually indicate a person was struggling to breathe.'

'Suffocated.' She was clearly stunned, though the rest of our group were nodding like I had just confirmed what they had suspected all along. 'You're sure.'

I reminded myself of what Pavlik would say. Which, naturally, was far less than I already had said. But I did add his caveat: 'Nobody can be absolutely certain until the autopsy. But—'

'You're sure.'

'Pretty much,' Sarah said.

'But why?' she demanded, tears welling in her eyes. 'If it was simple robbery, the thief would have run. But to put your hands around a person's throat and . . . why?'

Lita obviously hadn't tipped to why I had a sodden pillowcase in a plastic bag. I struggled with whether I should enlighten her now, but if I didn't Cabot would.

'Whoever it was suffocated her with a pillow,' I told her.

She closed her eyes and then opened them. 'Why does that seem better somehow? The fact she didn't have to look her killer in the face.'

'It was probably easier for the killer,' I told her. 'But I'm pretty sure Kate was unconscious when she was suffocated.'

'Didn't feel a thing.' She said it bitterly and then seemed

to gather herself. 'But, again, why would somebody do this? As you say nobody up here even knows Kate.'

'Except us, of course,' Gloria said. 'And some of us liked Kate more than others.'

'Oh my God, can we get out of here?' Faith exploded. 'I have no interest in playing *Clue* with the rest of these people.'

'Faith, please.' Jerome had been sitting quietly, his face drawn. 'You may not have cared about Kate, but I did.'

Faith opened her mouth and then closed it again.

'Kate was killed with my pillow,' Lita said, struggling to understand. 'In my room. What was she doing in there?'

'I'm so sorry.' Cabot sat forward, suddenly stricken with guilt. 'It's my fault. I told Kate that you said to go ahead and start without her. She was concerned that she didn't have the syllabus and I said maybe it was in the box you sent ahead.'

'When was this?' Lita asked.

'I'm not sure,' Cabot said. 'It was after you told me you were running late because of the rain and would be here about seven thirty.'

'We need to make a timeline and list of where everybody was when,' I said. 'We arrived at maybe five thirty?'

Sarah nodded. 'Kate said it was just after six when she started her talk and that had to take, what? A half hour?'

'Felt like more,' Harold said. 'She wouldn't let me go have a smoke.'

'No smoking on the property,' Cabot said, with a glance at Lita.

'We also had a discussion about the fact there is no cell service or Wi-Fi and that took a while,' Tien said. 'It had to be more like six forty-five when Kate left to gather her papers – presumably including the syllabus.'

Clare raised her hand. 'She said we would convene in fifteen minutes.'

'But she never came back?' Lita asked, sitting forward. 'Why didn't somebody go look for her?'

Guilty silence, since the truth was that we were happy to have her gone – and not talking at us – for a while.

'I started back to ask her about dinner but got distracted

somehow,' Sarah volunteered. 'I don't remember exactly why—'

'The phone rang,' I reminded them.

'Oh, yes,' Cabot said, turning. 'It was you, Lita.'

'That aborted call,' she said. 'I should have known it wouldn't get through. I could barely hear you. But at least I can check to see what time I placed the call.' Standing to fetch her purse, which she had left with the duffel by the door, she took out her phone and held it up. 'Seven fourteen.'

'After that we decided to make sandwiches and start the fire and that's when the lightning struck the chimney,' I told Lita as she sat back down.

'And you were all in the dark when I arrived.'

'And still are, sadly,' Cabot said, getting up and retrieving his coat from the back of the chair. 'Let me get back to work on that generator.'

'I'll go with you,' Faith said, seeming to want out of the room. She glanced at Jerome as she followed Cabot to the door, but he wasn't looking at her.

'You can take my rain jacket,' Lita told her, nodding at Cabot. 'It's in the closet.'

He opened the closet door and retrieved the coat.

'Oohh, Burberry,' we heard Faith breathe as she pulled it on.

'Just to complete the timeline,' I said as the door closed behind Faith and Cabot, 'I think it was just after seven thirty when we found Kate's body, right?' I should have checked the time.

Sarah was shaking her head. 'More like quarter to eight. Lita arrived around seven thirty, then Jerome came back with the lanterns and then you and I went to look for her.'

'A full hour after she left us then,' Tien said. 'Wow.'

'I should be able to confirm . . .' Jerome pulled his eyes away from the door through which Cabot and Faith had disappeared and took out his phone. 'Yes, the first photo I took was time-stamped eight-oh-eight, so that jibes.'

'I didn't think to ask you to take photos until we moved everybody out of the room.' Another blunder.

'We never did eat and now it has to be going on nine,'

Harold muttered to Gloria. 'For some reason every time somebody says the word "syllabus" I get even hungrier.'

'You're thinking of syllabub,' she said, patting his arm. 'British dessert thingy. You've probably seen it on my cooking shows.'

'Ah, yes.' He settled back.

I knew what a syllabus was, but I was still hungry. 'Maybe we could make those grilled cheese sandwiches now.'

'Tomato soup and grilled cheese for dipping,' Tien said, hopping up. 'It was my backup for lunch, because I planned roast chicken with lemon orzo, and red-wine-glazed beef short ribs for our two evening meals here. I'm afraid that's not going to happen, given the power outage and . . . all.'

'You're killin' me,' Harold said, rubbing his somewhat rotund tummy. 'But I do love me a good cheese toastie.'

'You stay, Maggy,' Clare said, as I got up. 'I'll help Tien.'

I started to sit back down but Sarah had already appropriated the whole chair. I went to take Tien's seat instead but hesitated. 'I should write this all down. Does anybody have paper and pen or should I go get some?'

'There's probably some in my room,' Lita said, standing up. 'Though . . . would you mind coming with me, Maggy?'

'Of course not,' I said, taking a lantern from the table to light the way.

Swinging open the door to the guest wing, I let her precede me into the hall. When she hesitated, I cocked my head. 'Are you sure you want to go in there?'

'I'm sure I *don't* want to go in there,' she said, and steeled herself before pulling open the door.

There was a part of me that expected Kate's body to be gone like none of this had ever happened. But no, she still lay on the floor.

'I'm sorry.' Lita averted her eyes. 'It's horrible for her to be just lying there like this, broken and bloody. Can't we cover her with something?'

'No,' I said. 'Whatever blanket or sheet we used could transfer evidence to the body. False – or at least misplaced – evidence.'

'You do know about these things,' she said, following my lead to stay on the perimeter of the room. 'Everybody else, too, seems really . . . well, for the want of another expression, into it?'

I flinched. 'Yeah, I'm sorry about that.'

'Don't get me wrong, I'm glad you're here,' she said, touching my shoulder. 'In fact, I need to tell you something. That's why I suggested we get the paper. Which' – she peered around the room – 'is here somewhere.'

'Don't worry about that now.' I set the lantern on the dresser, careful to keep it away from the blood evidence. 'What did you want to tell me?'

'How well do you know this Faith girl?'

The question surprised me. 'Not at all, really. I just met her here. I don't know how long she and Jerome have known each other, but Kate might—' I stopped.

'I know,' Lita said. 'I forget she's dead, too, and she's laying right there in front of us.' She still didn't look.

'I saw you and Faith talking after we found Kate,' I told her. 'I know she told you about her book on grieving and loss and how she thought it might help you, but I don't blame you for shutting her down. It wasn't the time nor the place.'

'Book?' She seemed surprised.

'Faith writes inspirational books. She told me that she hopes your publishing company—'

Lita was looking at me like I was crazy. 'But I don't have a publishing company. I mean, I'm an investor in the *Observer*, but I did that for Kate. And the paper doesn't publish books, so far as I know.'

'If it did,' I said, 'Faith could have approached Kate instead of you. Or had Jerome do it. She didn't have to come up here.'

'But she came to meet me.'

'So she said, though she also said she didn't want to leave Jerome alone with Kate.'

'This is hardly alone.' Lita glanced inadvertently at the body on the floor, before looking back up at me. 'Faith was jealous of Kate?'

'There was gossip when Jerome went to intern for Kate. You know, older woman taking a young photographer under her wing. I goaded her about it.' I swallowed hard. 'But I don't think there was anything to it.'

'She never said anything to me about him,' Lita said. 'If that means anything.'

It didn't anymore. One way or the other. 'So what were you and Faith talking about, if it wasn't the book?'

'That's what was strange,' Lita said, cocking her head. 'She has this idea that we're related. Second cousins or something.'

That had come out of nowhere. 'And are you?'

She shrugged. 'Not that I know of. But according to her, the same Marvin Payne who lived here—'

'Your grandfather?'

'Yes, my grandparents were Berte and Marvin. Anyway, Faith says that Marvin had a daughter out of wedlock before he and Berte married and had my father.'

'Then your father and that daughter were half-siblings,' I said. 'And Faith is her daughter?'

'Granddaughter, but to be honest I was so upset about Kate I didn't take it all in.'

'I can't believe she would choose that moment to talk to you about it.'

'I know, but I had the sense it had been building up. She had texted me, but I'm afraid I just ignored it. I had no idea she would be here, and I do get a lot of people contacting me, wanting—'

'Money?' I said, feeling a little sheepish about our own plan. 'But do many actually try to claim they're long-lost relatives in this day and age? They would have to know that DNA can prove or disprove it in an instant.'

'You would be surprised.' She shrugged.

'Do you think this has something to do with Kate's death?'

'I honestly don't know,' she said, rubbing her hand over her forehead. 'I just thought you should know. Especially since, as you say, Kate was killed in my room.'

'True.' I pursed my lips. 'But all of us here, including Faith, knew you hadn't arrived yet, so it couldn't be a case of mistaken identity.'

'I know,' she said. 'But . . .'

'But?' There was something she hadn't told me.

'If somehow she found out . . .' She let that sentence fade off, too.

'Found out what?'

She met my eyes. 'I don't have a husband or kids. Or any relatives at all, at least that I know of. But I do have a will that leaves several bequests to charity, of course. A hospital in New York, an animal shelter, a school.'

'And the rest?'

'Goes . . . or would have gone, to Kate.'

TEN

'You do know what that means?' I asked. We were still standing by the dresser in Lita's room, still trying not to look at Kate's body on the floor of that room.

Lita's face paled in the lantern light, the freckles standing out in stark relief. 'That my will was the reason Kate was killed? The fact that she's a beneficiary?'

'That, too,' I admitted, 'but of more immediate concern, it could mean that your life is in danger.'

Her mouth dropped open.

'There's nothing we can do for Kate,' I said, 'but we can make sure that you're with one of us at all times until the police get here. Which I hope will be first thing in the morning.'

'One of you?' she repeated. 'Listen, I don't mean to be paranoid—'

'Oh, no,' I said, 'be as paranoid as you like. It's healthy at this point.' As far as I was concerned it wasn't unreasonable to fear for your life when your life, indeed, was in danger.

'Well,' she said, her face reddening, 'the fact is that one of you – maybe Faith, but we don't know that for sure – killed Kate. And even if it was Faith, we don't know she acted alone.'

'I certainly wouldn't leave you with Faith. Or Jerome, even though I would trust him with my life.'

She looked alarmed at that.

I put up my hands and waved her off. 'But not with your life, of course.'

'What about the rest of them?' Lita asked.

I rubbed my forehead, not sure how honest I should be.

'Don't get me wrong. I know that Kate wasn't easy.' She laughed. 'She's been bossing me around for most of my life. I don't think she knows . . . knew how she comes off sometimes.'

I sighed, leaning with my backend against the dresser. I couldn't avoid seeing Kate's body in that direction, but maybe it was time to stop avoiding it. 'I've known Kate for maybe fifteen years, so certainly not as long as you have. At times, I even found myself liking her.' I couldn't help equivocating even more. 'A little.'

'But . . .' Lita turned so she was also facing Kate.

'She seemed to be getting progressively . . . meaner.' I held up a hand. 'I don't use that word lightly. But she was using the paper and her opinion pieces almost as a weapon. People were becoming afraid of her.'

'And fear begets hate,' Lita said sadly, turning away from her friend. 'She must have been so lonely.'

'I'm sure she was,' I said. 'But that didn't stop her. I know you wrote the syllabus for the workshops up here, but do you know what she wanted people to write about?'

'These creative prompts?' She made a face. 'I didn't really understand what that was.'

'Neither did the participants until they got up here. What she wanted was for people in the group – Harold, Gloria, Clare, even me and Sarah – to take hurtful episodes in our lives and write about them. Probe them, exacerbate them, make them even worse than they had been.'

'I still don't get it,' Lita said, wrinkling her nose.

'Probably the best illustration is Harold,' I said. 'He was a driver for Brookhills County. Garbage trucks all year round, but also snowplows in the winter.'

'He was a driver, past tense?'

'Yes,' I said. 'I won't go into detail, but one morning Harold left his snowplow unattended, and somebody was killed.'

'That's horrible,' Lita said.

'It was and, as it turns out, it really wasn't his fault. But Kate wrote a scathing editorial and Harold was fired – or took early retirement, if you want to position it the way the county did.'

'And Kate expected Harold to write a story about it?' She tapped her fingernail on the dresser. 'You don't suppose she was trying to help him to exorcise his demons?'

'Kate was Harold's demon.' I was getting angry at the now dead editor all over again. 'How about this one? Gloria's elderly husband Hank was killed in a hunting accident, accidentally shot by the man he was hunting with. Kate insinuated in an editorial that Hank was drunk. And what happens when we get up here? Kate tells Gloria to write a story in which she, Gloria, and this hunting partner plotted to kill Hank because they were having an affair.'

'Oh my God,' Lita said, hand to her face. 'Vintage Kate. I'm sure she had no idea how insensitive she was being.'

And I was equally sure that Kate was completely aware, but I had bad-mouthed Lita's dead friend long enough. So I kept my mouth shut, despite wanting to ask how Lita would feel if the shoe was on the other foot and Kate suggested using her parent's drunk-driving accident as a prompt.

'But if everybody disliked Kate so much,' she said now, 'why did they come up here this weekend?'

Fear? Curiosity? To kill her?

'I've been asking that question all weekend.' I stopped. 'Geez, it's still Friday night, isn't it? It seems we've been here for days.'

Lita dipped her head and then raised it. 'Have you considered the possibility that one or more of these people – your friends – may have come here to kill Kate?'

Sure, that possibility had raised its ugly, suspicious head. I was me, after all.

But these were my friends and, though I was willing to talk through the possibility of an accidental panic-killing with Sarah, I wasn't about to share that with Lita.

'Come here expressly to kill Kate? No.' So let's talk about Lita's friends, instead. 'What about Cabot?'

'What about Cabot?' Lita seemed astonished. 'He worked for my grandparents before they died, and he didn't even know Kate.'

'And he's not in your will?'

'No, I told you who's in my will. Cabot received a bequest from my grandparents and I pay him a good salary and give him a free place to live,' she said. 'It's a pretty cushy job.'

I wondered if Cabot felt that way. 'Well, this probably isn't getting us anywhere. We have a timeline of sorts – now we need to write it down and see where everybody was from six forty-five, when Kate left the room, to when Sarah and I found her body. Then we'll know for sure who to trust.' If anyone.

'Which means we still need paper, I guess,' Lita said, opening and closing the top drawer. 'There must be some somewhere.'

'Maybe on the shelves?' As I crossed to them, I saw that most of the books must have been there for years with a few newish novels and autobiographies tossed in. There was also a crammed pencil holder, textbooks, yearbooks, a small can of paint and stacks of discolored photographs. 'Was some of this your grandparents'?'

'Most of it,' she said, joining me. 'I just left what they had on the shelves and added my stuff to it.'

'Well, I don't see any pads of paper.' Turning, I caught sight of the cardboard box Sarah had kicked. 'Did you put any notebooks or pads of paper in the box you sent ahead?' It seemed like something the conference would supply, maybe even with their very own Payne Lodge Writes logo imprinted on them.

'My secretary packed the mailing boxes, so I'm not sure what's in that particular one.' She stopped short, as she bent down to look at it. 'The box hasn't been slit open.'

I had noticed that too. 'I guess Kate didn't get that far.'

We observed a spontaneous moment of silence.

'I saw a letter opener in the pencil jar on the shelves,' I said, going to get it and moving the box into the light in order to slit the tape.

'No syllabuses that I can see,' I said, peering in. 'But there are notebooks and pens.' With the logo on them as I had suspected.

'Good,' Lita said, taking a stack of notebooks from me. 'Now, let's go back and see who . . .'

'Could have done it,' I finished.

The buttery smell of toasting sandwiches filled the main lobby as we returned.

'Oh my God,' Lita said, as I held the door for her. 'I didn't realize how hungry I am. Though how can I even think about that, given what's happened?'

'We still have to eat,' I said, glancing around to see only Sarah, Gloria, Harold and Jerome in the chairs by the fireplace. 'Where is everybody else?'

'Tien and Clare are still in the kitchen,' Harold said. 'Hopefully they'll be out soon with a big pile of sandwiches.'

'You could go help,' Gloria said, elbowing him.

'Well, yes. Guess I could.' He hefted himself up and started for the kitchen.

'Is he limping?' I asked, settling into a chair as Lita did likewise. 'What happened?'

'His sciatica is acting up,' Gloria said. 'Or so he says.'

'You don't believe him?' I intended to ask questions about anything out of the ordinary.

'No,' Gloria said, looking surprised. 'Why wouldn't I believe him?'

'Maggy probably thinks he hurt himself leaping out of our window,' Sarah said.

'You know me too well,' I said with a rueful grin. 'Where are Faith and Cabot? Not back yet?'

'No,' Jerome said, his expression dark. 'I don't know what's going on there.'

Lita and I exchanged looks.

'How long have you and Faith been going out?' I asked Jerome.

'Almost a month.' He was still brooding.

'Interesting.' Lita caught my eye.

'Why are you two doing that?' Sarah demanded.

'Doing what?' I asked.

'Exchanging meaningful glances.'

I glanced at Lita.

'Stop it!' Sarah snapped.

'You can tell them,' Lita said. 'In fact, it's probably the best time, since Faith isn't here.'

'What's this all about?' Jerome asked.

I could tell he was angry with Faith, but also felt protective in some way.

'Faith lied to us,' I told him. 'Or at least she lied to me. She said she was here because she wanted to meet Lita.'

'That's right,' Jerome said, standing up and turning to Lita. 'To see if your publishing company would publish her new book.'

'As I told Maggy' – Lita ran her hand through her short blonde hair – 'I don't have a publishing company.'

'And even if she did,' I continued, 'that's apparently not why Faith is here.'

'Oh, she has some crazy idea I'm involved with Kate, if that's what you mean,' Jerome said. 'I told her it's not true.'

'But it would give her a reason to dislike Kate,' Sarah said, now exchanging meaningful looks with Lita and me, too.

'You mean, dislike Kate enough to kill her?' Jerome asked incredulously, as Harold emerged from the kitchen with a plateful of sandwiches.

'Well, somebody killed her,' Sarah said, helping herself to a sandwich as Harold passed her with the plate. 'And the fact is that most everybody here disliked Kate on some level, even hated her.'

Harold was about to set the plate on one of the coffee trunk tables and nearly dropped it.

'Steady there,' Jerome said, reaching out to level the plate. 'I'm sure that's not true in your case.'

'No, it is,' Harold said, restacking the diagonally cut sandwiches. 'I mean, not like I'm going to slit-her-throat kind of hate—'

'Or suffocate-her kind?' Sarah asked, just to be sure.

'No, not that either,' Harold said. 'I just think she's an opportunistic bitch who likes to torture people and will do anything to sell papers. Or would do anything.' He glanced over at Lita and colored up. 'Sorry.'

'No, I . . .' She cleared her throat. 'Maggy was telling me about Kate's mean little "creative prompts—"'

'More like probes than prompts,' Gloria said. 'How would you feel if somebody brought up the most devastating event in your life and twisted the knife? Even worse, wanted you to twist the knife?'

'I wouldn't do it,' Lita said, raising her chin. It trembled just a bit.

'Well, we didn't know that was her plan until we got here, now, did we?' Gloria said, standing to face her, fists balled. 'I thought this was a good chance to get away together,' she hesitated, and added, 'all of us, on her dime.'

More like our dime – Sarah and me.

Now it was Lita who flushed. 'I'm so sorry, Gloria. Maggy told me what Kate suggested about the death of your husband.'

'Well, aren't you just a wealth of information, Maggy?' Gloria said, glaring at me as she went to sit back down. 'Are you two thinking I killed Kate? Or that Harold and I did?'

'I don't suppose Harold was Hank's hunting partner?' Sarah asked.

'Of course not,' Gloria snapped.

'Honestly,' I told Sarah, 'you're nearly as bad as Kate was.'

'Listen,' Lita said. 'I'm well aware that Kate would do anything, almost, for a story. Or to make herself important. And that might have been partially my fault.'

'Because you own the paper?' I asked.

'Own the majority share,' she amended. 'And it wasn't like I was pressuring her for profits. I could have cared less, but I think Kate wanted to prove to me that she had made a success out of it.' A tear just escaped from her right eye. She swiped at it. 'It was a matter of pride for her.'

'She was proud,' Jerome said, his own eyes looking a little watery. 'And more vulnerable than she ever let on.'

'I haven't seen that side,' I admitted, 'but then I didn't know Kate in the same way either you or Lita did. We've always been adversaries in some way.'

'She said a journalist's role is to ask questions people don't want to answer and raise issues they prefer to keep buried.' Jerome rubbed his eye with his fist. 'And whatever her faults, she helped me a lot in my career when no one else believed in me. I would have done anything for her.'

'She was a good writer, too,' Harold said, a little shame-faced. 'An excellent writer, actually. I want to be a good writer, too, so I was willing to take the shit. It's as simple as that. I'll go get plates and napkins.' He went back to the kitchen.

'And soup?' Gloria called, getting up to go after him. 'Are we still having soup?'

'Harold is right about the writing, you know,' Lita said with a little smile as the kitchen door closed. 'Kate had a gift for storytelling from early on.'

'But I'm still trying to understand about Faith,' Jerome said, moving to Gloria's chair which was next to mine. 'You believe she came here to kill Kate *and* meet Lita?'

'I don't know about killing Kate,' I said. 'But Faith did want to meet Lita, like she said. Just not because she wanted to be published by her.'

'She came to tell me that we're related,' Lita said, leaning toward us. 'She and I. I'm not sure whether I believe her.'

'I swear,' Jerome said, shaking his head, 'she told me nothing about this.'

'Was the planning for this weekend already in progress when you met her?' I asked.

He thought about that. 'Yes, it had to be, because when Faith asked me if I knew Lita, I told her about the retreat.'

'You said you've been going out for about a month,' I said. 'Where did you meet?'

'The *Observer*.'

'She came to the newspaper?' Sarah asked. 'It's a hole-in-the-wall office for a weekly rag.' She raised her hand to Lita in apology. 'Why would she do that?'

'She was looking for a writing job,' Jerome said. 'Kate told her pretty abruptly that she wasn't hiring and, when Faith kind of teared up, I suggested we go for a cup of coffee.'

'That's really sweet.' Tien was carrying a heavy white soup tureen and set it down on the second trunk. Clare followed her with bowls and spoons, Harold with plates and napkins and Gloria brandished a silver soup ladle.

'But did she really want a job or was she snooping?' I posed. 'I mean, if she was researching Lita online, she would probably be able to tell that she was an investor in the *Observer*.'

'Maybe she was doing both,' Sarah said. 'If Faith got a job with the paper, she might logically think it would give her access to Lita, not knowing she was hands-off.'

'Possible,' Lita said, waving off Tien's offer of soup. She did help herself to half a sandwich, though. 'Does Faith live in Brookhills?'

All eyes turned to Jerome. 'She has an apartment in Milwaukee. If you're asking if she's originally from south-eastern Wisconsin, though, I couldn't swear to it.'

He picked up a sandwich and then went to set it back down on the chest.

'Here you go.' Harold slid a plate underneath it and then straightened, rubbing his back.

'Thanks.' Jerome seemed to be struggling with this new information. 'Are you telling me Faith started dating me because she wanted to come here?'

'No, no,' I assured him.

'No?' Sarah raised her eyebrows. 'This weekend was by invitation only.'

'She might have thought that dating Jerome would give her access to Lita,' Clare said, passing a bowl to Tien to fill using Gloria's ladle. 'Since she didn't get the job.'

'That's true,' Sarah said. 'And when he told Faith about this event, I'm sure she jumped at the chance of coming.'

'She did,' he admitted. 'Practically begged me to get Kate to let her come.'

'Come with *you*,' Tien emphasized. 'Part of the *Observer* family, so she'd have greater access.'

'Little did she know this was such a podunk event,' Sarah said. 'She could have walked right in and shot Lita without anybody raising a hand.'

The victim in question gasped.

'I think what Sarah means—' I started.

'What Sarah means,' my partner said, taking the bowl of soup Tien passed her and dipping the corner of her sandwich. 'Mmm.'

We all sat and watched her chew.

'What?' she said, after she swallowed.

'You were going to explain what you mean about Faith

being able to walk in here and shoot Lita,' I reminded her sweetly. 'Because apparently I couldn't do it well enough, despite spending the last three-plus years explaining practically every word that comes out of your mouth to our customers.'

'Wow, a little pent-up hostility there.' Sarah wiped her mouth. 'What I meant was that if this was some big conference with a lot of attendees and speakers, she might not have gotten close to somebody like Lita. But here . . .' She shrugged.

'I'm still missing why she would want to shoot me,' Lita said, frowning.

'Oh, I can tell you that.' Having relinquished her ladle duties, Gloria was ready to jump back into the conversation. 'You said that Faith believes she's related to you. You're a rich woman and, as Maggy said, Faith was probably doing research on you. Assuming she came up with the same facts that seem to be public knowledge amongst us here, she would know that you have no other living relatives and, therefore, she could shoot you and claim the estate.'

'Not if she killed her,' Harold corrected. 'You can't benefit from committing a homicide.'

'Slayer rule,' I said, nodding. 'It's a US law of inheritance that you can't inherit the estate of a person you've murdered.'

'I'm not sure why you both know that,' Lita said, wiping a buttery hand on a napkin. 'But I'm gratified there's a law like that. It makes perfect sense.'

Sarah had finished slurping her soup and put the bowl down. 'Obviously, I used "shooting Lita" as an illustration. Faith wouldn't do that.'

'Thank you,' Lita said. 'That makes me feel—'

'No, Faith would be sneakier than that. She would either kill you in a way that looks to be an accident, or she would pin it on somebody else. That way she still could inherit.'

Lita swallowed hard, probably trying not to upchuck her half a grilled cheese. 'But that only works if I died intestate, right? I have a will.'

'Of course you would,' Tien said, filling a bowl for herself. 'People who have money make wills. Faith had to realize that.'

'But that may be where Kate's death comes in,' I said.

Everybody turned to me, but I was looking at Lita, 'Do you want to tell them?'

'I guess I'll have to now,' she said and sighed. 'Kate was my beneficiary.'

'Wow,' Jerome said. 'That was generous of you. I mean, if Kate had lived to inherit. And you died.' He shut his mouth, since he was very obviously making a mess of things.

I eyed Jerome. My young friend was not at his best at the moment, and understandably so. His mentor was killed, and his girlfriend apparently was using him and had disappeared with another man. Even so, I felt like something else was off.

'But Kate did die,' Tien was saying as she took the chair on the other side of me with her soup. 'And if Faith killed her, she knew perfectly well that she was killing Kate, not Lita, because Lita hadn't arrived yet.'

'But now that Kate's dead,' I said, nodding my head to encourage her. 'If Lita should die and Faith can prove she's related, Faith could inherit Lita's estate. But if it had been the other way around, with Lita dying before Kate, then Kate's heirs would be next in line.'

'That's genius,' Tien said, her eyes wide.

'Glad you think so,' Lita said. The woman was more than a little shell-shocked. 'I don't suppose anybody smuggled in a bottle of wine? I could really use a glass right now.'

I was a little surprised at the question, considering the lodge's no-alcohol policy and what Kate had told us about the accident that killed her parents. Still, I wasn't one to judge and, besides, nobody was driving anywhere tonight. 'I did.'

'Not me,' Gloria said, shaking her head. 'I brought bourbon.'

'Do you want red or white wine?' Sarah asked Lita.

'Red,' Lita said in a little voice.

'Who has red – can we have a show of hands?'

Mine and Tien's went up.

'I've got red, too,' Sarah said, standing. 'I'll get that and Maggy's from our room.'

'You have a corkscrew?' Tien called after her. 'There's none in the kitchen, as you might expect.'

'You kidding?' Sarah said over her shoulder as she pulled open the door to the hallway. 'I never leave home without one.'

ELEVEN

In the end, two bottles of Pinot noir, one Cabernet, one Sauvignon blanc, one oaky Chardonnay, a bottle of bourbon, a bottle of brandy and Jerome's six-pack of Spotted Cow farmhouse ale were produced.

'I have peppermint schnapps, too,' Harold said, as he sipped his brandy from a water glass. 'If anybody wants some.'

'Before we get too schnockered, let's get this timeline down in writing,' I said, gesturing for Sarah to take a pen and one of the notebooks. 'Put down "Five thirty, arrival."'

'Five thirty-ish,' Clare corrected.

'Most of the times are going to be "ish,"' I said. 'We'll just stipulate that.'

'You write, Maggy,' Sarah said, passing the writing implements on to me. 'We'll all give you times. It'll go faster.'

'Want to get back to your wine?' I looked up at her with a grin. 'Though you haven't put it down.'

'Write,' she said, gesturing with the glass.

Ten minutes later, I read out what I'd written:

5:30 p.m.	Arrival
6 p.m.	Kate gathers us by fireplace and speaks
6:45 p.m.	Kate leaves to get syllabus, says we'll reconvene in 15 minutes
7:13 p.m.	Sarah offers to find Kate to ask about dinner
7:14 p.m.	Aborted call from Lita

I looked up. 'Do you know where you were when you called?'

Her nose wrinkled. 'Not exactly. But it would have been in the stretch of road where I thought there might be service. Maybe about three miles out?'

'That matches up with what Cabot thought,' I said, noting it. 'So . . .'

7:14 p.m.	Aborted call from Lita approx. 3 miles out
7:25 p.m.	Cabot goes to start the fire – lightning strike, power goes out
7:30 p.m.	Lita arrives

Clare raised her hand. 'It was seven thirty-one. I remember looking at my phone.'

I changed it.

7:31 p.m.	Lita arrives; introductions
7:35 p.m.	Jerome and Cabot go out to get lanterns, start generator
7:40 p.m.	Jerome back with lanterns Sarah and Maggy go to find Kate and tell her Lita has arrived
7:45 p.m.	Sarah and Maggy find Kate's body

I chewed on my lip. 'It had to be a few minutes later. We must have spent a good ten minutes in our room and checking out the others before we went into Lita's.'

'So it was seven fifty,' Sarah said, a little irritably. 'Like you said, most of this isn't exact.'

I made the change and set down the notebook. 'Either way, we waited way too long before going to look for Kate. Maybe we should see where Cabot and Faith have gotten to.'

Jerome held up his hands in double stop signs. 'Not me. I'm betting they're in Cabot's cabin and I don't necessarily want to see what they're doing.'

'Cabot's cabin?' I repeated. 'Where is that?'

'Behind the garage. It's one of the three cabins on the property.' Lita had downed a glass of Pinot and seemed considerably calmer. 'The only one, really, that's been cleaned up at all.'

'He's been gone a while,' I said. 'Didn't he go to start the generator?'

'Yes, and it is on,' Tien said. 'At least it's powering the refrigerator and freezer in the kitchen.'

'What about the lights?' I asked. 'We've been using the lanterns and our phones. Has anybody tried them?'

'No.' Sarah rolled her eyes and got up. 'Anybody know where the switch is?'

'There's one by the front door and one in the café,' Tien said. 'Next to the door to the kitchen.'

Sarah flipped the latter, and the track lighting in the ceiling flickered on.

'Now don't we feel stupid,' I said, leaning over to extinguish a lantern. 'Are we sure it's the generator? Maybe all the electricity is back on.'

'Afraid not,' Sarah said. 'I have my phone plugged into this outlet by the counter and it's not charging.'

'The outlet could be defective,' I suggested. 'Try another.'

Sarah obliged. 'Nope.'

I had an idea. 'The landline is back there, too, right?' I said, getting up to join her behind the café counter. The phone was almond-colored with the wireless handset Cabot had used to try to answer Lita's call.

'It needs electricity, remember?' Sarah said. 'And like I said, apparently these outlets aren't hooked up to the generator.'

'But the kitchen refrigerator and freezer must be,' I said. 'We'll unplug one of them, plug the phone into that outlet and call nine-one-one.'

'Great idea,' Clare said.

But behind the counter, I had already found a snag in my plan. 'The telephone line is too short,' I said, holding up the cord that ran from the phone's base to the jack in the wall. It was only about six feet. Not long enough to reach the kitchen.

I stepped into the kitchen to look for another telephone jack, but came up empty. The freezer was in the far corner of the room, humming away. The refrigerator and the outlet it was plugged into were closer, but not close enough. 'Damn.'

Harold had followed me in. 'How about we leave the phone where it is and run an electrical extension cord to the plug? Assuming we can find one long enough.'

'What do you think?' I asked, surveying the distance. 'Fifteen feet?'

'I would say so.'

Jerome stuck his head in. 'I think I saw a box of cords of various types in the room at the back, the one with the lanterns and the washers and dryers. There might even be a longer telephone cord.'

Perfect. I loved having options.

'We should check the generator anyway,' Harold said. 'If Jerome is right and Cabot is otherwise occupied, it could run out of fuel.'

'True,' Jerome said, as we returned to the main room. 'The generator is outside the laundry room or whatever they call it, but Cabot said he had to get the gas from somewhere else.'

It would be nice if the man was here to help us. 'Do you know where that might be, Lita?'

'The garage, I suppose. The gravel drive goes past the lodge here and then around back to the garage. Cabot's cabin is there, too, like I said.'

'Then who wants to go with me to get the cord or cords, check the generator and make sure Faith and Cabot are at his cabin?' I asked. 'We can also pick up gas, if we need it, from the garage.'

No hands went up.

Jerome sighed. 'I'll go. Faith obviously didn't care about me anyway, so seeing the two of them do the dirty shouldn't bother me.'

'*Inflagrante delicto*,' Gloria said, and slapped Harold's back. He winced.

'Are you sure you want to?' I asked Jerome.

'I'll go,' Sarah said, popping up.

'No,' Jerome said. 'I'm—'

I raised my eyebrows. 'A guy?'

'Well, yes. But also kind of responsible for Faith being here.'

'Which is why Sarah and I will go,' I said, and went to peer out the window. Our attention might have been diverted from the storm, but the rain was still coming down just as heavily. 'Does anybody have a spare slicker? I didn't bring my raincoat.'

'*You* wore hot pants,' Sarah said, flinging an arm over my

shoulder and walking me to the door. 'We wouldn't expect you to have anything as practical as a raincoat.'

'There are slickers in the closet by the front door,' Lita said. 'Will you two be OK? I could come with you.'

'We'll be fine,' I said, opening the closet door to pull out the slickers. I handed Sarah hers. 'We just follow the gravel driveway around the house so we can't get lost. We'll stop at the generator room and then continue to the garage.'

'Get another bucket if you can,' Clare said. 'So we can switch them out when we empty this one.'

'Will do,' I said, going back to the circle of chairs by the fireplace to retrieve a lantern. 'Will we be able to tell which cabin is Cabot's?'

'It's closest and has a straw wreath on the door,' Lita said. 'The others are deeper into the woods.'

'Gotcha,' I said, and opened the door.

Sarah preceded me out and stopped to put up her hood as I closed the door behind me and did the same. 'It's silly, but it kind of choked me up when you mentioned my shorts,' I said.

'Because you're sentimentally attached to your hot pants?' she asked, leading the way.

'Because Kate gave me crap about them.' I tilted my head down to keep the rain off my face. 'And now she's dead and will never give me crap again.'

'But I will,' Sarah said. 'And even if I die this weekend, I promise I will come back to haunt you and give you posthumous crap.'

'You're so thoughtful,' I said. 'And a wordsmith, as well.'

'Thank you.' A gust of wind hit us as we rounded the back corner of the house. 'There it is,' I said, pointing at a small frame room with a flat roof that appeared tacked onto the back of the log lodge.

Hurrying to get out of the wind, we flung open the door and stepped in, pulling down our hoods to look around. No Cabot or Faith, but there were two washers and three dryers, one of which looked non-operational, since the drum was pulled halfway out. Shelves with soap and boxes of what appeared to be cleaning supplies lined the room. One shelf was vacant except for a plastic storage box; probably the lanterns had been there.

'Where's the generator?' Sarah asked.

I hit myself on the head. 'Duh. Jerome said it was outside. If it's a gas generator it would asphyxiate anybody in here if it was running.'

'Let's look for the cords first,' Sarah said, pulling boxes off the shelf and opening them.

'Jerome said he saw them,' I said, setting down the lantern. 'So . . . yes, here.' I had taken down the plastic storage box and was digging through a tangled mess of cords.

'Is this a telephone cord?' I asked, holding it up. 'I can never tell the difference between them and the ethernet ones.'

'The ethernet ones are bigger and wouldn't be here,' Sarah said, taking it from me. 'Because there is no ethernet.'

'Good point. Think that's long enough to reach into the kitchen?'

'Looks like the longest one here,' Sarah said. 'But maybe we should take this electrical extension cord just in case.' The orange cord took up most of the box.

'That has to be fifty feet,' I said.

'Nah, probably thirty,' Sarah said. 'Which is perfect.'

I would take her word for it. 'Do you see a bucket for Clare?'

'In the utility sink,' Sarah said, pointing to a plastic tub. 'Bring it over and I'll coil the cords in it.'

I had to admit, Sarah was pretty handy to have around. 'Ready to go back out?'

'Yup,' she said, raising her hood and grasping the handle of the bucket.

Reclaiming my lantern, I pulled my hood back up and pushed open the door with my hip. As I stepped out, the wind grabbed hold of the door before I could block it open for Sarah and slammed it closed in her face. 'Oops. You OK?'

'Barely,' her voice said through the door.

'You want to come out or have me come back in?' I asked, switching the lantern handle into my left hand.

'Come in,' she said.

Puzzled, I wrestled the door open and stepped back in. 'What's wrong?'

'Being almost killed by the door reminded me of the person you almost hit in the hallway just before we found Kate's body. I mentioned that to the rest of the group, but you obviously didn't want me to ask who was in Kate's room at the end of the hall, imitating her voice.'

'It seemed pointless,' I said. 'Faith, assuming it was Faith, is not going to own up. All asking the question would do is alert her to the fact that we know it wasn't Kate in there.'

'Which she has to know, since we found Kate's body mere minutes later.'

'Another reason not to alert her.' I went to the door. 'You coming?'

'Yup.'

I gave the door a mighty shove and successfully held it open for Sarah this time so she could follow me out with her bucket. Leaving the door to slam in the wind, we rounded to the other side and found yet another add-on, this one an open-sided carport structure sheltering the generator.

'Still put-putting along,' I said, sticking my head in. 'There's a gas can here.' I hefted it. 'Empty. We should see if we can get another in the garage.'

'Is there a way to see how much gas is left in the generator?' Sarah asked.

'Probably,' I said. 'But I don't know how. I don't see anything obvious.'

'A touch screen maybe?' Sarah suggested, ducking to see in herself.

'I think this thing was born before touch screens,' I said. 'It looks pretty basic.'

'Sure makes a lot of noise,' Sarah said putting her hands over her ears. 'Grab the empty gas can. If the garage has a gas pump, we can fill it.'

'Garages have their own gas pumps?' I asked, trailing after her to the driveway.

'Maybe,' she said, struggling against the wind. 'Out in the country, working farms sometimes have their own tank for filling the tractors and stuff. Or at least they used to.'

'How do you know so much about farms?'

'My aunt and uncle had a dairy farm when I was a kid. But that was a long time ago.'

'A very long time ago. That must be the garage,' I said, pointing to a large structure.

'What gave it away? The gravel driveway ending at the big ol' door?' Sarah shifted the bucket with the cords in it to her other hand.

'Is that heavy?'

'Yeah, want to trade?' she said, holding it out.

'I'm not the one who had to have a thirty-foot monster cord,' I said, glancing around the corner. 'You see a door somewhere?'

'Other than this big one I just remarked about, you mean?'

'Well, yeah,' I said. 'I don't see any way to open the big door, do you? No touch pad, not that we would know the code anyway. We probably should have asked Lita. And we don't have a remote, so—'

'Here you go.' Sarah reached down to grasp the horizontal handle and lift the door open.

'Well, that was anticlimactic,' I said. 'But you are a wonder at this country stuff. Maybe we *should* start a coffeehouse up here. You can run it. I'll come and visit sometimes.'

'Are you done, Chatty Cathy?' Sarah was standing inside the garage next to a beat-up Toyota Corolla.

'Chatty Cathy?' I said, stepping in to join her out of the wind and the rain. I flipped down my hood. 'You really are dating yourself.'

'It's an expression. I never had the doll because it was considerably before my time.'

'Nineteen fifty-nine to nineteen sixty-five, though a British version was sold into the seventies.' I was looking around the garage. 'No gas pump.'

'A gas pump – key word, gas – would be outside, Sherlock. It's kind of like the generator. Not something you would want inside.'

'I suppose not,' I said, going to the back wall, which was lined with cluttered shelves. 'Here are some more gas cans, though.' I picked one up, identical to mine, then another and another. 'All empty.' I set my can on the shelf with its friends.

'I suppose we could siphon gas out of the car if we had to,' Sarah said, setting down her bucket to lift a clear siphon hose off a hook on the wall. 'If there's gas in the Corolla.'

'We have our van, too,' I said. 'And Jerome's car.'

'Hopefully we won't get to that point,' Sarah said. 'If the power is back on tomorrow morning, we can drive out of here as long as we haven't drained all the cars of fuel.'

'There is the matter of Kate's death, you know. There will be a police investigation by whatever force has jurisdiction up here.'

'Probably the county sheriff,' Sarah said.

'Sadly, not my county sheriff.' I sniffed. 'I miss Pavlik.'

'It's been less than twenty-four hours,' she pointed out. 'I would think being reunited with your favorite Pinot noir would have softened the blow.'

'It didn't,' I said regretfully. 'You know, even if the sheriff up here doesn't prevent us from leaving, there's the matter of the tree across the driveway. We'll need to move that somehow.'

'Or we can just pile into Lita's rental,' Sarah said. 'It's on the other side of the fallen tree.'

'Every word of wisdom that comes out of your mouth amazes me more,' I said, putting my arm around her shoulders. 'Next zombie apocalypse I want you on my side.'

She shook me off, going to the door. 'Where did Lita say Cabot's cabin is?'

'Behind the garage.' I pointed at the bucket she had left inside the door. 'Planning to leave that here?'

'Actually, I think I will until we check out the cabin,' she said, going to retrieve it. She pulled the door down and set the bucket in front of it and under the eaves, so it wouldn't fill with water prematurely.

'I think I see a light flickering,' I said as we rounded the corner of the garage. 'There.'

The cabin was about twenty feet behind the garage, surrounded by towering pine trees that disappeared into the rainy night sky. The only reason we could see the frame structure at all was that the light was on and the branches of the evergreens were sparse close to the ground.

'Norway pines,' Sarah said. 'It's hard to see at night, but they're beautiful trees.'

Who was this woman? 'I can see how someone could disappear up here if they wanted to.'

'The Others,' Sarah said, and a shiver went up my spine. I couldn't see her face, since she was leading, but I hoped she was smiling.

'Think we should make noise?' I asked Sarah as we got closer to the cabin. 'We don't want to surprise them.'

'Because you're afraid they're naked or that they'll shoot us?'

'Either,' I said. 'And especially both.'

'I say we just knock on the door. They've been out here a long time so they should have their clothes back on by now. And who shoots somebody who is polite enough to knock?'

'The Others?' we said in unison.

I laughed, but I still wasn't sure if Sarah was kidding.

Following my partner up the single porch step, I saw the straw wreath on the door. Right cabin, though, as Lita said, no others were in sight anyway. 'You going to knock?'

She did. Then she knocked again. And again.

'Either they're hiding or not here. Only one way to find out.' I reached past her to try the door and it swung open.

I hesitated. 'Cabot? Faith?'

No answer and Sarah and I exchanged looks in the lantern light.

'You have the lantern,' Sarah said. 'You go first.'

'There's a light source in here someplace,' I said, stepping into a living room. The room was furnished with what looked like castaways from the lodge, right down to a matching phone on the counter. An oversized blue and burgundy plaid couch, square barnwood coffee table and navy easy chair faced a fieldstone fireplace. The long flashlight lay on the coffee table, still on. To one side of the room was a small kitchenette with a café table and two chairs and, to the other, a closed door.

'Bedroom must be through here,' Sarah said, reclaiming the

flashlight and going to stand at the closed door. She tapped on it with the light.

'I have a bad feeling about this,' I said, when there was no answer.

'Me, too.' She turned the knob and swung the door open.

The bed was made and empty, except for an opened tote bag at the foot of it. On the dresser stood a wine bottle and two glasses.

TWELVE

'I really thought we were going to find a body in here,' I said as I bent to read the label on the wine. 'Pinot noir. Central coast of California.'

'Can you tell if it was opened recently?' Sarah asked.

'Not really, without drinking it.' I was examining the glasses, being careful not to touch them. One of the glasses was half full, the other nearly empty. 'And I'm not sure that's a good idea.'

Sarah nudged the bag on the bed with the back of her hand. 'Think it's OK to go through this?'

'Probably not,' I said. 'But look in the kitchen and see if there are plastic bags we can use over our hands.'

'No need.' She had the closet door open now and leaned down to pick up something. 'Here's a dry-cleaning bag.' She thrust it at me.

'You want me to do it,' I said uncertainly, glancing at the tote.

'Of course. You're the one who's been touching virtually everything, including Kate's body.'

She was right. And if I did accidentally touch something, the local police only had my fingerprints to exclude if they deemed the cabin a crime scene. Or a continuation of the crime scene inside the lodge.

'It's a Tumi,' I observed, sliding the thin plastic over my hands before going to lift out a pair of jeans and a blouse. A bra and panties were on the bottom of the bag. 'A change of women's clothes.'

'So either Cabot is a cross-dresser and two-fisted drinker or the clothes are Faith's?'

'Can I get back to you on that?' I asked, handing her back the plastic bag.

'Actually,' Sarah said, as she went to toss it on the floor. 'I think I may have my own answer.'

'Are you just going to throw that on the floor?' I asked.

'I'm leaving everything as it was,' she said. 'I would have thought you'd support that.'

'I do. I guess.' Though it just went against my nature. 'So close the closet door and let's go.'

'Well, we know for sure that Faith was here,' Sarah said, not moving.

'Why's that?' I asked and turned to see her holding a dripping Burberry rain jacket. The jacket Lita had lent to Faith.

'What are you thinking?' Sarah asked, as she followed me out onto the porch.

'That thanks to you, we have evidence that Faith was here,' I said, turning. 'And that you got your fingerprints on it.'

She ignored the last. 'The two wine glasses were a bit of a tip-off, too.'

'They were,' I said, frowning. 'Like I said, I was really expecting a body when we walked into that bedroom.'

'It's your nature,' she said. 'But whose body?'

'I suppose Cabot's, if Faith is our killer. Or Faith's, if Cabot is.'

'Don't forget about the Others,' Sarah said. 'They could have killed both of them.'

'There is no Others,' I said, and then thought I would double-check. 'Right?'

My partner illuminated her face from below with the flashlight, classic horror style. 'Right.' She lowered it. 'So where are Cabot and Faith?'

I let out my breath in a groan. 'Being me, I do have to consider the possibility that they've absconded together, having conspired to kill Kate and maybe to still kill Lita.'

'Or that one or both of them is dead, just not here.'

That, too. 'The most innocuous answer is that they returned to the lodge and we missed them somehow.'

'I suppose they could have,' she said. 'Either when we were in the laundry room or the garage.'

'Or there's another route back that we don't know about.'

'Possibly. What else is out here?'

'Two other cabins.' I shrugged. 'Somewhere deeper in the woods and I sure don't intend to try to find them tonight.'

'Agreed,' she said. 'Let's think about this. Cabot goes out to work on the generator and Faith volunteers to go with him. Could they have set it up ahead of time?'

'Maybe,' I said. 'We know that Cabot did get the generator started, so what happened after that? They fool around in Cabot's cottage?'

'Bad form for Cabot, don't you think? I mean, he works here and he's boinking the guests?'

'Bad form or not, there's the open wine bottle in the bedroom with two glasses,' I said. 'I don't see how we get around that.'

'True,' Sarah said, starting away from the door. 'Let's go pick up my bucket at the garage. Even money says Faith and Cabot are back at the lodge as we speak. Boinked or not.'

But they weren't. The rest of the group, though, were still gathered around the fire.

'You're sure Faith and Cabot didn't come back?' I said, perching on the edge of my former chair.

'We've been sitting right here since you left,' Tien said. 'Drinking, yes, but there's no way we missed somebody coming in the front door.'

'Assuming they came in the door,' Harold pointed out. He was sipping a clear liquid. I didn't think it was water.

I frowned. 'Why would they enter through a window?'

He shrugged. 'I don't know. Why was your window open?'

I didn't have an answer for either question.

'*Why* don't I go have a peek in the guest rooms?' Gloria said, setting down her juice glass of bourbon. 'I'll check the windows and knock on the walls. Who knows? Maybe there's a door we don't know about.'

'If there is, I don't know about it either,' Lita said.

'Can't hurt to check,' I told Gloria, thinking at least it would get her up and moving. 'Take Harold with you.'

Gloria turned around. 'Why? I'm perfectly capable.'

'Because you're drinking bourbon and he's drinking peppermint schnapps,' I said. 'If there are two of you, odds are one will remain upright.'

Gloria glared at me.

'Also, because somebody killed Kate.' Sarah apparently didn't want to get on Gloria's bad side again. 'And two other people are missing.'

'Best to stay in pairs,' I told them. 'For now.'

'Faith and Cabot are in a pair,' Jerome said. 'Presumably.'

'Pairing up only works if one of you isn't the killer,' Clare said. 'Trios would be safer.'

'She's right.' Gloria rubbed her chin. 'How do I know the killer isn't Harold?'

'Or Gloria,' Harold said defensively.

Retired pharmacy owner and retired truck driver exchanged suspicious looks.

'So go alone,' Sarah said, waving them off. 'Or, Clare, go with them if you want. Just scream if somebody hits you so we don't trip over your body.'

Gloria cocked her head. 'Coming, Harold?'

'Right away.' The two left.

Clare stayed put, nursing her white wine.

I turned back to the group. 'If Faith did kill Kate—'

Jerome started to protest, but I held up a hand.

'I know you don't want to believe it, but we have to consider it.'

'If Faith killed Kate, then . . .' Sarah invited me to continue.

'Then what about Cabot? Did she go outside with him in order to kill him, too? And why?'

'Maybe he caught her doing something suspicious,' Sarah suggested.

I glanced over at Sarah with an unspoken question, and she nodded. 'As Sarah told you, we saw somebody in the hall just before we found Kate's body.'

'What I didn't tell you,' she took up, 'is that there was somebody in the room at the end of the hall. The room that was assigned to Kate.'

'Who?' Lita asked, sitting up straight.

'We thought it was Kate,' I explained. 'In fact, it sounded like Kate when she answered us.'

'We heard her through the door though,' Sarah reminded me.

'What did she say?' Clare asked.

'She said, "mind?" when we tried the door. Then she slammed it closed and locked it. Said she was changing.'

'But you didn't see her?' Lita asked.

'No, but we told her through the door that you were here,' Sarah said, rubbing her chin.

'And?' Lita asked.

'She grunted.'

'Sure sounds like Kate,' Tien said.

'That's what we thought,' I said, 'until we found Kate dead, not five minutes later.'

'Somebody imitated her voice,' Clare said. 'Who could do that?'

I shrugged. 'We thought maybe Faith. She parroted something that Kate had said earlier in that same bitchy tone.' I raised my hand to Lita. 'Sorry.'

She shook her head. 'It does fit, though, doesn't it? With everything else we've found out about Faith.'

I nodded. 'The question remains, just where *is* she? And Cabot, for that matter. I'm sure you don't want to believe it, Lita, but is it possible that he was in it with her?' If there was an 'it' to be in?

'You think they both took off?' Tien asked, before Lita could answer. 'But how? We're all stuck here.'

'True. There's a tree down, blocking the end of the driveway, and the van and Jerome's car are parked up here.' I turned to Lita again. 'There's also a Toyota in the garage, we saw.'

'That would be Cabot's,' she confirmed. 'I just can't believe he would be a part of this scheme.'

I looked at Sarah. 'You said before that we could get out of here tomorrow morning without moving the tree.'

'By piling into Lita's rental on the other side of it . . . ohh,' Sarah said, tipping to it. 'Maybe that's what one or both of them did.'

'There's only one way to find out,' I said. 'Walk down the driveway and see if the car is gone.'

'Or we could just call for help,' Sarah suggested, getting up to go to the door for the bucket she'd left outside.

'Oh, good,' Clare said, going to take it from her.

'I need these first.' Sarah pulled out the heavy electrical cord and then tipped the bucket to spill the lightweight telephone cord.

'Well, done, you two.' Tien went to untangle the phone cord and held up an end that had a small white box. 'This is a telephone extension cord, see? It has a jack on so we can also use the cord that's already there. Together they should be long enough to reach the kitchen.'

'You mean I didn't have to lug this?' Sarah said, tossing the big orange cord on the floor by the closet.

'The electrical cord? Probably not.' Tien plugged the smaller phone cord into the extension and, stringing the line behind her, carried the phone toward the kitchen. 'Can somebody get the door?'

I went to swing it open. 'Is it going to make it?' I asked as the others trooped in behind us.

'Yup.' She set the phone on the counter and unplugged the refrigerator from the electrical outlet, replacing it with the phone plug. 'All set! You want to do the honors, Maggy?'

'Maybe Lita should,' I said, turning to her. 'After all, it's your property. I don't even know what the address is.'

'I guess I should, though I've never called nine-one-one from here before.' She took the receiver from Tien.

'Just tell them that there's been a death,' I told her. 'They may ask you if you know who the deceased is. They'll also want to know who you are, where you are and maybe whether you think there's any further danger to you or anybody else.'

'You have done this before,' she said, trying to hand me back the phone. 'Please.'

'I—'

'Please,' she said again.

I took the phone and put it to my ear. 'There's no dial tone.'

'I think you have to hit the little green telephone button,' Clare said. 'It's lighted – that's a good sign.'

'Duh.' I pushed the button as directed. 'That did it.' I punched in 9-1-1.

And waited.

'There is nine-one-one service up here, isn't there?' I asked Lita.

'Well, yes. I'm sure so.' Lita didn't look so sure. 'Maybe there's a phone book in one of the drawers in the café.'

'Good idea,' Tien said, as Lita went to look. 'We can find the police or sheriff department's direct number.'

'Or just hit "operator,"' Sarah suggested. 'Have them connect you.'

'Great idea,' I said, pushing the red phone icon and then the green again. 'I can't believe I've forgotten how to use a telephone other than my cell.'

Hearing the dial tone, I went to push '0' as the tone cut out.

'Nothing is happening,' I said, ear still to the phone.

'Maybe there has been a zombie apocalypse,' Sarah suggested. 'Or the Others cut the phone line.'

'Don't be silly,' I said, pushing red and then green again. 'It's just' – I took the phone away from my ear – 'the dial tone is gone.'

'There *is* a speaker on that phone,' Sarah said, nodding to another button, this one with a loudspeaker on it.

'Fine. So now you all can hear what I can hear.' I pushed it. 'Absolutely nothing.'

We tried reconnecting the cords. We tried using the electrical extension cord and not using the telephone extension cord. Nothing.

'You're sure you had a dial tone?' Sarah asked.

'Yes. And then I didn't,' I confirmed. 'I think it cut out just as I went to dial the operator.'

'Probably a lot of lines down.' Harold had returned, with his positive attitude and minty-fresh breath. 'Storm must be getting worse.'

'I assume you didn't find any secret panels or open windows?'

Gloria answered. 'No. Though this one' – she hitched her thumb at Harold – 'insisted on knock-knocking on every wall.'

'What do we do now?' Clare asked.

I was starting to feel claustrophobic, the full log walls of the place closing in to crush me like in some bad movie. 'We walk down and check out the car. We have the big flashlight now.'

'Yeah,' Sarah said, hefting it from the table where she had set it. 'Why wouldn't Cabot have taken this with him wherever he went?'

The answer, of course, was that he was dead, but I wasn't saying it. 'If the car is there, one of us could drive out and get help.'

'I'm not sure I would drive anywhere tonight,' Harold said, shaking his head. 'And I'm a professional.'

'Even walking down won't be easy.' Lita looked dubious. 'It's not a driveway in the city sense. It's got to be close to a half mile long and there was already standing water in parts when I came up.'

Jerome stood abruptly, apparently needing to get out as badly as I did. 'Then we had better get going now, while we've got a bit of a lull.'

It was true that the wind and rain had died down since Sarah and I had come back in.

'Thank you, Jerome,' I said gratefully, pulling my slicker off the hook by the door. 'You coming, Sarah?'

'I don't think so.' She was standing at the side window. 'Does it look weird to you?'

'Weird?' I was already at the door, so I opened it and stepped out. 'It's quiet – not even raining right now. It's a good time to go.'

'Kind of eerie quiet, though,' she said, coming out herself. 'And have you seen the sky over there?'

'Over where?' Jerome joined us.

'You should be able to see it around this corner,' she said, leading us to the side of the lodge where she had been looking out the window. 'See?'

We saw. The sky, even in the dark, had a greenish glow to it.

'I've never seen that at night,' I said. 'But during the day when the sky gets green it can mean severe weather.'

'You mean more severe than we've already been having?' Jerome folded his arms against the cold. 'Maybe it's dawn that we're seeing through the storm clouds.'

I realized with a start that I didn't have any idea what time it was.

'It's not even midnight,' Sarah informed us. 'And besides, that direction is southwest. The sun rises in the east.' She turned to me. 'What do they teach kids these days?'

I think Jerome flushed, but in the green light I couldn't be sure. 'I know where the sun rises. I just didn't know what direction that' – he pointed at the glow – 'was or what time it was. It seems like we've been here more than five or six hours.'

I had to agree with him on that. 'Anyway,' I said, waving them back around to the front door. 'I think we had better wait a bit before setting out.'

'Why?' Jerome asked, hanging back as we got to the door. 'We have a break in the storm.'

'Maybe,' I said, 'but it could just mean the storm is gathering strength.'

'To do what?' Jerome asked, holding both his hands out. 'We've already had intense rain, thunder, lightning and high winds.'

'Spawn a tornado,' I told him, as the wind swirled and picked up, big plops of rain beginning to fall. 'Or maybe sleet or—'

'Ouch,' Jerome said, backing away as he rubbed his head. 'What was that?'

'Hail,' I said, watching the white ball of ice bounce away. 'Golf-ball size, from the looks of it.'

Sarah pulled open the door and we ducked back inside just as all hell broke loose.

THIRTEEN

'I think you're wrong.' Sarah was standing at the window again.

'About the tornado?' I asked. 'Maybe so, but I still wouldn't stand at that window, as you keep telling me. Changing air pressure could blow it right out, not to mention flying debris or hail.'

'The hail is what you're wrong about.' Sarah had a blanket around her shoulders. 'I would say it's more fist-sized than golf ball.'

'Subjective,' I said. 'Whose fist?'

'Mine,' she said, balling it up to faux-threaten me as she turned. 'Want to argue?'

'Fist-sized it is then,' I said, returning to the group that had reassembled by the fire.

'Maggy is right. Better to use absolute terms.' Harold was poking at the fire. 'Maybe hardball or softball. I would vote for hardball.'

'Just as long as it's not soccer,' Tien said, standing up to warm her hands. 'Are we going to need more wood?'

'Maybe so,' I said. 'You would expect them to keep a stack by the door, wouldn't you?'

'Rats,' Gloria said, and our heads all swiveled her way. 'Or mice. They live in wood stacks, so you don't want them too close to the house. It's like inviting the buggers in.'

'That makes perfect sense, even if it's inconvenient at the moment.' I had a thought. 'Did we plug the refrigerator back in?'

'I did,' Tien said, going to sit back down. Odd as it was, we gravitated to the same chairs we had originally, like assigned seats in school.

I shivered. 'Where is the wood then? I didn't see it in the laundry room or garage, did you, Sarah?'

'It was stacked outside the garage, against the back wall,' she told me. 'Probably soaking wet by now.'

'Great,' I said. 'Guess we'll start burning the furniture.'

Lita's chin went up, and then she waved her hand. 'Sure. Why not?'

'I was kidding,' I said, wondering if we needed to worry about her mental health. Any more than the rest of us, that was. 'I'm going to get a blanket from my bed. Anybody else?'

'I'm putting on another layer,' Clare said, getting up to go to her room.

'I already took the blankets from our room,' Sarah said, snuggling.

'And you're using both of them?'

'No, yours is wet,' she said. 'I left it on the floor to dry out.'

Thoughtful. I stood up. 'I'll see what blankets I can rustle up for *everybody*.'

Sarah didn't rise to that, but Lita did, literally.

'I'll go with you,' she said, seeming to have to push herself upright. It couldn't be easy losing a friend and now she had to consider the possibility that her caretaker had a part in it. Or that he was dead himself. 'There's a linen closet.'

'Great,' I said, opening the door for her to precede me into the hall. 'Is there a light switch?'

'Here,' she said, flipping a switch on the wall by the doorjamb. The hallway went from black to gray, making me wonder if I should go back for the flashlight. I was pretty much done with the damn lanterns.

'That light fixture didn't throw much light even when we weren't trying to run it off a failing generator. But here's one linen closet,' she said, stopping at a cabinet between Harold and Jerome's room and Tien and Clare's. 'The blankets in here seem to be mostly cast-offs that even my grandparents had retired.'

'They'll be warm regardless,' I said, pulling the olive drab blankets out one by one to make a stack. 'Wow, these are heavy.'

'Wool, I'm sure,' she said. 'So they will be warm, if a little smelly and moth-eaten.'

The stack was up to my nose now and I gave a sniff. 'Musty with a tinge of mothballs, but we're not choosy at this point, right?'

No answer.

I shifted the pile in time to see her open the door down the hall that had been assigned to Kate. 'Lita?'

'There's a chest of drawers with linens in this room,' she called back to me. 'I'll see if I can come up with something better.'

'I think these will be fine,' I protested, but she had already ducked in. 'I'll take these out and be back to help you,' I continued, mostly for my own benefit.

Too late, I realized I had taken too many blankets and didn't have a free hand to turn the knob of the door to the main room. 'Hello,' I called. 'Can somebody get the door?'

I could hear voices, but none of them seemed to be in reply. So I kicked the door. 'Hey!'

Nothing. As I went to kick it again, it was pulled open abruptly and Sarah was standing there. With her blanket. 'For God's sake, Maggy. 'You really were born in a barn.'

'You're questioning my manners?' I asked, pushing past her to get into the room. 'I got blankets for everyone, not just for myself.'

Hearing that, the group crowded around to relieve me of my burden, blanket by blanket.

'Oh, dear,' Gloria said, pulling back as she realized she was about to take the last one. 'What about you?'

'Lita is getting more,' I said, twisting around to look through the still open door to the hall. 'She—'

'I thought we weren't going to leave her alone?' Sarah said, coming up alongside me.

We weren't. And I shouldn't have. 'She was just there. I thought she would be right out. Come on.'

Since I hadn't directed the last to anyone in particular, the entire herd followed me down the hall.

'This one,' I said, stopping at the door. 'Lita said there was a linen chest.' As I swung open the door, a gust of rain and wind swept into the hall from the darkened room.

'Damn,' Sarah muttered, as she reached in to flick the light switch. 'Has anybody ever replaced a lightbulb in the place?'

'Lita?' I called.

'Here.'

From the light escaping into the room from the hallway, I could just make out the blonde woman, sitting dazed on the floor by the bed, holding the back of her head.

'What happened?' I slid Kate's duffel bag over and helped Lita sit on the edge of the bed. Sarah closed the window.

'I'm not sure.' Lita took her hand away from her head and I could see blood on it. There was also a trickle of blood coming from her nose. 'The window was open, and I went to close it. Then nothing.'

'Maybe the window swung and hit you?' Clare looked overstuffed, like she had on three sweatshirts. Which she probably did.

'It's a double-hung window,' I reminded her. 'It slides up and down, not swings in and out.'

'Maybe you slipped on the wet floor?' Tien suggested. 'Though it would be quite a coincidence given what happened to Kate.'

'Who opened the window in the first place?' Jerome said, craning his head to see and then ducking back out of the room again.

'It was closed when Maggy and I checked all the rooms,' Sarah said.

'I honestly don't know,' Lita said. 'I'm not sure what happened.'

'You're soaked,' Gloria said to Lita. 'You must be freezing. Where is this linen cupboard?'

'There.' Lita pointed to the chest on the far wall.

'Did you see anybody?' I asked as Gloria retrieved a blanket and came back to tuck it around Lita's shoulders.

'No one,' Lita said, shaking her head back and forth. 'Why? Do you honestly think Faith is still out there? Why wouldn't she just leave in the car, like you said?'

Unfinished business?

I was saved from answering by Jerome's return. He handed me a damp towel from the bathroom for Lita's head and dropped a bigger dry towel on the wet floor under the window.

Then he sat down next to Lita. 'I obviously didn't know Faith as well as I thought, but it's hard to believe she's a psycho killer out there stalking us.'

All I knew is that I was glad I *hadn't* killed a hummingbird. Not that I ever would, you understand. I was even having second thoughts about that mosquito.

'Maybe I just did fall,' Lita said.

'If you did, you fell backwards,' I told her, 'because you hit the back of your head. But your nose is also bleeding.'

Surprised, Lita swiped at her nose. 'It is?'

'When I came in you were sitting up on the floor by the bed,' I said. 'Do you remember what direction you fell when you went down?'

Lita closed her eyes, thinking. Then she shook her head. 'No. It's just a blank.'

'Do you remember leaving me in the hall to come in here?'

'Yes. You were taking those old smelly blankets and I said that I thought there were some others in the chest of drawers in here, so I went to get them.'

'And?' Sarah prompted.

'And I opened the door and went to turn on the light, but it didn't work. I could tell the window was open, though, obviously. It was freezing and the rain was coming in. I intended to close the window, and I think I got that far, but . . .' She held out both hands, palms up, one bloody.

And here I was, still holding the towel Jerome had brought for her. 'Here,' I said, handing it to Lita. 'Hold this to your head. It's still bleeding.'

She obeyed. 'If somebody hit me, they must already have been in the room when I came in.'

I frowned. 'But if somebody took shelter in this room, they would have closed the window once they were inside. Why leave it open?'

'Maybe she heard the two of you in the hall and opened the window to leave?' Tien suggested.

'I was back here, too,' Clare said. 'In my room, getting another sweatshirt.'

'So then it's possible that Clare or I just startled her,' Lita said, seeming relieved. 'That would mean I'm not the target. That I just got in the way.'

I was regarding the double-hung window. 'Nobody touched the window, right?'

'No,' Harold said. 'But we probably should close it if we don't want this wood floor to be ruined.'

'Harold,' Gloria scolded. 'I think there are more important things than the floor right now.'

'Well, I know,' he said, uncomfortably. 'But this is a nice room and there's no sense in letting things get damaged unnecessarily. Maggy can always take a picture for the police.'

That actually was a good idea, so I pulled my cell out. 'I should have turned off roaming. My phone is nearly dead, probably looking for a cell tower that doesn't exist. I don't suppose anybody has a charger that doesn't use electricity?'

'I have a crank one,' Harold said, ever helpful. 'Takes a bit of elbow grease, though, and a phone isn't good for much up here anyway.'

'Just camera and flashlight,' I agreed, though I still didn't want to be without one. 'Sarah, can you take a couple shots with your phone? Also, of Lita's head wound.'

She did the window first and then turned to Lita. 'Can you take the towel down?'

'Of course,' Lita said, obliging and then tilting her head down so we could see. 'Is it still bleeding?'

'Yes, but it appears to be slowing down,' I said, looking carefully at the bloody welt across the back of her head. 'Was there anything outside the window when you went to close it? Or anybody?'

'How could there be?' Sarah questioned. 'Faith was inside the room hitting her.'

'Someone was,' I said. 'That doesn't mean there wasn't a second person.'

'You mean Cabot.' Lita's face screwed up like she was going to cry and then she seemed to gather herself. 'I just can't get my head around the possibility that Cabot is involved. And that he would hurt me.' She turned to Jerome. 'Any more than you can believe it of Faith.'

Which made me think. 'Did you search Faith on the web when you met her?' I asked Jerome.

'No, why would I?'

'You're kidding.' This was from Tien. 'It's the first thing I do when I meet somebody.'

'Maybe women do more research than men?' Which was stupid. Knowledge is power. And safety.

'Nah, I'm not saying I don't do it,' Jerome admitted. 'It's just that Faith told me when we met that she didn't do the Internet. She texted a bit but that was about it. She's kind of old-fashioned like that.'

'Or using a fake name,' I suggested.

'Yeah,' he said, slowly. 'Maybe that, too.'

'It's not your fault.' Gloria, who had been fairly quiet until now, put her hand on his arm. 'Faith used you to get to Lita and Kate.'

'Presumably because *she* did her Internet research,' Sarah said.

'Don't blame Jerome,' Lita said, struggling to her feet. 'He trusted her like I trusted Cabot. For all we know, Faith used Cabot, too, and got information on me from him.'

Now there was a possibility.

'I know Cabot worked for your grandparents,' I said, standing to join her, 'but how well do you really know him?'

Her smile was a little sheepish.

'So you . . . dated?' I asked, lowering my voice.

'He was – is – very good-looking. But it was only when I was up here. It didn't mean anything.'

'To you, it didn't.' But maybe Cabot had other expectations.

'I think I would like to lie down in my room,' she said, moving to the door.

'You can't,' I said, laying my hand on her arm. 'Kate—'

She closed her eyes, and I could feel the shudder that enveloped her body.

'What about this one?' Jerome suggested. 'I've mopped up the floor and if Maggy says it's OK to close the window it should be fine.'

I nodded and he slid the sash down.

'Is it safe for Lita to be in here alone?' Clare asked me.

'I can stay with her,' I offered, and Lita nodded gratefully.

'And you can fight off two determined killers?' Sarah asked.

'No, but I can make sure the window is locked and scream loudly,' I said. 'I would think all of us could use some sleep tonight. It's well after midnight now.'

'One-fifteen,' Clare confirmed wearily.

'I wouldn't bother with the assigned rooms unless you want to,' I said. 'Except presumably your bags are in them.'

'Anybody want to share mine?' Sarah asked. 'Maggy's bed is free.'

'And wet,' I said. 'With no blanket.'

'Besides, Sarah,' Tien said, moving away and up the hall, 'you snore.'

'Do not.'

'Do so.'

FOURTEEN

'Thank you for this,' Lita said. 'Sure you don't want to share the bed? It's a queen and I, for one, don't snore.'

'Nobody thinks they snore.'

Jerome and I had moved the overstuffed chair from Lita's room to this one. The chair wasn't quite as big as those around the fireplace, but it was plenty comfy, and I had a warm, non-smelly blanket from the chest of drawers to cover me. 'I'm fine here.'

'Probably a good call,' she said, wrinkling her nose as she slid into bed. 'I'm not sure Cabot changed these sheets. Good thing I still have my clothes on.'

Hmm. I'd noticed earlier that the bedspread was wrinkled and now the sheets were in disarray. Had somebody been sleeping in Mama Bear's bed?

'And for what it's worth, Cabot says I don't sn—' Lita stopped and sniffled. 'I was going to say Cabot says I don't snore, but that's pretty ludicrous right now, isn't it? Or maybe the word is pathetic.'

'Was the relationship more than you let on just now, with everybody around?' I asked.

'More than an occasional up-north booty call? Yes, it was more. Even to me. I really liked the man, though we weren't going to get married or anything, if that's what you mean.'

'It was, actually.' In addition to the chair, I had commandeered Cabot's flashlight and now I shut it off. 'It was your Tumi bag in his cottage.'

A hesitation. 'I . . . kept a bag there. Cabot was more comfortable in the cabin than here in the lodge, in my bed.'

I wondered why that was. 'Is it possible he did want more?'

'Like my estate?'

'Maybe. It might give him reason to get rid of Kate.' I shook my head in the dark. 'Though why now? Better to woo you, marry you and then kill Kate if he hadn't already convinced you to change your will.'

A giggle from the bed. 'I can't believe you said "woo."'

'I watch a lot of old movies.'

'That's kind of nice.' Silence. 'What's Cabot's connection to Faith?'

'I don't know,' I admitted. 'But I would bet Faith isn't her real name. I mean, an inspirational writer with the name Faith? Come on.'

'Maybe it's her pseudonym, if she really is a writer,' Lita said. 'Though, if it is a pen name, I'm surprised she didn't tell me.'

'Yet she claimed she was a real Payne by blood if not by name. P–A–Y–N–E, of course.'

Another giggle, this one a little sleepy. 'Like I haven't heard that one before.'

'Sorry,' I said, stretching. 'Though Payne Lodge does invite bad jokes.'

'I know.'

'Maybe Faith did use Cabot to get information on you, like she did Jerome,' I said. 'But how would she and Cabot have connected in the first place? Unless she found out he worked for you and came up here to seek him out.'

I had a better thought. 'Or, if Faith *is* related to your grandfather, she still may live up here. Maybe she and Cabot knew each other from school, like you and Kate did in Chicago. Maybe they even had a romantic relationship.' I giggled this time. 'Not that you and Kate did.'

Lita didn't dignify that with a reply.

'Sorry, I'm just spit-balling here,' I said apologetically. 'I thought if Faith saw you as a threat to her relationship, the attack on you now would make some sense, beyond the inheritance angle. But the thing is—'

A not so gentle snore interrupted me.

I awoke, startled. I had pulled a copy of *Strangers on a Train* by Patricia Highsmith from the bookshelves in Lita's room when we moved the chair and had barely gotten to the page when Guy met Bruno – on the train, naturally – before I nodded off.

When I awoke, the flashlight I'd been using for a reading light under the blanket lay beside me still on. I switched it off, though my worries that Lita would be bothered were apparently groundless – the woman was out like the proverbial light. And, for the record, she did snore. Though next to Sarah, Lita was a minor leaguer. In fact, her gentle snores as the rain pattered against the window had reassured me. She was still alive.

But something certainly had awakened me. I reached for my cell phone to see what time it was; but that, of course, was stone dead. Your own damn fault, I said to myself. You should have turned off roam—

A sound at the window stopped me.

Must be a branch, I told myself. Blown by the wind and rubbing against the house. Except I wasn't hearing much wind now. Nor seemingly was there hail or even sleet. Just the unrelenting drumbeat of the rain.

There it was again. Scratching – almost metal against glass.

I shivered, pulling the blanket closer. 'It's like that scary slumber party story about the couple whose car stalls near a prison. A murderer with a hook for a hand has escaped, but the boyfriend convinces the girl to lock the car and wait for him while he goes for help. She falls asleep, dreaming fitfully of a homicidal maniac scratching at the window. Morning comes, but still no boyfriend and when she unlocks the car and climbs out, she finds a bloody hook hanging—'

'*What* are you talking about?' Lita was no longer snoring.

'Sorry,' I said. 'I heard a sound, and I was saying it sounded like metal on the window glass. I was being fanciful, though. I'm sure it was just a branch rasping against the lodge.'

'And who were you saying this to?' Lita was sitting up now.

'Myself.' And I felt 'myself' blush. 'I guess I'm just nervous. When Pavlik isn't home, I talk to my sheepdog, Frank. But he's not here either.'

'So I have the pleasure of being startled from a dead sleep by your monologue.'

'I . . . well, yes.'

She yawned. 'OK. If you're done, I'm going back to sleep now.'

'Yup, all done.' I stage-yawned.

'Good.'

Silence.

Then the rasp came again. Lita shot up. 'What was that?'

'See? I told you I heard something.'

She caught her breath. 'It moved.'

'What moved? Did you see something out there?' I would switch on the flashlight, but I wasn't sure it would enhance our ability to see what was outside. But it would most certainly make it easier for what was outside to see in.

'The window – it moved. I could swear . . . there!'

Sure enough, the upper pane of the double-hung window seemed to shudder.

'I'm getting help,' I whispered.

We weren't two girls at a slumber party, after all, and we certainly weren't alone.

I slipped off the chair and onto the floor, crawling on all fours to the door to the hallway. Opening it quietly, I stuck my head out and saw Jerome snoozing on the floor. He was sitting, back against the door of the bathroom and facing straight down the length of the hallway to the open door into the main room. Bless him.

'Jerome,' I hissed.

His eyes opened.

'There's somebody outside our window.'

He popped up and signaled he was going out the front and around. As I returned to the room and Lita, I heard the front door softly close.

Lita was out of bed, huddled in the corner formed by the wall and my chair, gaze fixed on the window. She had *Strangers on a Train* in her hand.

Staying low, I joined her. 'Going to throw—'

'If you say "throw the book at her," I swear I'll scream.' She was trying to keep her voice low and light, but there was a quaver.

'Not me,' I said. And then: 'Jerome is going out there to look.'

'Oh my God,' she said a little too loudly and clapped her hand over her mouth. 'I don't want anybody else hurt,' she whispered.

'Including us, I assume.'

'Well, yes.'

That was when the window jerked down in one abrupt movement, and I screamed.

'What the hell did you think you were doing?'

Cabot Foxx was half-sitting, half-lying in a chair by the dying fire. The rest of the group was awake and gathered around, including a damp but heroic Jerome.

Cabot was even wetter than Jerome. A lot wetter. And bloody.

'We do have a front door, you know.' Lita had gone to fetch blankets and now draped one over Cabot's shoulders and handed another to Jerome before sitting down on the next chair.

'Give him a chance to explain,' I suggested, putting my hand on her shoulder.

She shook me off. 'It was my room he was trying to get into.'

'Actually, it was Kate's,' I said. 'And I was in it, too.'

'I didn't think anybody would be in there,' Cabot said, pulling the blanket tight. 'I woke up in the woods. That Faith woman' – he rubbed the back of his neck – 'I think she must have drugged me.'

'Sure she did,' Lita said, upping the snarky meter. 'And then did she force you to perform unnatural acts?'

He glanced toward the fire and then back to face her. 'No, but she did come on to me.'

Jerome took a deep breath and sat down across from him, setting aside his own blanket. 'How about you start from the beginning? You and Faith went out to start the generator and we never saw you again.'

'Yeah, yeah,' Cabot said, leaning forward. 'She said she wanted to help. I figured it was just to make you jealous, but . . .' He shrugged.

'You were all right with that, I'm sure,' Lita said.

'Oh, for God's sake,' he said, flinging a hand out irritably, 'I was fixing a frickin' generator in the middle of a storm with eight strangers and a dead body in the lodge I'm responsible for. Why wouldn't I welcome a little company?'

Jerome gave a little nod. 'Fair enough. What was wrong with the generator?'

'Ah, you know. It's been sitting for a while,' Cabot said, feeling the back of his head. 'Fuel wasn't getting to the carburetor. I took care of that and got it started, then told Faith I needed to find more gas or maybe siphon it out of the old tractor or the Corolla.'

Sarah shot me a triumphant look.

'She went with you?' I asked.

'She said she wanted to see my cabin first,' Cabot said, turning to Jerome. 'I know she's your girlfriend. But, like I said, she was all over me.'

'She's not my girlfriend,' Jerome said tightly.

'But that doesn't let you off the hook,' Lita told Cabot.

'You're the caretaker here,' Sarah said. 'Bad form to boink the guests.'

'I didn't boink her,' Cabot said.

'But you did show her your cabin.' Sarah was nodding knowingly. 'Prelude to a boink.'

'Great movie title,' I told her. 'Now can we let Cabot tell us what really did happen?'

The caretaker cleared his throat as we all turned back to him expectantly. 'Well, I . . . umm . . . showed her around and when we got to the bedroom' – he slid Lita a sheepish look – 'she asked if I had anything to drink.' He turned to Lita. 'You know, because the lodge doesn't have anything, alcohol or wine-wise.'

'It does now,' Tien said under her breath.

'And?' I encouraged Cabot.

'And I happened to have a bottle of wine.'

Lita's grandparents' teetotaling didn't apparently extend to the staff.

'So I opened it,' Cabot was saying, 'and then I went to the kitchen and got glasses.'

'You have wine and a corkscrew in your bedroom?' Sarah asked. 'Good form.'

'It was screw-top,' he said, cocking his head as if trying to understand her.

I would have told him not to bother trying, but I had very little sympathy for the caretaker at the moment.

'But you did have a bottle of wine in your bedroom.' Lita was keeping him on that hook.

'Well, yes. For, well . . . next time, you and me . . .' His hand gestured between the two of them.

She glared at him, even as Sarah turned to me and said in a low voice, 'They're a couple?'

'Lita doesn't seem quite sure what they are,' I told her. 'And from the sounds of it, neither is Cabot.'

'Not-so-young love.' Sarah grinned.

I turned my attention back to the main event.

'What kind of wine was this?' Lita was asking. 'You know, the one that you supposedly keep in your bedroom for me?'

It didn't seem relevant to our current situation, but I guessed Lita was entitled to her cross-examination. Besides, none of us were going anywhere.

'Pinot noir,' Cabot said. 'You know, your favorite.'

'It's everybody's favorite,' she said, folding her arms. 'That proves nothing.'

'Your point is further illustrated by the fact that three of us brought Pinot here,' Sarah said.

'You have wine here?' Cabot asked. 'Could I—'

'If you were drugged, I'm not sure that's a good idea,' Clare said, shaking her head.

'I have peppermint schnapps,' Harold offered, getting up to retrieve the bottle from the café, where we had stashed all the booze. 'It's practically not alcohol.'

'It's practically disgusting,' Gloria told him. 'Get the brandy for him instead, that's medicinal. And bring me a bourbon.'

'Isn't it a little early to drink?' Clare asked, checking her watch. 'It's five a.m.'

'Depends how you look at it,' Harold said, pouring the brandy and bourbon, plus a schnapps for himself. 'I'm thinking we're still drinking, rather than we're about to start up again.'

He handed Cabot his, then sat down next to Gloria with theirs.

'I still don't think it's a good idea,' Clare said in a small voice. 'I mean for Cabot. God knows what Faith gave him and how it will react.'

Cabot had raised the glass to his lips and now hesitated. 'You think it could kill me?'

'Maybe not kill you,' Clare said, 'but without access to medical care right now, is that a chance you want to take?'

He looked at the amber liquid and then downed it.

Time to steer us back on track. 'Anyway, Cabot. You said you went to get wine glasses in the kitchen, leaving Faith in the bedroom with the open bottle of wine. What makes you think she put something in it?'

'Well, now, I had one glass of wine, and I couldn't feel my feet.'

Interesting.

I frowned. 'But if Faith tampered with the wine while you got the glasses, she had to put whatever it was she used in the bottle. Didn't she drink the wine, too?'

Cabot gave that some thought. 'She picked up her glass, I know, but . . . well, I got distracted after that.'

'I just bet you did,' Lita said bitterly.

'But where would she have gotten anything to put in the wine?' Tien asked. 'Most people don't travel with poisons.'

'But they do with drugs,' I said. 'Jerome, do you know if Faith is on any medications?'

'I don't think so.'

'Her bag is on the bed in her room,' I said. 'We should check to see if there's anything in it.'

'She and Gloria are in the room next to mine,' Clare volunteered. 'Want me to go get it?'

'Please,' I said, a little irritated I hadn't thought to do it earlier. 'It's a floral duffel.'

'I'll go with you,' Tien said, getting up to follow her.

I watched the door close behind them and turned back to Cabot. 'What did you do after you couldn't feel your feet?'

'Yeah.' Sarah wanted in on the interrogation. 'You said you woke up in the woods. How did you get there?'

'I honestly don't know.' He rubbed his head. 'I felt my feet go numb and then it's like it worked its way up and everything went black.'

'Was Faith still there?' I asked.

'Yes,' he said, thinking back. 'I think she was talking but I couldn't understand what she was saying. When I woke up, though, she was gone and I was in the woods, soaked and bloody. Probably got banged up when she dragged me out there.'

Sarah looked skyward. 'Dragged you out there? That girl is maybe six inches shorter than you and fifty pounds lighter.'

'That's true now, isn't it?' Cabot said, rubbing the back of his head. 'Then maybe I just wandered out there? Sure took me awhile to get my bearings and find my way back though.'

'Why do you keep rubbing your head?' I asked.

'I have a headache. Probably whatever she gave me.' He glanced at Lita. 'Does Rohypnol give you a headache?'

'You're asking me?' she snapped.

'Well, yes,' he said, sliding down in his chair. 'I mean, you're a woman and all.'

'Which means she's had experience being roofied?' Sarah asked. 'That is kind of offensive.'

'I'm sorry.' Then he wisely shut his mouth.

'You should be,' Lita muttered.

'Turn around,' I told Cabot.

'Why? What are you going to do to me?'

I stood up. 'I'm going to exam your head.'

'Good idea,' Lita said sarcastically.

'No, really,' I said. 'Let me see the back of your head, Cabot.'

'Can you hand me the big light?' I asked Jerome, nodding to the coffee table where I had set the flashlight.

As he handed it to me, Cabot's head swiveled toward me apprehensively.

'Don't worry,' I said, testing the weight in my hand. 'It would make a good weapon, but I'm not going to hit you with it.'

He didn't seem so sure, but he turned back around anyway, and I shone the light on the back of his close-cropped head. 'I thought so.'

'You thought what?' Lita asked reluctantly.

'He's been hit on the head. Looks like with something similar to whatever you were hit with. Something long and straight.' I pointed to a line, akin to a scratch, but deeper and bloodier, bruising already showing around it.

'Long and straight,' Sarah repeated. 'Like a fireplace poker?'

We all turned to look at the one leaning against the hearth.

'The poker will have my fingerprints on it,' Harold said for maybe the tenth time. 'I stoked the fire, remember?'

'Believe me, we couldn't possibly forget it,' Gloria said wearily. 'And nobody is accusing you of anything except bringing that goddamned schnapps here.'

'We don't even know if the poker is the weapon.' I had poached more plastic bags from the kitchen and was using one on each hand to place the poker on the trunk coffee table. 'I don't see blood on it.'

'Too bad we don't have luminol,' Sarah said. 'It's dark enough in here, we might be able to see the blood glow even without an ultraviolet light.'

'Next time I'll pack it,' I said, wondering what was taking Tien and Clare so long. 'The weapon could be anything with a straight edge, though. It doesn't have to be the poker.'

'Golf club, tire iron, fishing pole.' Harold again. 'We could test them all.'

I frowned. 'I don't see how a fishing pole would do it, but yes to the rest.'

'There's a tire iron in the garage.' Cabot seemed to be nodding off. 'I sure don't remember being hit with one though.'

'Because you were drugged, remember?' Lita said sweetly between clenched teeth.

'I—'

'I still don't understand why you were at the window instead of coming in the front door,' Jerome said.

Cabot groaned. 'I know, but one of you is a killer. And I was just assaulted – maybe by that same person or another person entirely. I needed to get Lita out, but there was no way

I was just going to walk in the door. I knew Kate was dead, so figured that room was empty and I could get in without anybody seeing me. Assess the situation.'

Lita laughed. 'Who do you think you are? The Equalizer?'

'Think about it, honey,' he said, holding out his hands to her. 'This band of nut jobs descends on the lodge and before you even get here one of them is dead. A few hours later, another of them comes on to me and drugs me.' He winced. 'And, I guess, assaults me with a tire iron.'

'He's decided that sounds better than a poker,' Lita told us.

Cabot cocked his head. 'The tire iron was a whole lot more accessible out there than this poker was.'

'He has a point,' Sarah said. 'But what did Faith do? Snatch it in the garage and stick it up her sleeve so she could carry it into the cabin without his seeing?'

'No sleeves – she was just wearing overalls. But I suppose she could have gone to get it after he had passed out,' I suggested, standing up. 'I'm going to see what's keeping Clare and Tien. I meant for them to bring out Faith's suitcase, not go through it back there.'

As I finished, the door swung open.

'We found something.' Tien was holding a pill bottle gingerly and set it down on the trunk.

'What is it?' I asked, leaning down to read the label as the hall door closed. 'Xanax. Prescribed to' – I twisted my head to look at our hostess – 'Lita Payne.'

'I did have a bottle here,' Lita confirmed. 'In the medicine cabinet.'

'We found it in Faith's bag,' Tien said.

'But how did it get there?' Lita moved to pick it up and I stepped in front of her.

'Better not to touch it. You'll obscure Faith's prints.'

'You think she took it from the cabinet?' Lita asked.

'Xanax is benzodiazepine. It's for anxiety, but an overdose can put you into a coma, especially mixed with alcohol.' Harold seemed to be speaking with authority as he put down his glass. 'I was prescribed that after my snowplow incident, and I was mighty careful.'

Gloria patted his shoulder.

'I know what it is,' Lita said a little indignantly, and then her eyes widened. 'You think she used my pills to drug Cabot?'

'But the pill bottle was still in Faith's bag and she hasn't been back in the house since they went outside together,' Harold said.

'The bottle is nearly empty.' Tien nodded her head toward it.

'It wasn't when I left it in the cabinet,' Lita told us.

'So Faith poured some pills into the pocket of her overalls,' Sarah said, pulling at her own jacket pocket. 'Carrying around a prescription pill bottle would draw attention, especially if it wasn't hers.'

'But that means she planned to kill me,' Cabot said. 'Before she left the lodge.'

'Or drug you,' I agreed, chewing the inside of my cheek. 'I—'

'But that's not the worst thing,' Tien said. 'Clare? Are you OK?'

Nothing, but as Tien started back toward the hall, the door swung open.

'I'm sorry.' Clare's face was green, and she was dangling something in a plastic storage bag. 'I had to throw up.'

She set the bag on the coffee table.

In it was an eight-inch-long chef's knife sticky with blood.

FIFTEEN

'Who travels with a chef's knife?' Sarah asked. 'Especially one covered in blood.'

'Nobody,' I said, looking at Lita. 'Do you think she got it from the kitchen?'

'Seems too new,' she said, turning to Cabot. 'Have you seen it before?'

'No,' he said. 'Everything in the kitchen is pretty much the way Berte left it. And Marvin died just a couple days after she did.'

'That's what happens with long-time couples,' Gloria said, nodding. 'We see it at the Manor all the time.'

'I hate that place,' Harold muttered.

'It's an expensive knife,' Tien said, turning to Jerome. 'Was Faith a really good cook?'

'I don't know,' Jerome said, a little impatiently. 'But what does it matter anyway? Nobody has been stabbed.'

'Thank God for small favors.' Lita sounded seriously spooked.

'Yet it's covered in blood,' I said.

'It's not blood.'

Jerome's voice was barely audible.

'What?'

'I said, it's not blood on the knife,' he said, standing up to snag the bag and pull out the chef's knife. He held it up. 'It's paint. The rest of it is sitting on the shelf of . . . the room Kate was killed in.'

The can of paint I'd seen on the bookshelves. I'd assumed it had been there for years. 'I don't understand.'

'Join the club,' Sarah said sourly.

Jerome collapsed into his chair, still holding the knife. 'It was Kate's idea. A staged murder mystery—'

'In which Kate was the victim?' I asked.

He nodded. 'Only Kate and I were in on it, as far as I knew.' He turned toward Lita. 'Did she say anything to you?'

She shook her head wordlessly.

'I'm not surprised,' Jerome said. 'She wanted to wow you, along with the rest of the group. I was supposed to brief Cabot, but I never got the chance.'

'So Kate wasn't supposed to die fictionally at the time she died in real life?' I asked.

'Not then,' Jerome said. 'The whole idea was for Lita to be here when we staged her death and take part in solving the mystery. Kate thought she'd get a kick out of it and maybe they'd incorporate it in the next retreat.'

'Which was why Kate was so agitated she was late,' I said. 'It also explains why Kate was so vicious about the stories she wanted you to write,' I said to Harold and Gloria.

'She was setting up motives,' Jerome confirmed.

'More than we already had?' Harold asked.

Gloria elbowed him.

'I told her it was cruel,' Jerome continued. 'But she said that when the game was over and the mystery was solved, everyone would have a good laugh about it.'

She had overestimated everyone's sense of humor, apparently.

'But somebody killed her before she could pull it off.' Sarah was sitting forward on her chair.

'Where does Faith fit in?' I asked.

Jerome colored up. 'She was helping me. Kate didn't want me to bring her, but I told her Faith was a midwife and could pronounce death before Maggy got to her.' He threw me an apologetic look.

'Fat chance of that happening,' Sarah said. 'Maggy can smell 'em a mile away.'

Lita looked sideways at me.

'I know,' Jerome said. 'I fully expected to have to pull Maggy aside and fill her in. Maybe you, too, Sarah.'

'None of us are idiots,' Gloria said. 'We would have seen through it immediately.'

Jerome lifted his shoulders and then dropped them again, miserably.

'Is Faith really your girlfriend?' I asked. 'Or was that a set-up, too?'

'Oh, yes,' Jerome said, and his face changed yet again. 'Or at least she was.'

'So as far as you were concerned,' I continued, 'Faith was going to help with this mystery skit, but she was mostly coming here to meet Lita in hopes of getting her book published. That's all true?'

'As far as I knew,' Jerome said, crossing his heart. 'The thing about Faith being jealous was to give her a motive to kill Kate, too.'

Ahh. 'Was it her knife?'

'Mine,' he said. 'We put the paint on it before we left home, and she was going to stash it in the library so Kate could place it next to her body. I had already put the can of paint there for her to splash around.'

Gloria was right. We would never have fallen for it.

'Stupid,' was Harold's comment.

'Why don't I make coffee,' Tien said, getting up. 'It's getting light out.'

'Great idea. I have the regular beans in my suitcase,' I told her. 'I'll get it.'

Cabot roused. 'No caffeinated beverages—'

'Oh, shut up, Mr Pinot.' This was from Lita.

'You might be being too hard on him,' I whispered as I passed her.

'He's an idiot.'

I couldn't dispute that.

I had moved my bag to the room Lita and I had slept in, so I went there to pull the beans out. Returning to the hallway with my five-pound bag of beans, I opened the door to the bathroom.

The windowless room apparently backed up to the laundry room. Harold and Gloria had checked for secret panels, but I wanted to take a look myself. This room, unlike the others in the house, had drywall nailed over the logs of the walls, presumably because of the moisture endemic in any bathroom.

Opening the medicine cabinet, I found the usual aspirin, antacids and cold tablets. Most had expired. There was another prescription for Lita – an antibiotic – and a number of old bottles belonging to her grandparents.

'I need to get rid of those,' Lita's voice said from the door. 'You're not supposed to flush them, though, and I haven't gotten around to taking them to a drugstore for disposal.'

'I've got a ton I should get rid of, too,' I said, closing the mirrored door.

'Do you want to know what the antibiotic was for?' she offered. 'Bladder infection.'

'I wasn't going to ask.' I smiled. 'But you're supposed to take it all.'

'I know.' She sighed. 'What a mess. Why in the world did Kate want to impress me with this murder act?'

'Because she wanted you to partner with her?' I suggested.

'I'm already doing that with the newspaper.'

'Silent partner,' I reminded her.

'But I didn't think she would want my involvement. I just wanted to pay her back for what her family had done for me, letting me live with them after my parents died. I'm not sure you know about that.'

'I do,' I said. 'But I think you hit on it earlier. As much as Kate enjoyed the autonomy, at the end of the day, she was lonely.'

'It does sound like she had more enemies than friends.'

'By her own design it felt like,' I said. 'But you knew Kate better than anybody. Maybe she hoped that this new project' – I waved at our surroundings – 'would be something you could do together and rekindle your friendship.'

'It never went out. It was just long distance.' A silence as she turned to go back down the hallway, then: 'I missed her, too.'

When I took the bag of beans to Tien in the kitchen, I gave Sarah the high sign to follow and bring Jerome.

'Well done,' I said, when both appeared.

'We've worked together for years now,' she said. 'I get you.'

I grinned. 'Thanks.'

'Not that I want you, you understand.'

'Absolutely.' I handed the beans to Tien. 'I hope there's a grinder.'

'I will grind them with mortar and pestle if I have to,' she said. 'I need coffee. We all need coffee.'

'And we will all be grateful to you for making it,' I said. 'But let's talk as you do.'

'Are you sure you want me here?' Jerome asked. 'I wouldn't blame you if you didn't trust me.'

'You told us the truth,' Tien said.

'Eventually,' I added. 'What in the world were you thinking not 'fessing up the moment Kate's body was found?'

'Honestly?' He backed up against the sink. 'I was a little scared. Things were so out of hand. Kate was dead, Faith was acting weird. I felt like I was all on my own.'

'Not when we're around,' Tien said, giving him a hug. 'Now see if there's a grinder in the cabinet behind you.'

He did and came up with one. 'Electric,' he said, holding up the cord. 'We'll have to unplug the refrigerator again.'

'That's fine,' I said as Tien went to do that. 'We can also check the phone.' I nodded to the unplugged handset and base.

'I just did,' Tien said. 'Still out.'

'Meaning we're still stuck here,' Sarah said, 'assuming Faith took the car.'

'After the confrontation with Lita,' I said. 'And drugging and assaulting Cabot.' I frowned. 'I was much happier when I thought he was in on it. Do we really think Faith could do all this?'

'If she's a psychopath,' Jerome said, shaking his head. 'Maybe I will write a book: *I Slept with a Psychopath*.'

'Catchy,' Sarah said. 'Though I can't believe it hasn't already been written.'

'Titles can't be copyrighted,' Tien said. 'Kate taught me that. And each book is as different as its author.'

'Poor Kate,' I said, with genuine regret. 'I wish now that I had been nicer to her.'

Sarah shook her head. 'You realize that she didn't like you any more than you liked her.'

'Thank you,' I said, pretending to tear up. 'That helps.'

'Don't mention it,' she said, slapping my arm. 'Now what's our next step?'

'I don't think any of us wants to spend another night here,' I said. 'The rain has stopped, so I say we have coffee and toast—'

'I wouldn't plug a toaster in,' Jerome warned. 'I'm not sure how much amperage it draws and whether the generator can take it. The coffeemaker, too, for that matter.'

'No worries,' Tien said, lifting a metal pot with a glass knob at the top and a wire handle like our lanterns. 'There's a camp-style percolator I'm using on the stove, and I can pan griddle some buttered bread.'

'Like the grilled cheese sandwich except not a sandwich and without the cheese,' Jerome said, managing a smile. 'That actually sounds delicious.'

'Cinnamon and sugar on it,' Tien said.

'Everything is delicious with cinnamon and sugar,' I said.

'Now that you three have settled breakfast,' Sarah snapped irritably, 'can we talk about saving our lives? Those of us who still have them and have the luxury of talking, that is?'

Wow. Somebody needs her coffee.

'Absolutely,' I said, acting duly chastened for getting off topic. 'After we eat and when the sun is fully up, my plan is for all of us to troop down to the end of the driveway where the tree fell. If the car is still there, great. We'll pile in as many people as we can and—'

I broke off, realizing something I hadn't tipped to last night. 'Lita must have the car key, right? So that means Faith couldn't have taken it.'

'Unless Faith can hot-wire a car,' Jerome said. 'Which I wouldn't put past her at this point.'

Frowning, I went to the kitchen door and stuck my head out. 'Lita?'

'Yes.' She was still glaring at Cabot, who was awake, but now trying to see the reflection of the back of his head in the front window.

'Geez, she's right,' I said to Sarah, who had joined me at the door. 'He really is an idiot. Why didn't I see it before?'

'Because he's a handsome idiot,' she whispered. 'Takes awhile for the handsome to rub off.'

'Right.' I turned back to Lita. 'Where are the keys for your rental?'

'My what?' she asked.

'Your rental car. You brought the keys with you when you walked up last night, right? Where are they?'

'They'd be in your purse,' Gloria said. 'Where is it?'

'Next to your chair,' Lita said, pointing. 'But I'm not sure the keys are in there. I think I just left them there in the car.'

'You left your keys in the car?' I repeated, as Gloria passed her the bag.

'We all do that up here,' Cabot explained. 'It's not like there are car thieves cruising by, looking for something to steal.'

'Not much of anything cruising by,' Harold said, 'except maybe boats.'

Everybody stared at him.

'Because of the rain?' he tried.

'Never mind, dear,' Gloria said to him.

Lita was digging through her purse and now looked back at me and shrugged. 'Sorry.'

I ducked back into the kitchen. 'Great. Faith wouldn't have had to do any more than walk down the driveway, climb over the tree, get in the car and drive it away.'

'We don't have to walk down there, we can drive,' Sarah suggested, as Jerome and Tien worked on breakfast. 'Load up any chainsaws and axes and clear the tree if we have to. Then we grab our bags and get the hell out of here.'

'That, my friend,' I said, holding out my hand, 'is a plan.' We high-fived.

'This may be the best breakfast I've ever had.' Clare seemed fully recovered from her stomach upset, given the knife was covered with paint, not blood. 'The toast is delicious, Tien.'

We were back around the fire, which was little more than embers at this point and the morning light – sunshine, even – was streaming in the windows.

Tien grinned. 'Not quite my sticky buns, but it is bread, butter, cinnamon and sugar.'

'It is like the sticky bun,' Clare said. 'The top is caramelized. How did you do that? After you toasted the bread, you put it under the broiler?'

'I didn't have a toaster and the broiler is electric, so no to both. I just buttered the bread and sprinkled the cinnamon and sugar on before I put it face down in the frying pan. Instant caramelization.'

'Genius,' Clare said.

'Necessity,' Tien countered. She had a higher bar for genius.

'Well, now that we've had our breakfast, can we get out of here?' Sarah said.

'Shouldn't we clean up first?' Clare said, standing with her plate.

'No need,' Lita said. 'We'll take care of it later.'

In the bright light of day, it seemed that everybody – even Lita – was forgetting that Kate's body was still in the bedroom. And that she had still been murdered.

I wasn't terribly certain we would be allowed to leave today, though I also doubted we would be at the lodge. We would be staying wherever the county sheriff wanted us to stay. Hopefully wherever it was, though, would have electricity, and I would be able to call Pavlik.

'Make sure your bags are packed and bring them out to this room,' I told everybody. 'But we're going to leave them up here at the lodge for now.'

'Why?' Gloria had traded her tracksuit and fuzzy slippers of last night for navy pants and a flowered top.

'There won't be room in the van,' I said. 'Not with all of us, plus the equipment we'll need for clearing the tree.'

'I'll grab the chainsaw,' Cabot said, and then stopped. 'Hope there's gas in it.'

'Me, too,' Jerome said. 'Though we can always siphon from the Toyota, like you wanted to for the generator. I'll give you a hand.'

'Get the axes, too,' Lita called, then turned as the door closed behind them. 'Is that wise, do you suppose? Giving Cabot an axe?'

'You still suspect him?' I settled down next to her. Folks would be packing bags, using the bathroom and sharpening axes for a while. 'If Cabot wanted to murder us, he could have done it last night.'

'For all we know, there's an axe leaning against the house under my window, like in that story you told,' she said, and then shook her head. 'But no. I really don't think he's a bad guy. I just don't see him in the same light I did before, I guess.'

'The handsome wears off,' I said.

'That's very good,' Lita said, nodding. 'And so true.'

A hand slapped the back of my head. 'That's my line,' Sarah said.

'Actually, yours was "takes a while for the handsome to rub off." I paraphrased.'

'Ooh, I like Sarah's better,' Lita said with a smile. 'I suppose I should get my bag, too?'

'Yes, and don't forget the Tumi tote in Cabot's cabin if you want to take it, too.'

'Thanks for the reminder,' she said with just a trace of regret, as she stood. 'I don't imagine I'll be visiting there again.'

Sarah's eyes lit up. 'If you should ever want to sell this place, give me a call. I'm a real estate agent.'

'In addition to being a coffee maven,' I said.

'Well, isn't that lucky?' Lita said. 'If you give me your card, Sarah, I'll call should I make that decision.'

'She's not going to call, is she?' Sarah said as Lita went out the front door.

'Nope.'

SIXTEEN

Luggage assembled by the door, gas siphoned, and potty breaks taken, the nine of us wedged ourselves into the van that had brought seven of us up. Behind the bench seat in the back was one chainsaw, one can of gas and two axes.

Sarah's left buttock was on my lap. Tien was on the other side of Sarah's right butt-cheek and Lita was sitting to the left of me, butt free.

'A little tight, isn't it?' I said.

'We'll have my car for the ride back, too.' Jerome was riding shotgun.

'Plus, I won't be along,' Cabot said from the driver's seat. 'What about you, Lita?'

'I'm going with them to the sheriff's office,' she said a little stiffly. 'I'm not sure from there.'

'Well, I'll be here waiting when you get back,' he said.

'Oh, goody,' I heard her murmur.

'The sheriff will want to talk to him, so don't let him take off,' I said to her.

'Good, Cabot,' she said, a little louder. 'I probably won't be gone long.'

'Well done,' Gloria said, from the single seat in front of us. She was sitting on Harold's lap. 'Even the ones you don't want, you don't necessarily have to toss back right away.'

A fishing metaphor, I assumed.

'There it is,' I said, pointing toward the nearly three foot in diameter trunk of what Sarah had told me was a Norway pine. She was right that they were pretty trees – straight trunk with long dark green needles. The pine would make a great Christmas tree, but after seeing the magnificent thing fallen in the wild, it seemed wrong somehow to cut them down young to prop up in a house.

Still, we had to get this one out of the way.

Cabot pulled the van to a stop, grill-to-tree trunk and turned off the engine.

Being in the middle of the rear seat and sat-upon, I was the last to get out. 'Where did you leave the car, Lita?' I said, trying to see over what had to be ten or twelve feet of needled branches.

'On the gravel the other side of the tree,' Lita said. 'I remember specifically that I didn't want to get stuck in the mud.'

'This tree must be a hundred feet high – or now, long,' I said, surveying the length of the tree covering the driveway and extending into the woods. 'How did you get around it on foot?'

'I don't quite remember,' she said, standing on tiptoes and looking back and forth. 'It was dark, remember.'

'It may have shifted since it first fell,' Cabot said. 'Hopefully you didn't walk under it.'

'Let's go this way,' Harold said, pointing to the right. 'The branches start quite a way up the tree, so we'll just have to deal with the trunk.'

Harold, Lita, Jerome and I went right, toward the base of the tree. The lower twenty feet of trunk was devoid of branches and held away from the ground by the upper part of the tree, creating a lean-to we were able to squeeze under.

'Didn't Cabot just warn us about this?' I asked, ducking through after Jerome and Harold to look around.

'This must have been the way I went,' Lita said, following suit.

'Where did you leave the car?' I asked her.

'It was there,' she said, pointing at the gravel shoulder of the drive.

'Not here anymore, is it?' Harold said, going for a closer look.

I went to join him. 'It was raining when Lita parked, but not as heavily as it did later when that second line of storms came through.'

'With the hail.' Jerome had joined us. 'The car was parked on the gravel, so all Faith had to do was stay on it as she turned around and not go off into the mud.'

'The rain would have taken care of any tracks,' I said. 'I suppose there's no way to tell if she took off last night or this morning.'

'If she was smart, she waited until daylight,' Harold said. 'Less chance of getting stuck.'

'And we weren't going to be able to chase her down regardless,' I said.

'I'm so sorry,' Lita said. 'If I had only taken the key with me and locked the car.'

'It's not your fault.' Jerome was standing by the tree. 'But I guess I still hoped that—'

'Faith wasn't a killer,' I said. Thing was, somebody was a killer. Kate was dead.

'This is one big tree,' Harold said, as we ducked back under the trunk. 'Going to take some time to cut it up.'

Lita frowned. 'But we don't have to clear the whole thing, do we? Just cut up enough to move it off so we can get by.'

The rest of the group was debating the issue as we approached.

'Car's gone,' I told them.

'We know,' Tien said, waving. 'Cabot climbed up on the tree trunk and looked over.'

'A hunky caretaker, a chainsaw, and a corpse,' Sarah said in my ear as we watched Cabot take off his shirt and heft the chainsaw out of the van. 'Which one of these three things doesn't belong in a slasher movie?'

'None of the above,' I told her. 'Is he going to actually use that thing or just flash his pecs?'

As I asked the question, Cabot gave the starter cord on the chainsaw a yank and it revved right up, drowning out all conversation.

'Men do love their chainsaws, don't they?' Lita said in my other ear.

'They do.' Suppressing a grin, I walked away from the noise and back along the length of the tree toward where it had broken.

Harold was already there frowning. 'Well, I'll be damned.'

'You'll be damned if what?' While Harold could drone on

endlessly about the most mundane things, I had the time on my hands.

'Well, this tree.' He indicated the place where the tree had broken. 'If I didn't know better, I would say somebody took an axe to it.'

I felt a shiver crawl up my spine. 'What do you mean? Show me?'

Unaccustomed to somebody actually encouraging him to expound, the man beckoned me over. 'See here? Somebody notched it before it went down.'

'I don't quite—'

'There's a wedge-shaped piece cut out of both the part that fell down and this stump here.' He put his foot on it. 'You do that with an axe, so you know the tree will go that direction when you cut it down.'

'So the notch is cut on the side you want the tree to fall toward?' I asked, so I understood.

'You got it in one,' he said. 'Now this notch is toward the driveway, which makes sense if you're planning to clear it after you take it down. Just bad luck it came down in the storm, but they sure as hell shouldn't have notched it and left it standing. A tall tree like this, with all that weight of the branches and needles at the top. A high wind like we had last night will take it right down. That Lita is lucky it was already down when she came upon it or it could have fallen right on top of her car and smashed it.'

I was looking back to where the car had been parked. 'I don't think luck had anything to do with it.'

'What do you mean?' Harold squinted at me.

'I have a question for you,' I told him. 'And it's really important you answer me honestly.'

'All right,' he said, not sounding all that sure.

'You and Gloria. Were you in the room at the end of the hall on the right last night before we found Kate's body? The one with the queen-sized bed?'

'No,' he said automatically. 'I mean why would we be? I don't even know which room you're talking about.'

'I'm talking about the room Lita and I slept in last night. She said the sheets were dirty.'

It wasn't quite what she had said, but close.

He shrugged. 'What would I know about sheets?'

'You would know if you and Gloria did the dirty on them, I would expect.'

'Did the—'

'Stop it,' I snapped at him and then lowered my voice. 'I don't care if you two had sex in every room of the lodge. What I do care about is whether it was one of you that I nearly hit with the door when I came out of my room with Sarah. And, more importantly, whether it was Gloria who pretended to be Kate when Sarah and I knocked on the door a few minutes later.'

'I . . . Well, you should ask Gloria then.'

'You're afraid, aren't you?' I accused him. 'Afraid she's going to yell at you. What did she do? Make you pinky swear?'

'Make who pinky swear?'

I whirled around and confronted the senior in question. 'I'm asking Harold if it was the two of you in Kate's room early last night.'

'And what did he say?' Her eyes shifted to Harold and back.

'Oh, for God's sake,' I said. 'You two are consenting adults. The room is one of only two in the lodge that have a queen-sized bed.'

'I do have sciatica,' Harold said.

'Made worse by having sex last night,' I said, nodding. 'See? Was that so hard to admit?'

'My sciatica was actually made worse by you knocking at the door,' he said. 'I was kind of startled.'

'Startled? You fell off the bed,' Gloria said.

The thud we had heard. And maybe the grunt.

'Never did get to have sex,' Gloria continued. 'Probably won't for a month now, while his back heals up.'

'Getting old's a bitch,' Harold said, nodding.

'You slammed the door when Sarah opened it?' I asked Gloria.

'He was on the floor butt naked and I was the same but upright,' she said. 'What were we supposed to do?'

'Exactly what you did,' I said, grateful Sarah and I hadn't

been privy to that little scene. 'You did a fine imitation of Kate. I've been assuming it was Faith.'

'I've had a lot longer than that young lady to mock Kate.' Gloria crossed herself. 'May she rest in peace.'

'Was it you I almost hit with the door?' I asked.

'Me,' Harold said. 'I had just left my room.'

'And was coming to meet me,' Gloria said. 'I'd just checked that nobody was in the room. It's right across from the one Faith and I were assigned.'

It was all coming together. 'You changed clothes, didn't you, Gloria? When you arrived at Lita's room when we found Kate, you had your burgundy tracksuit on.'

'If anybody asked where I had been,' Gloria said, 'my story was that I had gone to change in the bathroom. Nobody asked, though.'

More shame on me.

SEVENTEEN

'You've lost your mind.'

'I have not. The last twenty-four hours was staged. Somebody wanted us trapped up here.'

I was driving Sarah and Jerome back up to the house in the van on the premise that we were going to bring down the luggage.

'What are you saying?' Sarah demanded. 'That the game Kate cooked up with Jerome went from a little innocent red paint and a planted knife to full on *Haunting of Hill House*?'

'The movie was *House on Haunted Hill*,' I said, 'not to be confused with Shirley Jackson's book *The Haunting of Hill House* and its adaptations.'

'Then there's *Clue*, both the game and the movie.' Sarah's voice was thoughtful. 'Faith's reference to it makes sense now.'

'I mentioned it to her when I was explaining Kate's plan to stage her own murder mystery,' Jerome said from the seat behind me.

Sarah twisted around. 'But when Kate was really killed, Faith didn't want to be part of the game anymore.'

'But what if there was a bigger game?' I asked, giving the van more gas to climb the alternately gravel and mud driveway. 'One that took advantage of the confusion Kate's original game caused.'

'You're confusing me,' Sarah said. 'We know that Kate brought us up here planning to fake her death, with the help of Jerome and Faith, to impress Lita. Are you saying it was also Kate who took it a step farther—'

'A big step farther,' Jerome observed.

'And knocked down a tree so we were trapped here?'

'Knocked down a tree?' Jerome repeated. 'That's the big step? How about dying?'

'She did look very dead to me,' Sarah admitted, glancing toward me in the driver's seat.

'Me, too.' I checked the rearview mirror. Jerome was staring out the window, like Faith or Kate – or maybe both of them – was going to appear on the side of the drive.

'Faith was totally weirded out,' he said. 'She expected Kate to be faking and when you said she was dead, she just assumed you were in on it. Then when . . . well, it's no wonder she flipped.'

'And we're absolutely certain Kate was dead,' Sarah said.

'You were the first one to point out her dead eyes,' I reminded Sarah. 'And both Faith and I checked for her pulse and pupil reaction,' I said. 'Even if we discount Faith for the moment, I don't think I could have been fooled unless Kate had superhuman abilities or was under the influence of some exotic drug.'

'Neither seems very likely,' Sarah said.

Jerome turned face-forward as we pulled up to the lodge. 'I see what you're saying, Maggy, but I'm not sure I trust anybody at this point. I would like to see Kate's body for myself.'

I had to assume the 'anybody' included me and I couldn't blame him, necessarily. I had been so sure I could trust Jerome, only to find out about the whole fake murder plot. And Harold and Gloria, too, kept quiet about something as important as who was in Kate's room last night. A piece of information I realized I hadn't shared yet with Sarah.

'. . . don't think anybody has been in that room since Maggy and Lita last night,' Sarah was saying as she got out of the car. 'There's no reason not to check. Right, Maggy?'

'Right,' I said, climbing out from behind the wheel and going to join her on the gravel walkway. 'By the way, I just found out who was pretending to be Kate just before we found her body.'

Sarah's head snapped back. 'You've been interrogating witnesses without me?'

'In this case, yes, though it doesn't seem to have much bearing on Kate's death.'

Sarah frowned as Jerome joined us. 'How can it not?'

'How can what not?' Jerome asked. 'And not what?'

I was sure that made sense, in some alternate universe.

Which, come to think of it, was very much where we seemed to be living. 'Harold and Gloria were fooling around in Kate's bedroom before Sarah and I found Kate's body. It was Gloria who slammed the door on us and pretended to be Kate.'

'I told you that all that's needed to imitate Kate is speaking loudly and rudely in clipped tones,' was Sarah's comment.

But Jerome seemed stuck on something else. 'Fooling around?'

'Sex,' I said, and turned to Sarah. 'You startled Harold so much he fell out of bed and that's how he hurt his back. Gloria hopped off the bed and slammed the door when you tried to open it. They were both naked.'

'Got to give the old gal credit,' Sarah said. 'I want to be her when I grow up.'

'You are already her,' I assured my partner, as I went to open the door. 'I tipped to who it was last night, when Lita said the sheets weren't clean.'

'Oh, ugh,' Jerome said. 'Did she—'

'Slept there anyway, in her clothes,' I said, shrugging. 'But I'm sure she was really exhausted.'

'What about the figure in the hall?' Sarah asked, as we stepped into the lodge. 'Was that Gloria, too?'

'Harold,' I said. 'Remember, Harold and Jerome's room is the first door on the left, across from Lita's room. He'd have had to pass our room to get to their tryst.'

'Tryst,' Jerome repeated.

'Gloria and Faith are on the end.' Sarah was nodding.

'Directly across the hall from Kate's, which was convenient for her.'

'Why not just do it—' Jerome was still trying to get a handle on senior love.

'In yours or the one Gloria shared with Faith?' I asked. 'They just have twin beds, of course. The larger beds are in Kate's and Lita's room.'

'Gloria had on different clothes when we found Kate,' Sarah said. 'Than when we arrived, I mean.'

'And, as you'll recall,' I said, 'she got there pretty quickly. Right after Clare, who came looking for Kate. We had ruined the mood, of course, so Gloria just helped Harold up and pulled on the change of clothes she had brought from her room.'

Jerome cleared his throat. 'So, umm . . . Gloria had a change of clothes in Kate's room?'

I nodded. 'Her whole overnight bag was in there,' I said, turning to Sarah. 'That's why you'll recall it was just Faith's bag on the bed in their room. That was to be Gloria's excuse, you see, in case anybody wondered where she had gone. She was in her room or the bathroom – both also clustered at the end of the hall with Kate's – changing clothes.'

'Like I said, my hero.' Sarah gave a side glance at Jerome. 'And I suppose Harold just—?'

'Got redressed and hobbled down the hallway barely in time to appear at the door behind Cabot.'

'So one mystery solved,' Sarah said, moving toward the guest hallway.

'Yes,' I said, following her. 'One mystery that, combined with Jerome's duplicity about Kate's murder game, completely confused—'

'Duplicity,' Jerome protested.

'Yes, duplicity.' I turned and held up my hands. 'I know, I know. Kate had sworn you to secrecy, but once she was dead, you needed to come clean. At the very least, to me.' OK, so my feelings were hurt.

'I'm sorry,' he said, joining us at the door. 'I'm not sure I can explain how everything seemed turned on its head in that moment. It's like I was in a—'

'Alternate universe,' I finished for him, touching his shoulder gently. 'And I get it. You said Faith flipped, too.'

'She did,' he said, rubbing his eyes. 'She said she had never touched a dead body before. I think that's why afterwards she was acting . . .'

'Like a psycho bitch?' Sarah guessed.

'I was going to say pissy,' Jerome said.

'If Faith was so traumatized,' I said, 'why did she – just minutes after touching what she told you was her first body – chat up Lita, trying to convince her she was her long-lost cousin? It doesn't add up.'

'I don't know,' Jerome said, shaking his head. 'All her lies.

It makes me believe there was some elaborate plan that I wasn't part of.'

Deception upon deception upon deception. Some that mattered and others that didn't, but all managing to confuse the larger picture.

'Look,' I said, stopping outside the first room on the right, the one marked *Private*. 'One thing at a time. First, we make sure Kate is dead and the body is still where we left it.'

'Ready?' Sarah asked, hand on the knob.

Jerome and I nodded.

'Ta-dah!' she called, pulling the door open.

EIGHTEEN

'Oh, God, the smell.' Jerome's hand was over his nose. We were standing in the corridor.

'Decomp,' I said. 'Also her bowels and bladder—'

'Yes, yes,' Jerome said. 'We get it. Kate is dead. Should I go back in and open a window?'

'Umm, no,' I said, and then with an apologetic grimace, 'animals.'

'Right.' His head bobbed. 'I'm sorry, Maggy. Sorry I didn't come clean right away with you right when Kate died. Last night was bad enough, but this—'

'No, I'm sorry.' I was feeling terrible. In my desire to tie up loose ends, not only had I given Jerome a small glimmer of hope that Kate might be alive, but also that Faith wasn't a murderer. He had lost them both, all over again.

But I couldn't do anything to change that.

'Well, Kate is most certainly dead,' Sarah said, waving us toward the main lobby. 'What does that do to your theory, Maggy?'

'Nothing, I'm afraid,' I said, rubbing my chin.

'But I thought you believed this whole thing was some fabulous murder mystery weekend that Kate dreamed up to impress Lita.' Sarah seemed angry that I hadn't been able to wave my magic wand and make Kate's murder go away. At least for Jerome's sake.

'To be fair to Maggy, that's the way it started out,' Jerome said, moving into the main room.

'If it was this good,' I said, following him, 'even I would have wanted to invest.' I shot Sarah a small smile. 'But what I said was that our being trapped here was no accident.'

She didn't smile back. 'The tree. That had to be Cabot, right?'

I bowed my head. 'He's the only one who had the time and knew how to notch the tree correctly. Unless Harold is wily enough to do it himself, and then innocently point it out to me knowing it would implicate Cabot.'

'It would explain the back injury,' Jerome said.

Sarah shook her head. 'You really don't want to imagine Gloria and Harold having sex, do you?'

'It's like thinking about my grandparents,' Jerome said. 'And the answer is no, but I agree Harold is a long shot.'

'Yet he hated Kate,' Sarah pointed out. 'Which means he had motive.'

'Last night we wrote down the timeline,' I said, gesturing them toward the seating area. 'But we never really nailed down where everyone was between when Kate left the room and when we found her body.'

'Opportunity, you mean,' Jerome said, taking one of the big chairs. 'When Faith disappeared with Cabot, we pretty much forgot about everybody else with motive to kill Kate and whether they also had the opportunity to do it.' He seemed grateful to move the spotlight off Faith.

'But they did,' Sarah said. 'All of us did. The lights went out, remember? Who knows where anybody was?'

'Let's talk about that,' I said, taking the notebook I'd used the night before and opening it to the page with the timeline.

Brushing a grilled cheese crumb off the cover of a second notebook from the stack, I opened this one to a blank page and picked up a pen. 'So Kate leaves at about six forty-five to get the syllabus she hopes is in the box that Cabot says is in Lita's room. At that point, the rest of us are all in this room, right?'

'Right,' Sarah says. 'Jerome, you and Faith were having an argument.'

Jerome nodded. 'And Tien was talking to Cabot, because when she left his side, Faith went over there.'

'Because you two were having an argument.' I was writing all this down.

'We had a long discussion, too, Maggy,' Sarah said. 'About our sponsoring this weekend.'

And about Lita possibly investing in Uncommon Grounds. Which seemed a long shot at this point.

'I pretty much lost sight of where everybody else was at that point,' I admitted. 'What about you, Jerome?'

'I flopped into a chair—'

'Brooding?' Sarah suggested.

'Yup. And I didn't want to give Faith the satisfaction of watching her flirt with Cabot, so I'm not sure when she left his side.'

'She wasn't with him when the phone rang,' I reflected, tapping my pen on the 7:14 notation. 'Sarah had just started back toward the guest rooms and Cabot said it was the landline ringing.'

'Clare was there, too,' Sarah said. 'And Harold, because he said Lita had probably slid into a ditch.'

'Tien suggested sandwiches, so she was there, as was Gloria, heading to the bathroom.'

'And then as Cabot went to light the fire, lightning struck and the power went out.'

'The lightning struck, the rock fell and the power went out,' I said, expanding my timeline. 'In that order.'

'Nit-picking,' Sarah said.

'Yes,' I agreed. 'Who can we account for then?'

'It was mostly voices at first,' Jerome said. 'But Cabot, obviously, because he had just tried to light the fire. The two of you, Tien.'

'Gloria, when the lightning struck,' I added. 'She was just coming out of the bathroom.'

'I didn't see Faith until after Lita arrived,' Sarah said. 'Everybody popped out of the woodwork then.'

'I don't remember that,' Jerome said.

'You and Cabot had gone out for the lanterns,' I told him. 'Clare, Tien, Gloria, Harold – they were all there.'

'And then Faith finally showed up,' Sarah said. 'And introduced herself to Lita.'

'That's right. They were talking when I came back with the lanterns,' Jerome remembered.

'Which is when Sarah and I went to look for Kate. Do you remember who was where after that, Jerome?'

'After you left?' He squinted, thinking. 'I think Harold said he was going to our room to get a jacket or something.'

'He got "something" all right,' Sarah said, elbowing Jerome.

A weak smile. 'I guess Gloria might have slipped out at that point, too.'

'Should we even be talking about Harold and Gloria?' Sarah asked. 'We know what they were doing and where they were doing it.'

'The two of them supposedly fooling around might be a red herring,' Jerome said hopefully. 'To explain why they were in the hallway at all.'

Sarah frowned. 'They both had motive, I suppose. Maybe one of the plots Kate suggested struck too close to home.'

'Sarah and I talked about this possibility before,' I told Jerome. 'That one of our group had an argument with Kate after she got so personal with her creative prompts.'

'And they killed her?' Jerome asked. 'Those story ideas were fictional. To give people a motive for murdering her. Fictionally.'

'You see, the problem is that nobody knew that fictional part,' I said, grimacing. 'Just you, Faith and Kate.'

'You think our game got Kate killed?' Jerome was appalled.

I tried to alleviate the increasing tension in my neck. 'I don't, but we have to consider all possibilities and eliminate those we can.'

'The idea is that the argument got out of hand,' Sarah told him. 'Kate fell and hit her head.'

'Then they picked up a pillow and smothered her instead of getting help?'

'You loved Kate.' When Jerome started to protest, I held up a hand. 'I'm not talking about that way. As a mentor. As a friend.'

'Other people were afraid of her,' Sarah said. 'She could destroy lives with her newspaper.'

'Already had,' I said. 'Ask Harold.'

'So they killed her because they were afraid of her?' Jerome seemed to be trying to understand.

'They panicked because they were afraid of her,' I said.

'Imagine it,' Sarah said. 'You've just argued with Kate,

maybe even pushed her, and she falls and hits her head. It's an accident, but Kate is merciless. She'll call the police and file a complaint against you.'

'And your life will become a nightmare,' I said. 'It's not unlike Terra scratching Kate at Clare's shop.'

'It's not?' Sarah was squinting at me.

'No, it's not,' I said. 'It was a scratch, but Kate says it was a bite and reports it. Suddenly Terra could be put down.' The thought made me sick.

'So now Clare killed Kate?' Sarah seemed confused.

'I sure would think about it if Kate threatened Frank or Mocha, but no.'

'Maggy's point, I think,' Jerome said, glancing over at me sympathetically, 'is that Kate could throw gas on a fire that was barely a spark.'

'And burn somebody's life down.' I sat back. 'Now I honestly don't think Harold, Gloria, Clare, Sarah or Tien did—'

'Maggy prefers her murderers to be strangers,' Sarah told him. 'Like Faith. And Cabot. Even Lita would be OK if she had been here, right, Maggy?'

'Absolutely,' I said. 'So what I want to do right now is recap where everybody was and when. Rule out who we can.'

'"When you have eliminated the impossible, whatever remains, however improbable, must be the truth,"' Sarah quoted. 'Sherlock Holmes.'

'Truer words never written,' I said. 'Back to when Kate leaves the room. We've accounted for Tien, Cabot, Faith and Gloria.'

'Clare was there when the phone rang and so was Harold,' Sarah said, raising her hand.

'But that was a half hour later, at seven fourteen.' I retraced the entry on my notebook, thinking. 'That's the only time we have for certain, isn't it? Lita showed us the phone.'

'When she arrived, too,' Sarah said. 'Clare said it was seven thirty-one.'

Now that was interesting.

'Why are we bothering with everybody else?' Jerome burst out. 'It's Faith who was missing from sometime before the phone call until you say she introduced herself to Lita.'

'That introduction was a little awkward,' I said. 'Faith seemed to think Lita should know her.'

'The long-lost heir thing,' Sarah said.

'Lita told me that Faith texted her, but she didn't reply.'

'That couldn't have made Faith happy,' Sarah said.

'No,' I said, with a glance toward Jerome. 'You came back with the lanterns fairly quickly. But I didn't see Cabot again until after we found Kate's body.'

Jerome nodded. 'We went to the addition at the back of the lodge where the laundry facilities and storage were.'

'That backs up to where the bathroom is at the end of the guest wing,' I said.

He thought about that. 'Yes, I guess it probably does. Cabot checked the fuse box first thing, but there was no juice coming in, so he had me take lanterns back to you in the lobby. He stayed to start the generator, which was around the side. I guess the gas for the unit was stored away from the house in the garage, so he would have had to go there to get that, as well.'

'But he came back into the lodge before he got it started,' I said. 'We were all huddled around Kate's body.'

'That's right,' Sarah said. 'And then he went back out to continue the work when we were doing almost exactly what we're doing now. Trying to figure out where everybody was when Kate died.'

'Uncomfortable subject for him?' I suggested.

'Faith went with him that time,' Jerome said.

I shut both notebooks and set down the pen. It rolled off, so I leaned down and retrieved it. 'Well, it doesn't definitively rule anybody out, but you're right, Jerome. We lost track of Faith from at least seven fourteen to around seven thirty-five, seven forty. Cabot was outside from seven thirty-five, when he left with you, until shortly after we found Kate's body at seven fifty.'

'That's not all that long, really,' Sarah said. 'The question is why did he come in only to go back out again?'

'Maybe he heard the commotion,' Jerome said.

'This is hopeless,' Sarah said. 'There were a lot of people who could have snuck away long enough to kill Kate.'

'There are,' I said, sliding the notebooks away from me. 'But I was thinking about who had the time and ability to fell that tree, and I keep coming back to Cabot. Also, Lita said it was about half a mile from the lodge to the end of the driveway where the tree fell. Do you think that's about right?'

'Almost exactly,' Jerome confirmed. 'I noticed when we drove down.'

'You really think Cabot engineered this?' Sarah asked me. 'I mean, I've started to think the lights are on but nobody's home.'

'What?' Jerome said, looking back and forth between us.

'Pretty, but not smart,' I translated.

'Oh, yeah. That I can believe.' Jerome settled back.

'I'm not sure I do, though,' I said. 'Yes, the pretty part. But I feel like Cabot, in particular, is playing a part. Somebody had to notch that tree and be ready to knock it down at the appropriate time.'

'It couldn't have been the wind that took it down?' Sarah asked. 'After it was notched, I mean.'

'Oh, it helped,' I said. 'In fact, a tree randomly falling to block the driveway could only trap us here if—'

'There was a storm and the electricity went out so we couldn't call for help,' Jerome said, getting it.

'This storm was certainly forecast,' Sarah said. 'I was getting weather bulletins all the way up here on my phone. Until we lost cell service, of course.'

'Cabot had up-to-date weather information when we arrived,' I said. 'Which means he was monitoring it before any of us got here.'

'Not surprising, given we all were driving up. But also not easy to do without the Internet or good cell service,' Jerome said. 'Though he did say there was a weather radio.'

'The power went off *after* the lightning strike.' I was thinking. 'You said Cabot checked the electrical box, Jerome, but did you actually see what he did?'

'I . . . well, no. His back was to me and he's not a small guy, so I couldn't see into the box.'

Sarah was watching me. 'Even if the lightning tripped the circuit, he might have been able to reset it?'

I dipped my head. 'If he wanted to. But if he didn't, would we know any better? We just assumed the power was out. You and I didn't even glance at the electrical box.'

'I'm disappointed in myself,' Sarah said.

'I'm disappointed in you, too,' I said, reaching over to punch her in the arm, before I turned to Jerome. 'Did you see a tractor anywhere?'

He shook his head. 'No, but like I said, I didn't go to the garage.'

'We did,' I said, gesturing to myself and Sarah. 'There was no tractor, just a car.'

'True. I can't imagine missing something that size, at least. But what's a tractor got to do with anything?' Sarah asked, frowning, and then light dawned. 'Oh, that's right. Cabot said he was thinking about siphoning gas from the car or the tractor.'

'And a tractor would come in handy for knocking down a tree,' I said. 'I'm betting it's sitting hidden in the woods somewhere.'

'Maggy has to be right,' Jerome said. 'Cabot is the only person who could have set this up beforehand. But why did he want to trap us here?'

'To kill Kate and Lita so his girlfriend Faith would inherit, of course,' Sarah said. 'Right, Maggy?'

'No wonder they looked so natural together,' Jerome muttered, shaking his head. 'They were a couple before we ever got here.'

'So the attempt on Lita was by Faith?' Sarah asked. 'Or Cabot?'

'Either or both,' Jerome said. 'They were both supposedly outside working on the generator, but Cabot could have left a window open so one of them could get back in and lay in wait.'

'How would they know that Lita would go into that room?' I asked.

Jerome shrugged. 'It was cold and when you and Lita started talking about blankets, Cabot would know instantly where they were stored. I'm betting they were watching us the whole time.'

Sarah liked this theory. 'One of them was probably hiding

in the shadows. They knew Lita would go to the window to close it and when she did, bam.'

I tick-tocked my head. 'And Faith is where now?'

'Duh,' Sarah said. 'When the attack on Lita failed, she realized the jig was up and took off in Lita's car. We know that.'

'Do we? Why didn't Cabot go with her?' I asked. 'Why the lame scratching-on-the-window act?'

'Because he's an idiot,' Sarah said.

'That's what Lita said.' I was chewing my lip. 'Though none of us had that opinion of him earlier.'

'Maybe he's playing stupid now, so we don't suspect him,' Jerome said irritably. 'Or so if Faith is caught and implicates him, he can claim it was all her and he was tricked into helping.'

'Not bad,' I said, 'but I don't think Faith is going to get caught.'

'Because she's smarter than Cabot?' Sarah suggested.

'No. Because Faith is dead.'

NINETEEN

'So Cabot Foxx killed Faith,' Jerome muttered, as he stomped down the gravel path and around the corner of the house. The initial shock of my statement had been replaced by anger.

'I'm not sure what's worse,' I said in a low voice to Sarah. 'His girlfriend being a murderer or being dead.'

'Neither is good.'

Yup.

'But why would he do that?' Jerome demanded, turning.

'Good question,' Sarah said, a little breathless as we caught up with him. 'As the Payne heiress, Faith was the goose that laid the golden egg. Without her Cabot gets nothing.'

'We don't know that Faith, or whoever she was, is the heiress,' I said.

'That's true,' Jerome said, opening the door to the laundry/storage room. 'Hell, for all we know, Cabot could be the one who is related to Lita.'

'Ugh. They're sleeping together,' I said, stepping in. 'Where's the fuse box?'

'There.' Jerome pointed to a gray metal box on the wall the room shared with the lodge.

Crossing to it, I swung open the door. 'It's got fuses.'

'Isn't that why it's called a fuse box?' Jerome asked, coming to look over my shoulder.

Sarah elbowed us out of the way. 'Maggy is an elephant and says fuse box, when she actually means breaker box, which is the modern equivalent.'

'My house has circuit breakers,' I admitted. 'You flip a switch. These are old-fashioned screw-in fuses.'

'They are,' Sarah said, examining them. 'But the only ones that are screwed in all the way are labeled kitchen outlets and ceiling lights.'

'Bastard!'

Both Sarah and Jerome turned to regard me.

Sarah lifted her eyebrows. 'You think this guy is involved in killing Kate and maybe Faith, and this is what gets you mad?'

'It was just all those lanterns and cell phone flashlights,' I said sheepishly. 'Got on my nerves.'

'Whatever floats your boat,' Sarah said, turning back to the box. 'Or sinks it.'

'So how did he manage to shut off everything when the lightning struck?' Jerome asked. He was looking over Sarah's shoulder now.

'Well, this big block' – she pointed to a black rectangle with a handle – 'will shut down everything if you pull it out.'

'But he was inside, lighting the fire,' I pointed out, just for kicks. I thought I knew exactly how it had been managed, but I needed one last piece of the puzzle to fall into place.

'I'm not an expert,' Sarah said, 'but could the lightning strike blow out all the fuses without damaging the circuits? If so, when Cabot was supposedly out here starting the generator, he could have been at the fuse box instead, screwing new fuses into the circuits he wanted to work.'

'You're saying the generator is just sitting there huffing and puffing and doing nothing?' Jerome asked, hooking his thumb toward the thing outside.

'Not anymore,' Sarah said, cupping her ear. 'From the lack of noise, I'd say that generator ran out of gas sometime during the night.'

Another red herring, as Jerome would say. 'Can you tell if the rest of the fuses were blown?'

'They have little glass windows at the top,' she said, pointing. 'If the metal inside is melted or the glass is discolored, the fuse is probably blown.'

She was squinting at one after another as she spoke and now straightened. 'They look good to me, so maybe he replaced them and just didn't screw them in all the way.' She took care of that problem with a few twists.

'Maybe so,' I said.

She turned. 'You have a better explanation?'

I shrugged, and Sarah's eyes narrowed. 'What's next, Chief?'

'Well, there's nothing else in here.' I had been opening and closing the doors of the washers and dryers. 'We should move onto the garage.'

Closing the door, we crunched down the gravel driveway to the garage.

'What are we looking for?' Jerome asked.

'Something smaller than a breadbox, judging by the fact that Maggy was checking the washers and dryers,' Sarah told him as we reached the garage. 'The man did have a chainsaw.'

I snuck an uncomfortable glance at Jerome as I reached for the handle to pull up the garage door. The young man seemed to be steeling himself.

Sarah ducked in and went straight to the Toyota to try the door. 'Not locked, no surprise.' She leaned in. 'Nothing here.'

'And what are we looking for?' Jerome asked again.

'Faith's body, of course,' Sarah said. 'Can you pop the trunk, Maggy?'

I leaned in and obliged.

'Nothing here,' Sarah said. And then to Jerome, 'Would you rather not be here?'

'No, I'm fine,' he said, looking anything but. 'I want to help. Besides, we've been up here awhile. Cabot could get suspicious and I wouldn't want him to find you here alone.'

'You're going to beat him up for us?' Sarah asked.

'Jerome did a great job rousting him outside the window,' I told her.

'I would love the chance to beat him up,' Jerome said, lifting his glasses and repositioning them on his nose. 'Don't let these glasses fool you.'

I smiled and patted his arm. 'I certainly wouldn't want to tangle with you.'

'Don't worry about Cabot,' Sarah said. 'It'll take him some time to clear that tree. Besides, we have the van, so he'd have to walk up.'

'He would,' I said. 'How long would that take? About ten minutes?'

'Maybe eight at a brisk pace, but Lita was right about the standing water and mud along the way.' She straightened up from her examination of the Toyota's trunk. 'Where to next?'

'Cabot's cabin,' I said. 'And then the other two cabins, which hopefully are around here somewhere.'

Circling the garage, we found Cabot's cabin just as we had left it. Wine bottle and glasses still on the dresser.

'Was the wine drugged?' Jerome asked, looking at the glasses. 'Or did Cabot make that up?'

'I think the wine was drugged,' I told him. 'But I'm pretty sure it was Faith who drank it, not the other way round.'

'But Cabot was acting logy,' Sarah said. 'Was that just an act?'

'An act or, if he was smart, he took a couple Xanax so it would show up in his system, if any tests were done.'

'Is he that smart?' Jerome asked.

I shrugged.

'But it was Lita's prescription,' Sarah pointed out, and then had a thought. 'That was Lita's Tumi bag here, wasn't it? Cabot could have filched her pills from it.'

'Lita did tell me she stayed over quite often.'

'Bet that relationship is in the rearview mirror,' Sarah said sourly.

'I'll check under the bed,' I said. 'Sarah and I already checked this closet. Jerome, why don't you do the pantry in the kitchen?'

I got down on my belly and looked under the bed. 'An old ironing board, looks like, but—'

'No body.' Sarah was prone on the floor next to me.

'Two of us don't have to do this,' I said, swiveling my head toward her.

'No,' she said, 'but I just thought of something. This tree that Cabot pushed over, that trapped us here. He had to do that before Lita arrived, right? So maybe he felled it right after Jerome drove up.'

'Jerome and Faith were the last to arrive,' I said. 'And Cabot was outside, because he brought in Faith's bag.'

'Maybe Cabot decided he couldn't wait any longer to do it.' Sarah was silent for a second. 'You don't think Lita is involved, do you? I can't think of any motive she would have for killing Kate. They were friends.'

'No,' I said, shaking my head awkwardly given our

positions on the floor. 'Lita is as much a victim in all this as Kate.'

'There's something behind this pantry door,' Jerome's voice called from the kitchen. 'Something on the floor that feels heavy. I can't get the door open.'

'Let me help,' I said. And then to Sarah, 'Good talk.'

'Nothing under the bed but dust and an ironing board,' I told Jerome, dusting off my hands. 'It won't budge?'

He had the door open about six inches. 'No, I . . .' He put his shoulder to the door and gave it a shove. 'I think it's giving . . . yes . . .'

There was a thud inside and a rumble.

A single potato rolled out.

'Sack of potatoes in the pantry.' I closed the door behind us, taking the time to center the straw wreath. 'And an ironing board under the bed.'

'So it was a waste of time. But you really didn't think he would hide Faith's body in his own cabin, did you?' Sarah was glancing around. 'Now where are these other cabins? Cabot was pretty eager to tell us how they weren't renovated, don't you think?'

'I do think.' I pointed down at the gravel in front of Cabot's cabin. 'As for where they are, I say we continue to follow the gravel path, or what's left of it.'

'More mud than gravel,' Jerome said, trying to stay on the grass on either side of the track as it circled behind the cabin. 'This rain has made a real mess of things.'

'We could check for footprints on the path,' I said, following him, 'if it wasn't submerged under three inches of water.'

'Stop being babies.' Sarah was sloshing right on through behind us, splashing muddy water at the backs of the two more sensible members of our party. 'There.'

I twisted back to see where she was pointing. 'Where?'

'Chimney dead ahead.'

I followed her finger, vaguely in line with what we believed was the path. 'I see it.'

As the path petered out, we slogged through the wet undergrowth to get to the porch steps of the first of two small cabins in a clearing. I was still wearing the sweatpants I had pulled on just before we found Kate's body and they had wicked up the rainwater. I was wet to my knees.

'I think this might be a waste of time, too,' Jerome said, pointing. 'The porch is covered in mud and there are no footprints. Nobody has been here for a long time.'

'Which makes it a perfect place to cut up a body,' Sarah said, trying the door. It opened.

'Will you lay off the dismembering?' I said softly to Sarah as I followed her in.

She ignored that. 'We probably should have checked the chainsaw for blood before we let Cabot start cutting up the tree with it.'

Valid point.

'I know you think Faith is dead,' Jerome said, stepping in and looking around, 'but isn't it possible he's holding her somewhere?'

'It is,' I said.

'Faith?' Jerome called. 'Are you here?'

'She might be gagged,' Sarah told him. 'Go look in the bedroom.'

He nodded and disappeared through the door.

The cabin was identical to Cabot's but in much worse shape, the fieldstones of the fireplace falling off the wall without even the aid of a lightning strike.

'Nothing in here,' Jerome said, coming back.

I opened the pantry. 'Nothing here, not even a potato.'

'On to the next one?' Jerome asked.

I nodded, following him down the steps.

'You're sure we're looking for a body, aren't you?' Sarah asked me.

I nodded. 'Absolutely.'

TWENTY

The second cabin was empty, too.

'Where to now, Maggy?'

'The lodge. It's the only place left.'

'You really think he hid her there?' Jerome asked. 'That would be too dangerous, don't you think? We would have seen him.'

'Especially with acres of woods to choose from instead,' Sarah said. 'I know we've been searching structures, but it would make more sense to leave a body out here in a shallow grave. The animals will take care of the rest.'

There was that. But somehow, I didn't think so in this case, at least. 'A little sensitivity please, Sarah?' I said, nodding to Jerome.

Jerome waved it off. 'No worries. I'm past it. Really, Maggy.'

Sure he was. 'We can't search the entire woods, so I say we go back to the lodge. If nothing else, I would very much like to change clothes.'

'Good call,' Sarah said. 'I have to pee anyway.'

Lovely.

'Well, look who's here,' Sarah said, as we rounded the lodge to the front door, and she opened it.

Damn.

'Where have you been?' Gloria demanded, apparently speaking for the entire group. 'We thought you were going to pick up the luggage and drive back down.'

'We were sidetracked,' I said, counting heads. 'Where's Cabot?'

'He's still clearing the tree,' Tien said. She was back in her assigned seat.

'Some of us needed to use the facilities,' Harold said, coming out of the bathroom.

'Hey, watch it.' Sarah jumped out of the way of the door she'd been heading for herself, before it could hit her.

'Oh, sorry, Sarah,' Harold said. 'Didn't mean to bop you.' He swung the door back and forth on the brass hinges. 'These solid doors could do some damage.'

'I'm sure they didn't need to know why we walked back up,' Gloria told Harold, managing to slip into the powder room ahead of Sarah.

'And Lita?' I asked, growing more concerned. 'She didn't come with you?'

'I don't think she had to go,' Harold said, cocking his head. 'Why?'

'Then she's still down there with Cabot.' I had finished my headcount.

'Yes.' Tien had picked up on my stress level. 'Do you think she's in danger?'

'We think Cabot killed Faith.' Sarah was leaning against the bathroom door now, not willing to let her place in line slip away again. 'And one or both of them killed Kate for a clear shot at Lita's money.' She shrugged. 'Though why Cabot would get rid of Faith before she inherited, I don't quite understand. They really should kill Lita first.'

'So the answer to my question is, yes, Lita is in danger,' Tien summed up.

'Yes,' Jerome affirmed.

'Well, we had better get back down there then,' Harold said, starting for the door.

'Wait,' I said, waving my hands to stop them. 'Sarah doesn't have it quite right, but it's all conjecture so far anyway. Before I fill you all in, though, I just have to search—'

'I don't have it right, do I?' Sarah said accusingly, tilting her head at me.

'I—' I broke off. 'I need to show you.'

'Maggy thinks Faith's body might be here in the lodge,' Sarah said. 'Again, I probably don't have *that* right, but . . .' She shrugged.

'What about the outbuildings?' Harold said. 'That would be a lot more likely.'

'Already searched them,' Jerome said. 'All that's left is this building.'

'Then let's do it,' Clare said. 'Should we each take a room?'

'But don't you think somebody should go down to make sure Lita is all right?' Tien asked. 'I can take the van.'

'It's too dangerous,' I said, putting my hand on her arm. 'I need you here.'

Her eyes widened, but she didn't argue.

'Now,' I said, 'how about everybody starts by searching the room they were sleeping in?'

'Search under beds and in closets, if your room has one,' Jerome ordered. 'You know the drill.'

'I'll do the extra room, too,' Tien volunteered, glancing at me. 'The one Lita was attacked in.'

'Would you check to make sure the floor is all right?' Harold asked. 'That it hasn't started to warp? Though with today being a nice day, if the window was opened it might dry . . .' He shrugged.

We all stared at him for a beat.

'Right,' I said, reminding myself that he had brought me the most important clue to date, the notching of the tree. 'Sarah, if you can take our room, I'm going to check this one.'

'Suit yourself,' Sarah said, giving up on the bathroom for the moment to move off with the others. She was miffed with me, but she would get over it. This was one instance where I needed to show, not tell.

Because I could be wrong.

Alone in the lobby, I scanned the space. Gloria still occupied the powder room, but since there was no place to stash a body in there anyways, that left the coat closet. I swung open the door. Four or five slickers on hangers, as well as a couple old parkas. On the shelf was an assortment of stocking caps, gloves and scarves. The floor held a pair of yellow rain boots, a golf umbrella, an ice scraper for car windows and a small snow shovel.

Moving to the café, I bent to look on the shelves under the counter. All open, all holding what I'm sure Lita's grandparents would have called bric-a-brac and knick-knacks, along with odd pieces of china. There were no upper cabinets, no place to hide anything.

I turned to regard the massive fireplace, dismissing a body stuffed down the chimney à la Santa Claus. We had used the fireplace last night and it had been just fine. The chairs were overstuffed, but certainly not with a body.

I had my money on the coffee tables, saving them until now. Two heavy, metal-trimmed steamer trunks.

Sliding the notebooks and my pen onto a chair, I lifted the first lid, holding my breath. Games, I said to myself. Checkers, cards, dominoes. I pulled out a familiar box. *Clue* of all things. What else?

I dug deeper. Video tapes, VHS. A couple DVDs.

Reaching the bottom, I considered replacing everything, but instead let the top slam and opened the second trunk. This one had dishes in it. Bright turquoise pottery. Fiestaware – I'd have to show Clare.

Pulling the colorful cups, bowls, plates and serving dishes out of the trunk and setting them aside carefully on the floor next to it, I reached in and felt heavy plastic. Something wrapped in plastic, something that didn't feel like pottery. Something . . . soft. Like a body wrapped in plastic so it wouldn't smell.

I removed a stack of saucers. Whatever it was, it was bulky, but not big enough to be a body. Unless she was in pieces. There was also a . . . my nose twitched . . . familiar smell.

I pulled out the last dish and reached in to fold the plastic away from—

'Find something?'

I jumped.

Gloria was out of the bathroom, tucking her blouse into her pants.

'I'm not sure,' I told her, unaccountably glad for her company. 'It's something kind of soft, though, and . . .'

'Furry, looks like.' She reached in. 'Yup, I thought I recognized the smell.'

'You smell it, too?'

'Smell what?' Sarah asked, coming in.

'Taxidermy with a touch of cinnamon,' Gloria said, pulling

back the plastic to reveal a paw as the rest of the group joined us, too. 'Looks like a coyote or no, more likely a gray wolf. They're protected now, but they get to be fifty to a hundred pounds.'

'Taxidermy has a smell?' Clare asked, but then was distracted by a shiny object. 'Original Fiestaware!' She picked up a pitcher to examine.

'Sometimes it does,' Gloria said, answering the question Clare had asked. 'Used to be they used arsenic soap on the inside of the skin to preserve it. Museums have to be careful when handling the specimens because they can be dangerous.'

Goody. Had I touched anything beyond the plastic? 'Should I go wash my hands?' I asked Gloria.

'Can't hurt,' she said, shaking her head over the poor wolf. 'Homemade job, no doubt. The cinnamon was to cover up the smell.'

I loved cinnamon. Or at least I had.

'Ah, well,' Harold said, coming to look over our shoulders. 'Guess we should be glad the old folks were stuffing wolves and coyotes, not Great Aunt Martha, right?' He chuckled.

'Not a body then,' Sarah said, turning to go into the bathroom. 'Or at least not the right body,' we heard faintly through the closed door.

'I was so sure,' I said as the front door opened. 'But we still should look—'

'Look for what?' Lita asked, coming in.

'Thank God you're OK,' Tien said, rushing to her.

'Why wouldn't she be OK?' Cabot asked, stepping in behind her.

Tien's eyes went big. 'You, meaning both of you. It's dangerous work, using a chainsaw.'

'Oh, I thought you might mean safe from Faith,' Cabot said, eyeing Tien curiously. 'But she's long gone, I'm betting.'

'Maggy and Sarah think she's dead,' Harold said. 'We're looking for her body.'

'Here in the lodge?' Lita asked, puzzled.

Clare looked up from her treasure-hunting. 'They've searched everywhere else. Do you mind if I make you an offer on this Fiestaware? It's very nice.'

Lita blinked. 'No, not at all. But this search?'

'It is a long shot, admittedly,' Jerome said. 'One or the other of us has been in this room since we arrived. It would be a little tough to carry Faith's body past us to anywhere in the house.'

'Besides, the car is gone,' Cabot said. 'If Faith didn't take it, who did?'

I wasn't ready to answer that yet. 'I don't know. I just have a feeling there's a body here.'

'There is, in the bedroom,' Lita said a little angrily. 'Kate's.'

'A second body,' I amended.

'Have you looked in the freezer?' Tien asked.

The freezer. Tien had mentioned it more than once since the power went out, but she'd have stored the food she brought for the weekend in the refrigerator, not the freezer.

'There,' she said, leading us through the door into the kitchen and pointing semi-dramatically.

The white chest freezer stood in the corner of the room where I had seen it earlier when we plugged in the phone. A couple of old boxes were stacked on top. The thing probably measured six feet long, two and a half feet wide and three feet deep.

'Certainly big enough to freeze a couple deer carcasses,' Gloria assessed, as the rest of the group joined us.

'Or a few of those wolves and coyotes before stuffing them,' Harold said. 'Bunches of rabbits and squirrels.'

Thank you, Harold.

'Or a body.' I pulled the boxes off, wanting to lift the lid before anybody could stop me. But the thing wouldn't budge. 'It's locked. Where's the key?'

'No idea,' Cabot said, leaning against the kitchen door. 'Thing hasn't been used for years.'

'And yet it was one of the two things running in the kitchen before Sarah screwed in the fuses,' I said. 'Why would that be?'

'Yes, Cabot,' Lita said, turning on him. 'Why would that be?'

He just shrugged.

She pivoted back to me. 'Are you saying the electricity wasn't out at all? The fuses had just been tampered with?'

'It seems that way, but we can't be sure,' I told her. 'Somebody could have pulled out the main fuse block.'

'I'm not sure what that is,' Lita said, 'but Jerome does have a good point. There's no outside door to the kitchen here. How would Faith's body get in the freezer? Cabot – who I assume you think killed her and put her here – would have had to carry her past us.'

'This is ridiculous,' Cabot protested. 'Faith attacked me, not the other way around.'

'Jerome wasn't exactly right,' Gloria said. 'We all went to our rooms last night to sleep. The body could have been brought in here then.'

'That's a possibility,' I said, as Jerome caught my eye. Cabot couldn't have done any such thing, since Jerome had been sitting watch in the hallway last night with the door to the main room open while we all slept.

'That's true,' he said now, going along with it.

'Well, don't look at me,' Cabot said, holding up his hands. 'You saw me last night, when I made it back. I was drugged, in no shape to be carrying around a body.'

'So you say,' I said. 'Yet you refuse to give us a key to the freezer.'

'Don't need a key,' Harold said. 'I've got a multi-tool and these locks are usually just plastic.' He pulled a thing that looked like a large switchblade out of his pocket and sorted through a needle-nose pliers, wire cutters, knife, scissors, ruler, can opener and bottle opener before finally getting to what he was looking for.

He inserted the flat screwdriver and we heard a snap. 'Yup. There you go.' He swung up the lid.

We all peered in.

There was something very large on the bottom of the freezer, wrapped in the same heavy plastic as the stuffed wolf in the trunk.

'Oh my God,' Lita said, backing up.

I levered myself up on the side of the freezer to try to reach the plastic.

'Need help, Maggy?' Jerome was beside me.

I gave him a little smile. 'Please. If you're OK.'

'I am.' Eight inches taller than me, Jerome was able to reach low enough inside the freezer to pull back the plastic.

A generalized gasp and then: 'Who is that?' Tien demanded.

'It's not Faith,' Clare said. 'It's a stranger.'

'Not exactly,' I said, stepping back and turning to face the assemblage. 'Everybody? Meet Lita Payne.'

TWENTY-ONE

'You're not Lita Payne?' Cabot gasped, turning to Faux Lita.

'Drop the act, Cabot,' she snapped, the pleasant, freckled face suddenly not so pleasant. 'I'm not going down for this alone.'

'Who are you really?' I asked.

'Why in the world would I tell you that?' she demanded, advancing on me.

Jerome tried to get between us, but I held up my hand. I had expected a retreat from Lita, at least, if not from Cabot.

Since neither of them seemed to be going anywhere, I would work with it. 'Only so I have a name to use while I'm doing my big reveal. This is a mystery weekend, you know. It's only fitting.'

Her lips twitched, but she didn't answer.

'Fine,' I continued. 'If you prefer to stay anonymous, I'll just call you . . . Mary.'

'Mary is just fine,' she said, tilting her head. 'And I'm sure we're all anxious to hear what you have to say. Aren't we, Cabot?'

'Sure.' He had gone from a bad imitation of incredulous to downright surly.

'Good,' I said. 'Should we go into the other room, so we'll be more comfortable? This may take a while.'

'Lead the way.'

I would have been hesitant to turn my backs on the two of them if I didn't have Jerome and the rest of our gang trooping along behind them. Still, I was torn between hoping they would make a break for it and actually wanting my Hercule Poirot moment.

Everybody took their usual seats. I stayed standing, leaving two chairs open. Lita took one of them, but Cabot stood, hovering between fight or flight.

'Sit down,' Mary ordered, and he did.

'Guess we know who is boss,' Gloria muttered.

'Yes, I think Mary is probably the alpha,' I said. 'But I do believe she and Cabot really are a couple. Am I right?'

A single nod of the woman's head was my answer.

'I'm not completely sure of the whys of this game of yours,' I told Lita. 'But I think I can point out your mistakes.'

'Please.'

'Woman of few words,' Harold said. 'I like that.'

Gloria slapped him.

'First of all, the tree,' I said. 'Harold spotted it and I'm grateful to him.'

'Spotted what?' Cabot was querulous now.

'The notch you made to make the tree fall across the driveway.'

'Oh, for God's sake,' Mary burst out.

'It had to fall the right way,' he said. 'Nobody would notice if they thought it fell down during the storm.'

'But it didn't. You knocked it down with your tractor during the storm. That's why you were out there so much trying to start the generator or looking for gas or a cell signal. You had things to do.'

'But that doesn't make sense.' Clare held a Fiestaware cup on her lap. Maybe for protection or maybe because she loved it. 'That was all after Lita . . . Mary arrived. The tree was already down when she tried to drive in.'

'It's true that it was after Mary made her grand entrance, but she was here all along,' I informed them. 'There never was a long drive from the airport. No slog through the storm. Or even a car left parked at the end of the driveway.'

'A car that Faith, therefore, couldn't have taken.' Jerome closed his eyes.

'But how can you know that?' Tien asked.

'The timeline,' I said, picking up the notebook. 'The only two exact times we had on it referenced Lita: the seven fourteen phone call, which Mary took pains to show us, and the time the fake Lita arrived, which Clare confirmed was seven thirty-one.'

'So?' Cabot demanded.

'So both you and Mary told us the only place that call could have been made was three miles away. Plus, the walk up the driveway from where the car was supposedly left was another half mile.'

'There's no way anyone could drive three miles on that country road in a storm and then walk a half mile in seventeen minutes.' Harold was nodding in approval. 'No way at all.'

'Don't forget parking, pulling her bags out of the car and climbing around the tree,' I reminded him. 'With the bags.'

Gloria was puzzled. 'You're saying they killed Kate? But which one of them? When? How?'

'Team effort,' I said. 'Cabot set the trap by telling Kate that Lita had sent on a box for the conference and that it was in her room. When Kate went in to find it, Mary was waiting for her and hit her over the head, maybe with one of the books on the bookshelf. It wouldn't have left a mark or necessarily even knocked Kate off her feet, but it would have stunned her enough for Mary to smash her head into the dresser.'

'Which did knock her out,' Tien said.

'Exactly,' I said. 'Giving Mary time enough to suffocate her with the pillow, pull the case off and make her way to Kate's room at the end of the hall, where she climbed out the window. She must have lost the pillowcase somehow, or maybe she just hid it for Cabot to pick up and dispose of later.'

'He got the picking up part right,' Sarah said.

'That's why the window was open a smidge, when we went in that room,' Gloria said to Harold. 'We locked it, of course.'

Jerome caught my eye and rolled his. I suppressed a smile. 'That room was the only one with a smoothly operating window and lock. Mary could probably pull down the window from the outside, but she wouldn't have been able to lock it.'

'And then what?' Jerome asked. 'She just circles the house and shows up at the front door with her suitcase having supposedly walked up the driveway?'

'Yes, but first she makes that "dropped call" to let Cabot know Kate was dead and Mary was in position.'

'She had cell service?' Gloria sounded jealous.

'There was a landline in Cabot's cabin,' I said. 'It wasn't far and all Mary had to do was make the lodge phone ring and hang up. The rest was play-acting.'

Cabot didn't comment.

'Besides,' I continued, 'Mary needed to change into Lita's clothes.'

'But only after killing Kate,' Clare said. 'She wouldn't have wanted to get blood on that linen jumpsuit.'

I was nodding. 'That's why Lita's Tumi bag was in Cabot's cabin.'

'Way to go,' Cabot said sarcastically. 'Guess I'm not the only one who's not perfect.'

'Shut up.'

He did.

'Next,' I continued, suppressing a smile, 'Mary wanted to cut the electricity to cause confusion. She went back to the laundry room and pulled out the main fuse block in the electrical panel.'

'But the lightning strike,' Harold said. 'How could she possibly have timed that?'

'I think she was just waiting for a big clap of thunder or even gust of wind,' I said. 'The lightning strike on the chimney was just gravy.'

'But very theatrical gravy,' Mary agreed. 'Then what did I do, Maggy?'

'You circled the house wearing Lita's clothes and toting Lita's duffel.'

Gloria was shaking her head. 'Enters this house bold as brass, claiming to be the woman who owns it, and there's nobody left alive to say any different.'

'Because she's just killed Kate,' Jerome said. 'Was the attack on the fake Lita just to cover her tracks?'

'Partially,' I said. 'The original idea was to kill Kate, but stage it as an accident. She falls, hits her head on the dresser and dies. Everybody is sad and leaves never knowing the truth.'

'But then you and Faith saw the petechial hemorrhaging,' Jerome said, 'and realized Kate had been suffocated.'

'Exactly. But Mary is quick-witted, I'd even say wily.'

If I'd expected a response to the semi-compliment, I was doomed to disappointment. Mary just pursed her lips and stuck out her chin.

So I went on. 'She knew there had to be a change in plans and the best way to throw off suspicion was to be attacked herself.'

'In Kate's bedroom,' Clare said. 'Was that because of the window? Her assailant, presumably Cabot, could get out quickly?'

'Excellent guess,' I told Clare. 'It was because of the window, but Cabot didn't have to be in the room. In fact, Mary might just as easily have done it to herself.'

'But how?' Clare asked.

'The window. Mary used it to fake her injury, as Cabot faked his later. Remember the straight cut on the back of his head? Mary's was identical.'

'We thought it might be the poker or a tire iron,' Jerome said.

'I wasn't so sure,' I said. 'And then there was Mary's bloody nose.'

'I probably hit it when I fell.' Mary seemed to be enjoying this.

'More likely that when you brought the window sash down on the back of your head, it was a little too hard and you hit your nose on the sill,' I said.

'More likely the moron who was helping me did that,' she growled at Cabot.

I nodded to him. 'So you did help. You certainly would have had plenty of time after you killed Faith and supposedly got the generator started on that trip outside.

'One question, Cabot,' I continued. 'Is that generator actually powering anything? Because we realize now that after you put back the main fuse block, you unscrewed all the fuses but the two that controlled the lights and the kitchen sockets for the refrigerator and freezer. Couldn't have that freezer thawing.'

He didn't answer. Which was my answer, of course.

'Was Faith in on this?' Jerome asked. 'Or did she accidentally become a target when she told Lita – or Mary – that she was an heir?'

I shook my head. 'I'm sorry, Jerome. I know this will only make it harder, but Faith was exactly who she told you she was. An inspirational writer looking to be published. Mary made up the bit about her being a missing heir, so we would suspect her in Kate's death and the attempt on herself.'

'So they had to kill her.'

'I'm afraid so,' I said. 'I think Cabot drugged her wine with the Xanax he and Mary had found in Lita's tote. When they were about to stage the attack on Mary, he passed her the pill bottle through the window to plant in Faith's bag in the next room.'

'That was my idea,' Cabot muttered, nodding to himself. 'And a damn good one.'

'As was taking a couple of pills yourself,' I told him.

'I know, right?' He was nodding.

'Oh, for God's sake,' Mary/Lita said.

I was hoping to get more from Cabot. 'I thought we might find Faith tied up in one of the cabins today, but—'

'We really *were* looking for Faith then,' Jerome interrupted.

'And Lita, too. Faith was the only one I thought might be alive.'

'So when did they kill Lita?' Gloria asked.

'The day before we arrived,' I said. 'Kate said Lita told her she'd be here "yesterday," which was Thursday. I believe she did make it, only to be murdered and put in the freezer.'

I'd touched a nerve. 'Wrong on that one, Sherlock,' Mary snapped. 'She showed up Wednesday, a day early, and found the two of us in *her* room. In *her* lodge, she said. We had been living here for four years. Even before the old bastards died and here she comes, accusing us of having something to do with them dying like that. And saying we cashed the old man's pension checks.'

'Well maybe we did, one or two,' Cabot said, and shrugged. 'But they were both dead, and a man's got to live.'

'Did you kill them?' Harold asked. 'The old couple, I mean.'

'I had nothing to do with that,' Cabot said, holding up his hands. 'I liked them. And Lita.'

Hmm. 'Maybe you liked Lita a little too much?' I tried, jerking my head toward Mary. 'Or so *she* thought.'

'I never even met the woman,' she said now. 'Cabot wanted me to hide the couple of trips she made up here. But then this last time . . .' She shrugged.

'How long did you work for her grandparents?' I asked Cabot.

'For about two years before they died,' he said, rubbing the stubble on his face. 'I liked it here. Suited me fine, and then I met Meg and we fell in love, wanted our own place together.'

Ahh, sweet. And finally, I had a first name. 'Meg.'

'Moron,' Meg said.

'So you moved into Cabot's cabin?' I asked. 'I noticed the family touches. The straw wreath on the door. The ironing board.'

'The sack of potatoes,' Jerome added.

'Why shouldn't I?' she demanded. 'Nobody was up here. We lived in the cabin at first, but then we moved into the lodge.'

'Kate told Sarah that Lita's inheritance was hung up in probate for two years,' I said. 'You must have gotten pretty comfortable here.'

'Nobody ever even came up, except those couple times,' Cabot said. 'The estate was still paying me to keep the pipes from freezing and such. But then this newspaper woman talks Lita into opening this place up to conventions.'

'That wasn't going to happen,' Meg said, her nose starting to bleed just a bit. 'This is our home, not hers. This was never her home.'

'I just needed more time, I told you that, to bring her around. Show her how expensive it would be. But you wouldn't listen.' Cabot handed her his handkerchief. 'Things got out of hand.'

'She called us squatters.' A vein in her forehead was throbbing.

No wonder her nose was bleeding again. Her blood pressure was spiking.

'And fired me and threatened to call the sheriff,' Cabot explained.

'So you killed her and stuck her body in the freezer,' Tien said. 'Thinking what? Once we had all left, things would go back to normal?'

'It would have if you truly thought that Meg was Lita,' Cabot said. 'Lita would call, you know. Talk about Kate and their plans. Even gave me a list of everybody coming this weekend, so I could get the place ready. Your names and what you did and such. She was dead set on being hospitable to Kate's friends, even though she'd never met any of you.'

'She'd never met any of us,' I repeated softly. 'Except Kate.'

'Which is why Kate had to die, you see,' Cabot said, nodding, 'before Meg got here as Lita. It was supposed to look like an accident. Like Kate had tripped over the box and hit her head. Nobody would ever know.'

'And,' I said, 'the fake Lita, having lost her friend here, would "decide" not to open Payne Lodge with all its sad memories. Leaving the two of you free to continue squatting on the property.'

If I had expected to get a rise out of Meg for the word 'squatting,' I was disappointed yet again.

'Exactly,' she said coolly, 'except now there's no heir to bother us. Lita is dead and Kate is dead, and your Faith really wasn't an heir at all.' She directed this last at Jerome.

I felt my eyes narrow. 'Let's talk about Faith. We found the Burberry jacket – the real Lita's Burberry jacket, I assume – in the closet in the cabin's bedroom. I saw the little nod you gave Cabot, Meg, after you offered it to her. Was that when you decided she had to die?'

'Well, certainly not because of the jacket,' she said, 'but yes. Cabot knew what he had to do. I had already spun the yarn about the long-lost heir. We couldn't risk her coming back and saying I was a liar.'

'Which you are and a damn good one,' I told her.

'Thank you.'

'I half-expected to find her body in the freezer with Lita's,' I said. 'Why freeze one and not the other?'

'It was Cabot's bright idea to put Lita in there,' Meg said. 'I thought it was a risk, but he assured me it would be locked and the power to it would be on until we had time to dispose of her.'

'But Faith?'

'Like you said,' Cabot took up. 'There was no way I could

risk bringing her body in. Better to just leave it in the woods a ways out, where I knew you all wouldn't be tramping around.'

'How did you kill her?' Jerome's lips were tight.

'Suffocated her with the dry-cleaning bag,' Cabot said. 'Like I did Lita.'

I closed my eyes. Of course. 'Lita's own dry-cleaning bag, I assume, since I doubt you two get much dry-cleaning done.'

'The outfit I'm wearing was in it,' Meg said, smoothing the wrinkles of the jumpsuit.

'Got a little bloodstain there,' I said, pointing at a drip from her nose that had made it to her chest.

'You think you're so smart, don't you?' Meg snapped, swiping at it.

'You might try a little vinegar on that,' Clare told her. 'Works wonders on blood.'

'Why bother?' I told Clare. 'She'll be wearing a different kind of jumpsuit soon and I'm sure the matrons have plenty of experience getting blood out of them.'

'I'm not going to jail,' Meg said, standing up.

'You know that saying, "Nobody will hear you scream?"' Cabot said, making an effort at menacing as he followed suit. 'It's true up here.'

But Meg had been glancing around and now she shook her head. 'There are only six of them here. Where's the other woman? The snarky one.'

'Sarah,' I supplied. 'She went for help a half hour ago.'

'How did she do that?' Cabot asked. 'Walk? The van is here.'

'We do have another car,' Jerome told him. 'Mine.'

'The BMW?' Cabot asked, looking out the window. 'It's out there, too.'

'That's because Jerome keeps the keys in his pocket, not in the car. So when Sarah saw you walk up, she took your Toyota. The one in the garage.' I smiled at Jerome. 'The keys are in that one. That's the way they do things up here.'

'Then you'll give me yours, please,' Meg said, holding out her hand. Jerome dropped the key in it.

'And the van?' The hand came my way and I dug the ignition key out of my pocket and gave it to her.

'Now Meg unplugged the phone line last night when you were trying to call out,' Cabot said, backing toward the door.

'When I went to look for the phone book.' Meg smirked. 'Cabot finished the job permanently by cutting the wires outside.'

'I did.' Cabot gave a proud hitch to his jeans. 'So if you know what's good for you, you'll just sit tight here until we're good and gone. Never know what or who might be waiting for you out on these country roads. Maybe "the Others." Ooooooo.' He waggled his fingers.

'Is he kidding?' Tien whispered to me. 'They *are* the Others.'

Insane murderous misfits, hiding off the grid. Yup, met my definition. 'Maybe don't tell them,' I whispered back as Meg moved to the entry hall.

'We can't just let them go,' Jerome said, jumping to his feet. 'We can stop them.'

'No, you can't.' Cabot pulled a revolver out of his jacket pocket, still backing. 'You go start the car, Meg. I'll be right out there.'

She seemed to want to argue, but I think the gun won him points. For once, she did what he told her.

'I may not be as smart as Meg is,' Cabot was saying, as he continued to back toward the entry hall, 'but it honestly makes no difference to me whether I'm convicted of killing one person or six or seven, however many there are of you.'

'It'll be eight with Kate and Faith,' I told him. 'Unless you did kill Lita's grandparents.'

'Like I said, no difference to me.' He waggled the gun at Jerome. 'Stay back there, son. I—'

With a warrior-like yell, Sarah swung the powder room door open wide, smacking Cabot on the side of his head and knocking the gun out of his hand.

Jerome, who had been shadowing Cabot despite the warning, jumped on top of him, taking him to the ground. Clare threw her cup in the general direction of the melee, and Gloria sprang up and kicked the gun across the floor.

'Well done,' I said, as I heard a vehicle start up outside. Most likely the BMW, given Meg's tastes. 'Should we stop her?'

'Let the police track her down,' Sarah said. 'I'm exhausted and my butt fell asleep on the toilet. It was very tense waiting in that bathroom.'

'I'm sure it was,' I said, going to hug her. 'Thank you.'

'And thank Lita's great-grandfather, rest his soul.' Harold knocked on the door. 'Three inches thick, just like that Cabot said.'

'Guess what?' Brookhills County Sheriff Jake Pavlik asked, as I joined him and our sheepdog Frank and chihuahua Mocha on the couch. It was a tight squeeze. 'I have news on Margaret Wooster.'

'Who is Margaret Wooster?'

'Meg/Mary/Lita?'

Oh, yeah. It had been a couple of days.

'She was picked up trying to cross into Canada.'

'Thank God,' I said, snuggling up to him. 'I was afraid she was going to become one of those recurring villains, popping up every few months.'

'No chance of that,' he said, kissing the top of my head. 'You did good work up there.'

'Thanks. I can't take all the credit, though. I had an amazing team.'

'Ahh, the sign of a good leader. Giving credit where credit is due.'

I sighed. 'Speaking of credit, Sarah is having money problems. She was hoping to entice Lita Payne into investing in Uncommon Grounds so we could pay ourselves more.'

'Well, that's not going to happen now,' Pavlik said. 'What are you going to do?'

'The shop will pay her rent for the space in the depot, for one thing,' I said.

'That won't help your bottom line,' Pavlik said.

'No, but it's only fair. And it's a start.' I was quiet for a second. 'I don't suppose they've found Faith's body?'

Pavlik pulled me closer. 'Foxx isn't talking, but maybe they'll get something out of Wooster.'

'What they need to do is interview the two of them together,' I said. 'That's when they'll spill on each other.'

'Like I said, you are good.'

'I've learned from the best,' I told him, as Frank groaned and went to stretch, knocking Mocha off the couch. I patted the sofa for her to hop back up. 'So what should we do this weekend?'

'I thought maybe camping,' he said. 'Now that you've had a taste of Up North, I figured we'll take both dogs—' At his words, the sheepdog jumped down and disappeared around the corner, the chihuahua hot on his heels.

As for me, I went to open a bottle of Pinot and order a large pizza for four.

Peperoni.